Jane's Country Year

Also published by Handheld Press

Jane's Country Year

by Malcolm Saville

illustrated by Bernard Bowerman

with an introduction by Hazel Sheeky Bird

Handheld Classic 24

First published in 1946 by George Newnes Ltd.

This edition published in 2021 by Handheld Press
72 Warminster Road, Bath BA2 6RU, United Kingdom.
www.handheldpress.co.uk

ISBN 978-1-912766-54-3

2 3 4 5 6 7 8 9 0

Series design by Nadja Guggi and typeset in Adobe Caslon Pro
and Open Sans.

Printed and bound in Great Britain by TJ Books, Padstow.

Contents

Hazel Sheeky Bird is a research associate at the University of Newcastle. She is the author of *Class, Leisure and National Identity in British Children's Fiction, 1918–1950* (2014). She is researching and cataloguing the papers of Aidan and Nancy Chambers, held by Seven Stories, the National Centre for Children's Book, Newcastle.

Introduction

BY HAZEL SHEEKY BIRD

Malcolm Saville: Setting the Scene

Jane's Country Year (1946) is a perfect example of the many children's books about the British countryside that were published in the first half of the twentieth century. It begins with a key trope of children's books from the 1930s: a train journey. Following a long illness, we meet eleven-year old Jane who is put on a train in London by her parents and travels alone to Shropshire, to stay with her Aunt Kate and Uncle William on their farm to regain her health. Supported by friendly well-wishers, including the local rector, Mr Herrick, and his son Richard, George the stockman and Frank the shepherd, Jane, and the reader, are gently initiated into the ways of the countryside. Equally concerned with husbandry, rural life and heritage as well as nature observation, for many *Jane's Country Year* is the best of Malcolm Saville's many children's books.

Saville (1901–1982) was a prolific author, producing 80 books for children while also working in the publicity departments of major London publishers, Cassell and Company, Amalgamated Press and George Newnes. Writing warmly about both *Jane's Country Year* and Saville generally, the progressive children's author Geoffrey Trease observed that Saville was an author with 'an intense feeling' for the English countryside and that the novel contains the 'essential' Saville (Trease 1949, 56). The book was certainly roundly praised, both at the time of its publication and in the many children's books surveys, aimed at parents, librarians and teachers, published in the 1950s and 1960s. With its believable plot, strong sense of place and detailed observation of the natural world and country life, *Jane's Country Year* is an intensely realistic book, a quality that was increasingly praised in writing for children by the mid-twentieth century.

By and large, Saville is not greatly remembered as a nature writer for children. His reputation is rooted in the many series of adventure books that he wrote between 1943 and 1978 and is most associated with his Lone Pine novels. Beginning in 1943 with *Mystery at Witchend* and closing in 1978 with *Home to Witchend* (published in paperback by Armada) the Lone Pine books (eventually running to 21 titles) epitomise a particular type of book that was perennially popular from the mid-1930s to the 1970s: the holiday adventure novel. The first book introduces the Morton family: David, the eldest, Dickie and Mary, the twins, accompanied by their mother and Scottie dog, MacBeth, move to Witchend in Shropshire due to the war (Mr Morton is in the RAF). The Morton children spend the first part of the novel exploring the countryside, establishing the Lone Pine club, under a particularly large pine tree, and making friends with two other children who would become key figures in the series: Petronella Sterling, or 'Peter', who loves horses and lives nearby, and Tom Ingles, who is an evacuee from London now, like Jane, also living on his aunt and uncle's farm. As with many other titles in the series, and indeed as with many other series of novels by different authors, notably Enid Blyton, the children become embroiled in a mystery, in this case a spy plot. Subsequent novels would introduce other characters and the action would shift to other fully realised locations, including Rye, Hereford and North Yorkshire, but the basic formula remained the same.

By working within the adventure genre and by writing about the countryside, Saville was an astute judge of the mid twentieth-century children's book market. Both genres were highly popular during this period and Saville was adept at writing them. Saville's writing, however, along with that of Arthur Ransome, David Severn and Henry Williamson, for example, who all wrote diverse books, actually belongs to a wider canon of children's countryside writing. This predates the twentieth century; one that looked back beyond the Edwardian river bank of Kenneth Grahame's *The Wind in the Willows* (1908), encompassing fiction and non-fiction, dipping deep into Romantic, pastoral and Georgic poetry, and came to rest in the writing of the Victorian ruralist Richard Jefferies. Two of Jefferies' novels, *Wood Magic* (1881) and *Bevis* (1882), which refashioned memories of his boyhood on Coate Farm in Wiltshire, were foundational books for later children's authors. The first is a work of rural fantasy, the second recounts the adventures of two friends, Bevis and Mark, as they build rafts, make maps, wage war on other children, and explore the surrounding countryside. When *Bevis* was reissued in 1932 by Jonathan Cape, replete with illustrations and maps by E H Shepherd, illustrator of A A Milne's Pooh books from the late 1920s, it became a landmark book in children's literary culture. As for many children's authors of the time, *Bevis* was an enormously important book for Saville. We see Saville return to it time and again, either intertextually (Richard Herrick gives Jane a copy for her birthday, and Petronella Sterling is shown reading a copy in *Seven White Gates* [1944]) or through direct recommendation in his *Country Scrap-Book for Boys and Girls* (1944). Reading *Bevis* was a barometer for rightmindedness, which Saville encouraged through his own very different books.

It is useful to place Saville's work within the broader trends in early twentieth-century British children's publishing, because these impacted so significantly on both his critical reception and long-term reputation. As might be expected, there is no consensus view on the state of British children's publishing in the first half of the twentieth century. For many years, the period 1920–1950, in which Saville began writing, was largely viewed as a fallow period: an 'age of brass' sandwiched between the first and second 'golden ages' of children's books, running from 1850–1920 and 1950–1979 respectively. It has been argued that many children's books produced between the world wars were lacking in quality, often prized for their bulk rather than their contents. Certainly, children's publishing was hard hit by both paper rationing and the departure of creative and technical expertise in the war; it was not until the 1950s that children's publishing began to recover. The absence of realism in writing for children was also lamented by critics and Marcus Crouch's view in 1962 that this was a period in which children's reading was remote from the realities of everyday life has held sway until very recently. Kimberley Reynolds (2016), for example, has uncovered a canon of progressive and left-wing books for children published between 1910–1949. However, what is certain is that the quality of children's books was increasingly prioritised in discussions about what children should and should not be encouraged to read.

Spurred on initially by developments in children's book publishing in the USA and fuelled largely by increased advocacy for improved standards from librarians and teachers, British publishers began to give serious consideration to producing high quality children's books (Eyre 1952). Two events mark this shift in Britain: the founding of *The Junior Bookshelf*, a critical review journal, in 1936 and the foundation of the Carnegie Medal for children's books in 1937. From this point on, there were clear ways by which the 'best' children's books could be celebrated and shared, resulting in 'better' books reaching their readers. By the 1960s, newly increased public funding for libraries and schools helped British children's publishing reach new levels in quality, imagination and experimentation (Pearson 2013). Consequently, the literary quality of books aimed at children became increasingly important, at least to the adult gatekeepers who tended to buy them.

The issues of quality and reputation are complicated for Saville because he is best known for his many series of holiday adventure stories, which immediately set him in comparison with Arthur Ransome. The publication of Ransome's *Swallows and Amazons* in 1930 was a landmark in children's publishing, and Ransome is widely credited with creating the holiday adventure genre. Set largely in the Lake District and the Norfolk Broads, the Swallows and Amazons novels recount the gentle holiday adventures of three families of middle-class children: the Walkers, Blacketts and Callums. While three novels in the series are arguably fantasies, the novels essentially focus on realistic depictions of the children's sailing, camping, hiking and exploring. It is this low-key realism that sets Ransome's novels apart from the work of many authors, including Saville and Enid Blyton, who engineered thrilling spy plots and criminal gangs for their children to contend with while holidaying in the countryside. There was a clear preference in the reviewing press for stories that tended toward realism rather than sensation, with reviewers in *The Junior Bookshelf* tending to divide holiday adventure stories into two types: believable, and far-fetched. Time and again, commentators lamented authors' tendency to add far-fetched elements to holiday stories, the best-known example of this being Enid Blyton's Famous Five and Adventure series. It was, and remains, as Victor Watson notes, 'easy to ridicule' (Watson 2000, 103) the holiday adventure novel formula: as Eileen Colwell would famously ask of Blyton, 'But what chance has a gang of desperate criminals against three small children?' (quoted in Eyre 1952, 53). The formula was, however, solidly popular for most of the century and Saville apparently received 3,000 letters a week from young readers. We are told that Saville, ever the publicist, answered all his fan mail personally (quite a feat if true) and he certainly sent out regular newsletters to his fans (Doyle 1978). The popularity of Saville's books may have been partly due to their serialisation for radio broadcast. Many of his books were dramatised for the BBC's Children's Hour. Broadcast daily between 1922 and 1964, the Children's Hour, presented by a series of 'Aunties' and 'Uncles', was made for children aged between five and fifteen years, and offered listeners a mixture of commissioned plays, dramatisations of novels, short stories and music.

Despite Saville's popularity with readers and listeners, reviewers at the time often chose to overlook his books. For example, Kathleen Lines' influential survey *Four to Fourteen. A Library of Books for Children* (first published in 1950 and again in 1956), makes no mention of any of Saville's titles. Consequently, not only has there has never been a consensus view of Saville's work, opinion is often divided. Writing in 1970, children's author Rosemary Manning noted that Saville could not be regarded as a classic writer, but strongly disapproved of public librarians refusing to stock his books. For Manning, children's literature is 'surely what children read and enjoy', and that, as such, 'Malcolm Saville's work should have an honourable place in it' (Manning 1970, 90). Saville's writing was, then, frequently set outside the 'gold standard' of children's books epitomised by Carnegie-winning authors such as Ransome, with his later books rarely being reviewed. Like many authors of genre fiction, Saville has always occupied an uneasy position – beloved by his readers, but frequently criticised by those who were not his intended audience.

Jane's Country Year

Despite Saville's reputation resting largely on his more thrilling holiday adventure stories, genuine engagement with the English countryside and rural traditions was actually central to his writing and personal life. Saville would publish thirteen non-fiction books on the countryside, the seaside, exploring woods, growing food, as well as observing plants, flowers and wildlife throughout his career. The first, *Country Scrap-Book for Boys and Girls,* was published in 1944 and the last, *The Seashore Quiz,* in 1981, appeared a year before his death. *Jane's Country* Year adopts an unusual form. Geoffrey Trease described the book as 'didactic fiction' (Trease 1964, 56) because Jane's year-long convalescence at Moor End Farm is a framing narrative that gives Saville the space to teach children about nature, rural life and the workings of a farm. The book is divided into twelve chapters, one for each month of the year, and each chapter allows the reader to follow Jane's experiences through her eyes. In the second, expanded edition the chapters were followed by a short summary of all that Jane had observed in the natural world that month; in these sections Saville addresses his readers directly, using an overtly adult, didactic tone.

Jane, arguably, is not the main character of the novel, rather, it is the countryside that holds the reader's attention. By sending Jane to her relatives' farm, and focusing on farming life, Saville establishes a rooted, permanent connection between Jane, who is initially a city child, and the countryside. In doing so, he avoids a common trope of much countryside writing for children, including in some of his own novels, of the idea of the countryside as a tranquil and empty playground for the professional middle classes. In general, the lived experiences of British children in the countryside, particularly during the Second World War, including the many thousands of school children who worked on the land as evacuees or on school harvest camps (Mayall & Morrow 2020), are absent from writing for children. Saville, unlike many 'realistic' authors such as Ransome, did address the experience of being an evacuee in the countryside. Lone Piner Tom Ingles is evacuated to the countryside from London, and Saville shows that he neither likes working the land nor being forced to part with his family. Saville tells his readers that Tom is lonely in the countryside and Tom himself tells the Morton children that 'he didn't think much of it up here (Saville 1943, 31). His Uncle Alf also says that Tom sometimes 'wishes he was back in [...] "them blitzes"', but 'his house has gone and his mother's somewhere else with the baby and his Dad's somewhere else in the war' (30). *Jane's Country Year* is different as it was written and set after the war. Certainly, there are very few mentions of it and Jane has not been evacuated: she is convalescing. However, as we will consider shortly, *Jane's County Year* explores the emotional impact of long enforced separations on children, parents and surrogate parents, even if the image of urban children working the land is entirely absent from Moor End Farm.

Although the form of *Jane's Country Year* is unusual, it is not without its forebears. In the first chapter, Saville sets up a gentle teacher/pupil dyad between Jane and her slightly older and better-informed friend Richard. Richard Herrick is the middle-class son of the local rector and a day-pupil at a local school, with many opportunities to roam the local area birdwatching and so on. In using this personable pupil-mentor dynamic, we again see Saville's astute understanding of his readers' tastes and the contemporary children's book scene. Saville was drawing upon an earlier and highly popular series of children's books about the countryside by George Bramwell Evens, known as 'Romany', with titles such as *Out with Romany* (1937) and *Out with Romany by the Sea* (1941). These books used a similar pupil-mentor pattern as a means for writing about nature observation. Generally, they involved Bramwell Evens, accompanied by his dog, Raq, and a boy, Tim, who is about the same age as Jane, rambling around various parts of the countryside and chatting about what they saw. The popularity of these books with children led to copycat series, by figures such as Norman Ellison, or 'Nomad,' with both authors having extremely popular programmes on the BBC's Children's Hour. Romany and Nomad were benevolent, paternalistic figures, very similar to the narrator of the chapter summaries in the later edition of *Jane's Country Year*, who shared British country lore and natural history through a series of conversations with apprentice naturalists, usually boys. Nomad was accompanied on his rambles by a boy called Dick, again of a similar age to Jane. Both series, easily comparable to *Jane's Country Year*, are noteworthy for their unsentimental observations of both farming and the natural world.

We see this lack of sentimentality many times in *Jane's Country Year* and two episodes typify the way Saville writes about the precariousness of life. During the harvest in August, Jane is aghast when the farmhands shoot the rabbits that emerge from the sheaves of wheat, but her Aunt Kate simply says that 'we have to kill them else they would ruin the farm' adding, 'Don't worry, Janey! You'll like them in a pie' (158). Jane cannot quite reconcile herself to this, but we are not told whether she eats the pie. Then, in September, Jane stumbles across a group of dead shrews when out blackberrying with her aunt; she literally stands on a 'tiny furry' body that looks as though it 'had just laid down and died'. To her horror, she realises that the path is covered with them, and she runs to tell her aunt that she has found 'something beastly' (170). However, her aunt just says this is something inexplicable that sometimes happens, and then leads Jane away to finish picking blackberries. This matter-of-fact approach places *Jane's Country Year* within a very specific group of children's books, which includes Henry Williamson's *Tarka the Otter* (1927), that adopts an unsentimental attitude to the natural world.

While following established trends, *Jane's Country Year* offered readers new approaches. Saville's choice of a female protagonist is unusual in a book aimed at both boys and girls, but he was adept at writing strong female roles. Both Petronella Sterling and Jenny Harman from the Lone Pine series are credible, independent characters with fully realised personalities. *Jane's Country Year* is Jane's year of discovery. Richard Herrick remains in the background, appearing at intervals to dispense knowledge and accompany Jane on her explorations, but she is as often exploring and discovering on her own as she is under his tutelage. We can see Richard as a more child-friendly version of the Romany and Nomad figure, particularly for a modern reader. The figure of the benevolent male expert roaming the countryside freely with groups of children in tow is now anachronistic, but this trope has an honourable history in children's books about the countryside. In camping and tramping fiction or holiday adventure novels, such figures were central to the framework on which the action of the novels was built. In his Waggoner novels (1942–46) David Severn sent three sets of siblings on various country holidays with Bill 'Crusoe' Robinson, a young man in his early twenties whom the children befriend in the first book. In *Jane's Country Year*, the combination of knowledgeable male figures who support Jane (including Richard, the rector, Uncle William, George the stockman and Frank the shepherd) add to the book's realism, while affirming Jane's initially more submissive role in the pupil/mentor dynamic.

To understand Saville's intentions in writing *Jane's Country Year*, it is helpful to consider both the physical changes that took place in the countryside between and following the two world wars, and its symbolic relevance to British national identity. During and between the First and Second World Wars, the British landscape came increasingly to represent what was being fought for, and what British, or English, identity was based on. A desire for continuity with the past, rooted in the idea of a tranquil and immutable 'Deep England', led to much writing about the countryside, for children and adults, lamenting the physical changes that were taking place in the 1930s, notably the rapid unregulated building work that was consuming 60,000 acres a year (Lowerson 1980, 258–80). Books such as Clough Williams-Ellis' *England and the Octopus* (1928), commissioned by the Campaign for the Protection of Rural England, not only warned of the resulting physical erosion between the town and the city at a catastrophic rate, but also looked to children's education to ameliorate the damaging effects of increased tourism in the countryside. The founding of the Youth Hostel Association in 1929 and the Ramblers' Association in 1932 point to the widening of participation in open-air leisure pursuits in Britain in this period. Added to this, by the 1930s many urban Britons also enjoyed a rise in standards of living in real terms, which, when combined with the impact of the Holidays with Pay Act (1938), meant that more people than ever before looked to the countryside for their recreation.

It is striking that children's authors, including Saville, rarely acknowledged the significant limitations that were in place in terms of where people could go in the countryside. In the early 1930s, for example, only 1% of open moorland in the Peak District was accessible to the public (Curry 1994), and the first National Park in Britain would not be established until 1951. A tension was emerging between the demands for increased access to the countryside and the desire to protect it. This was certainly the case for children's writers, including Saville, who wanted to help children learn about and connect with the countryside, while also preserving it. The way they achieved this was to imagine the countryside as a private, exclusive space for the quiet, more contemplative leisure pursuits of the professional middle-classes (Bird 2013) such as hiking over lonely fells. Day trippers arriving in charabancs, having picnics and leaving rubbish behind, or mass groups of hikers singing 'I'm Happy When I'm Hiking' have no place in children's books.

To an extent, the illustration by Bernard Bowerman used as the front cover image for this edition mirrors the way the countryside was visualised in many children's books of this period. It is a variation on the 'monarch-of-all-I-survey' position, with the viewer, in this instance Jane, shown elevated above the landscape, which spreads out before her 'land-spanning' gaze (Pratt 1992). There are important differences, however, between Bowerman's illustration and the classic summit scenes that featured on covers of books such as the 1947 Penguin edition of Barbara Euphan Todd's *South Country Secrets* (1935). Euphan Todd's children are shown standing, one with hands on hips, looking out over rolling empty hills: Jane sees a patchwork of fields peppered with small farm buildings. In the foreground, almost directly below her, is a farmstead, most likely Moor End Farm, in the middle distance she looks onto a small cluster of houses around a single church and in the far-distance is the train line that brought her here at the start of the book. This is no empty playground or *terra nullius;* it is a populated and cultivated landscape, there to be understood and appreciated rather then taken over. Interestingly, it is also clearly winter; Jane is wrapped up in a knitted scarf and thick coat, and the trees are bare. Euphan Todd's children recline under bright blue skies, wearing only summer clothes. While some writers did send children into the countryside during winter, Arthur Ransome's *Winter Holiday* (1933) and Marjorie Lloyd's *Fell Farm at Christmas* (1954) being notable examples, most children's books were summer stories. Anyone who has ever camped in a tent in Britain would, probably, vouch for the sense in this. This illustration for *Jane's Country Year* signals that this is an unusual book. Jane's gaze surveys a populated countryside that is physically shaped by farming; one that exists beyond the very limited parameters of a summer's camping or tramping holiday.

In focusing on the life of Moor End Farm, Saville critiqued the popular idea of the countryside as a site of leisure and emphasised its economic importance. We see Saville return to this subject repeatedly by connecting the work of farmers to key events in the Christian and rural calendars such as Lammastide, St Swithin's Day and harvest, around which the book is structured. The inclusion of these celebrations, connected to the management and produce of the farm, not only reminds readers of their reliance on them, but also looks back to a time when the Church, the people and the land were in harmony. When Mr Herrick explains the significance of Lammastide to Jane, he tells her that, 'Once upon a time, Janey [...] when life was altogether simpler and when men and women in this country came to Church to say their prayers and to give thanks, they offered to God on this day a loaf baked of the newly gathered grain' (144). In case the lesson has not been fully absorbed, Saville reminds readers a few lines later that they should 'remember to be thankful for the bread you eat every day'. It was not uncommon for children's books during the war years to remind readers of the importance of British agriculture. As such, *Jane's Country Year* belongs to a small canon of children's books on farms and farming, both fiction and non-fiction, that sought to redress the dissonance between literary and artistic depictions of the countryside and the realities.

If we read *Jane's Country Year* alongside Saville's earlier book *Country Scrap-Book for Boys and Girls* it becomes clear that teaching children about the economic and symbolic importance of the countryside was a sustained focus in Saville's work. It covers much the same ground in that it teaches children about the British countryside, but as a work of non-fiction it lacks the framing narrative that gives *Jane's Country Year* the cohesiveness and emotional engagement of a novel. *Country Scrap-Book* includes chapters on 'The Farm', 'The Village', 'Animals of the Countryside', and 'Weather Signs', all of which are covered in *Jane's Country Year*. In the later edition the chapters are interspersed with poems by Keats, Tennyson, Browning and W H Davies, all extolling the beauty of the countryside. It was not beauty alone, however, that prompted Saville to write about the countryside. In his introduction to *Country Scrap-Book,* Saville reminded his readers that, 'there is no country in the world for which so many sacrifices have been made', and that 'one day the countryside will pass into your keeping to guard' (Saville 1944, 5). Tied to the physical countryside were the traditions and heritage that were rooted into rural life and that, for some, were the foundations of English, if not British identity. Saville uses a similar tone in the expanded edition of *Jane's Country Year* in short sections to close each chapter, offering a round-up of the new things Jane experiences each month. The tone of these sections is completely different to the novel and is akin to the more overt didacticism of Saville's *Scrap-Book*. So in September, we are told that, 'Jane went to the *Fair* and so should you because English fairs are a part of our heritage [...] Many old rural customs and habits are disappearing now and this is a great pity,' (Saville 1947, 200). Here Saville's voice emerges, revealing the assumed authority over his readers that is largely masked in the first edition.

Saville's authorial voice reveals much about his personal disdain for city-dwellers and his ideas about farm workers, both of which sometimes verge into caricature. We can see a fair degree of condescension in Saville's narrative voice in *Country Scrap-Book* when he writes that 'many foolish and ignorant people pretend to despise the slower-thinking countryman who has worked on the land all his life' and that 'I want you to realise that you cannot enjoy the country unless you try to understand the men and women who live their lives and make their living in the country' (Saville 1944, 24): people who are 'simple' according to Saville. A clear binary emerges between the town and the country, both in terms of the space and the people. Saville's *Scrap-Book* village is populated with 'jolly country people' who are 'quite unlike the rather worried-looking folk you see on the trams at home,' (Saville 1944, 31). These two figures, the 'simple' country yeoman and the worried town-dweller find their way into *Jane's Country Year* in the figures of George the Stockman and Jane's mother. When Jane sees George for the first time, looking from her bedroom window on her first morning, she thinks that he is a tramp: 'he looked so rough and wild […] He was wearing a very old and battered soft felt hat with the brim turned down and a sack over his shoulders. He was not near enough for her to see his face clearly but he looked very brown and quite old' (8). George is shown again and again in the novel to be a valuable agricultural worker, but Saville also describes him at one point as staring at Jane, 'with open mouth' (146). George is Saville's essential countryman, skilled and valued, but simple. Jane's mother is also something of an archetype: she is the ignorant, city dweller who wears the wrong shoes for exploring in the woods, worries that Jane is too weak to compete in village races, and is generally ill at ease in the countryside.

If we look closely at the month of August, we can see how Saville draws many of these themes together. The chapter begins with Jane waking, excited about her parents' arrival that day, setting out for an early morning walk. The first three pages of the chapter describe Jane running across the farmyard and through fields of wheat, oats and swedes; she thinks of the coming harvest that would bear the 'results of all [the farmer's] work,' and inhales the early morning smells of the countryside; 'the smell of mist, the smell of a farm and of animals, the scent of growth in the hedge and of distant blossom' (143). The world is bursting with life, symbolised by Sally the dog and her puppies, and the fields of 'glowing grain' (144) ripe for harvesting. The perfection of the scene is disturbed, almost from the start, by Jane's reflections. Running barefoot through the morning dew on the grass, she notes that 'her feet and legs were now as tanned as her face which had filled out and glowed with health and happiness. She laughed to herself as she thought how shocked her mother would be to know that she ran about now without shoes or stockings and never even caught a cold' (143).

There is a tension, one that becomes very apparent once Jane's parents arrive, surrounding her mother's attitudes towards Jane and, specifically, what she should and should not physically do. This would not be remarkable, attitudes to parenting do differ after all, and her mother is firmly rooted in the urban environment. She is literally out of place in the countryside, hence the wrong shoes. Thinking about her home in London, her 'real home', Jane reflects that 'the pavements would be hot in this weather' and that 'the High Road would smell of petrol and of hot tar', and that 'Mummy would fuss about leaving the house and locking everything up' (146). The comparison of the city to the countryside is unfavourable and Jane's mother clearly represents the worried-looking folk that Saville criticised.

Living in the countryside obviously has a positive impact on Jane's health. We see the fruits of this, also in August, when Jane takes part in a village race on Bank Holiday Monday and helps to bring in the harvest. In both instances, Saville shows her mother to be at odds with her daughter's abilities, fundamentally underestimating what Jane is capable of. It is important to remember, although it is easily forgotten by this point in the novel, that Jane's mother has nursed her through a debilitating illness – although Saville suggests that she was often 'too busy' to spend much time with Jane during her illness (2) – and has only rarely seen her recovering over the course of eight months. It is, therefore, natural that she is concerned for Jane. So, when Richard puts Jane's name down to run three races during the village gathering at Townsend, her mother is aghast and objects that she does not think she is 'strong enough'. Her fussing is positioned against Mr and Mrs Watson's reaction; they simply 'look at each other and smile' when Jane says she is well enough (150). Again, there are subtle tensions here; between the mother who no longer understands her daughter, changed physically and mentally through her time at Moor End Farm; between the mother and Jane's surrogate parents, Mr and Mrs Watson, who clearly understand Jane better than her mother and who love children despite having none of their own. Jane's mother, on the other hand, is a stifling figure. Saville never develops the implications of this tension between Jane's two sets of parents, but the Watsons see Jane as a permanent part of their lives. Later that day, Mr Watson observes that Mrs Watson and 'young Janey' could 'start some bees' so as to bring something to the village show next year. Jane's response is telling: 'Next year! Jane wondered if her uncle knew what he was saying and it was as well that she did not see her mother's face' (154). Viewing Jane's mother through a sympathetic lens, her fussing becomes an understandable attempt to assert her position as Jane's mother and primary carer.

Saville, however, does not view Jane's mother sympathetically and continues to portray her as being at odds with the very environment that has wrought such benefits for Jane. On the morning of the stooking, Mrs Watson tells Jane that she had 'better be wearing those dungarees I bought for you else you'll scratch yourself to bits'. Jane's mother responds with 'horror' saying 'Dungarees! [...] My Jane in dungarees like a . . . like a *workman*!' (155). It is impossible to know what really drives her mother's horror here. It may simply be the unladylike nature of the dungarees, but there is clearly an element of class bias to her objection. What she has failed to account for, because she remains at odds with country life, is that harvest time is a communal endeavour. Labour is not despised on the farm because without it there would be no harvest. Jane's mother, then, is a cautionary figure; she has become so disconnected from the natural world and the realities of country life that she simply does not know what to do with herself. There is hope though. Over the course of the two-week holiday, her mother starts to relax: 'she stopped worrying as to whether it was too hot or too windy or too wet or too tiring to go out of doors. The lines on her forehead disappeared and without realizing it she got a little sunburned and looked much nicer for it' (161). She is, though, always slightly ill-at-ease in the countryside and remains a figure indicating tension.

Although Jane's stay in the countryside is due to ill-health, rather than war, Saville sympathetically explores the impact of long, enforced separations between parents and children, such as that experienced through evacuation by Tom Ingles. By the end of the novel, Jane's feelings about returning to her 'real home' are ambivalent. The thought that she and her parents will return to Moor End goes some way to ameliorate her sense of sadness, but she remains torn. In December, the sight of primrose buds hidden under leaves reminds her that she will not be there in spring to see them bloom, prompting her to say, 'I know it's awful of me but I don't want to go home' (222). The arrival of Christmas is bittersweet; a cause of celebration and sorrow, as Jane prepares to say goodbye to the farm and her friends. For the adults, Christmas and Jane's departure has loomed in their consciousness for some time. In August, while Jane's parents are staying at Moor End on holiday, Mr Watson tells Jane that he, 'Can't think how we ever did without you, Janey girl! Can't think what we shall do after Christmas' (164). In contrast, when Jane's mother meets her on the train platform for the last time in the novel, she hugs her saying, 'I'm never going to let you go away again, Jane [...] This is the very last time. It's been too long' (225). Given Saville's earlier critical presentation of Jane's mother we could read this either as a sign of true maternal affection or a threat. Jane's father, always more sympathetically drawn, acknowledges the mixed feelings that Moor End arouses in them. His questioning, 'You won't mind coming home now, Janey, will you?' suggests his own vulnerability, rooted in the fear that Jane might want to stay in the countryside (230). Being the good girl she is, Jane reassures her father that, although it is difficult, she is happy to be going home. Saville's nuanced portrayal of the emotional impact of separation on children and adults remains in the background of the novel and is never allowed to overshadow Jane's time on the farm; however, it must have resonated with many readers and their parents at the time it was first published.

In *Jane's Country Year*, Saville offers readers an insight into farming life and the natural world that is rooted in discourses of English identity, and the preservation of the countryside and heritage. It is, despite its sustained critical neglect, a classic work of children's countryside writing that warrants recognition for its dedication to realism, its believably drawn main female protagonist, and its sympathetic portrayal of the impact of enforced separation on parents and children.

Works Cited

Bird, Hazel Sheeky, *Class, Leisure and National Identity in British Children's Literature, 1918–1950* (Basingstoke, 2013).

Crouch, Marcus, *Treasure Seekers and Borrowers* (London, 1962, 1963).

Curry, Nigel, *Countryside Recreation, Access and Land Use Planning* (London, 1994).

Doyle, Brian, 'Malcolm (Leonard) Saville' in *Twentieth-Century Children's Writers*, ed D L Kirkpatrick (London, 1978), 1081–3.

Euphan Todd, Barbara, *South Country Secrets* (London, 1935, 1947).

Eyre, Frank, *20th Century Children's Books* (London, 1952).

Lines, Kathleen, *Four to Fourteen. A Library of Books for Children*, illustrated by Harold Jones (Cambridge, 1950).

Lowerson, John, 'Battles for the Countryside', in *Class, Culture and Social Change. A New View of the 1930s*, ed. F Glover Smith (Brighton, 1980).

Rosemary Manning, 'A Book is a Book is a Book', *Signal* 3, September 1970, 81–90.

Mayall, Berry and Virginia Morrow, *You Can Help Your Country. English Children's Work During the Second World War* (London, 2020).

Pearson, Lucy, *The Making of Modern Children's Literature in Britain: Publishing and Criticism in the 1960s and 1970s* (Farnham, 2013).

Pratt, Mary Louise, *Imperial Eyes. Travel Writing and Transculturation* (London and New York, 1992).

Reynolds, Kimberly, *Left Out: The Forgotten Tradition of Radical Publishing for Children in Britain, 1910–1949* (Oxford, 2016).

Saville, Malcolm, *Mystery at Witchend* (London, 1943).

Saville, Malcolm, *Country Scrap-Book for Boys and Girls* (London, 1944).

Saville, Malcolm, *Jane's Country Year* (London, 1946, 1947)

Trease, Geoffrey, *Tales Out of School* (London, 1949, 1964).

Watson, Victor, *Reading Series Fiction: From Arthur Ransome to Gene Kemp* (London, 2000).

Williams-Ellis, Clough, *England and the Octopus* (London, 1928).

Further Reading

Butts, Dennis (ed), *Children's Literature in its Social Context* (London, 1992).

Carpenter, Humphrey and Mari Pritchard, *The Oxford Companion to Children's Literature* (Oxford, 1984).

Darling, F Frazer, *The Seasons and the Farmer: A Book for Children*, illus. by C F Tunnicliffe (Cambridge, 1939).

Edwards, Owen Dudley, *British Children's Fiction in the Second World War* (Edinburgh, 2007).

Giles, Judy and Tim Middleton (eds), *Writing Englishness, 1900–1950. An introductory sourcebook on national identity* (London, 1995).

Hunt, Peter, *An Introduction to Children's Literature* (Oxford, 1994).

McKibbin, Ross, *Classes and Cultures. England 1918–1951* (Oxford, 1998).

Walvin, James, *Leisure and Society, 1830–1950* (London and New York, 1978).

Works by Malcolm Saville (chronological)

Countryside books
Country Scrap-Book for Boys and Girls (London, 1944).

Open Air Scrap-Book for Boys and Girls (London, 1945).

Seaside Scrap-Book for Boys and Girls (London, 1946).

Jane's Country Year (London, 1946).

Small Creatures (London, 1959).

Malcolm Saville's Country-Book (London, 1961) – an updated revision and expansion of the *Country Scrap-Book* and *Open Air Scrap-Book*.

Malcolm Saville's Seaside Book (London, 1962) – a similar updated revision and expansion of the *Seaside Scrap-Book*.

See How It Grows: an introduction to gardening for boys and girls (London, 1971).

Eat What You Grow (London, 1975).

The Countryside Quiz Book (London, 1978).

Wonder Why Book of Exploring a Wood (London, 1978).

Wonder Why Book of Exploring the Seashore (London, 1979).

Wonder Why Book of Wildflowers Through the Year (London, 1980).

The Seashore Quiz Book (London, 1981).

Children's series fiction
Lone Pine (1943–1978)

Buckinghams (1950–1974)

Jillies (1948–1953)

Nettlefords (1951–1955)

Michael and Mary stories (1945–1957)

Susan and Bill stories (1954–1961)

Lucy and Humf (1959–1973)

For Jane Norris
(The Jane I know)

January

Jane woke slowly. For a long minute she lay drowsing with her eyes shut, wondering why the bed felt so different. She loved her own little bed at home and during her long illness she had got to know it very well; but the bed in which she was now snuggling was more like a nest, for she seemed to sink into its warm softness and could hardly feel a mattress under her. And this was not surprising for Jane's new bed was a feather bed!

The pillow was soft too and she was warm enough to realize that her nose, just peeping over the edge of the eiderdown, was very cold. She turned and stretched like a kitten and then put her hand out, rubbed her nose and opened her eyes. She blinked and opened her eyes wider on to a strange, new world.

The room she was looking at was as different as the bed and was filled with a weird, grey light. The window had changed its position and the bed had two big brass knobs sticking up at the end of black rods down by her toes. She glanced up next and saw that the ceiling, which sloped down towards the window, was crossed by two dark beams.

With a sudden shock of fright that started her heart thumping Jane sat up and then, as sleep fled, she smiled to

1

herself as she remembered where she was and slid back into the warmth of the bed. She remembered now that she was no longer at home and that this was her first morning at Moor End Farm, where she had come to live for a time with her Aunt Kate and Uncle William.

She closed her eyes blissfully again and because she knew that she was a beginning a new life to-day she began to think of all that had happened to her since her tenth birthday last August. She remembered how wet she had got that day running home from school; of how ill she had been soon after and how she had been whisked off to hospital and how nice it had smelled. And she remembered a doctor in a white coat and nurses and bright lights and milk pudding that she hated; and then, after a time that she couldn't remember so well, she went home again and spent a long, long time in her own bed in her own room. She had painted a lot and done jig-saw puzzles and tried to do some knitting and read books until her head ached. Sometimes she had looked out of the window, but there was not much to see except chimney pots and the bare branches of the poplar tree at the bottom of their narrow little garden. If only her room had been in the front she could have watched the people and seen the milk cart and looked for the man who pushed a barrow of vegetables up the street twice a week. But she had been forced to make do with the patch of wintry sky behind the chimneys and she had become very weary of the view.

Sometimes people had come to see her — Mummy of course whenever she wasn't too busy, and once or twice two of the girls from school — but she was lonely most of the time. She could not remember now all the private adventures and dreams which had comforted and helped her during those long days, but she did remember how frightened she had been when she had looked at herself in the mirror on her mother's wardrobe door and seen her dark eyes big in a pale face and her arms and legs so very white and thin. But she had got better and, although her knees had wobbled badly when she was first allowed out of bed, there came at last a Saturday when Daddy stayed at home in the morning and carried her downstairs and put her in the big chair by the fire. Then, when the sun came out, she had gone into the garden and after that came the adventure of learning to walk by herself again. Then the cough had come back and she had found herself in hateful bed for a time, but just before Christmas when she was up and about again nice Doctor Jones had put the peculiar pipes in his ears and listened to her chest and back, smiled at her over the top of his spectacles and said, 'A year in the country is what this young lady needs and what she must have. Fresh air, good food, no school till after Easter and plenty of running wild,' and then he had gone out of the room with Mummy and their voices had rumbled on in the dining-room for a long time and now here she was in a big, soft bed with brass knobs, in a strange farmhouse, come to live with a strange aunt and uncle whom she had not seen since she was a baby.

And now yesterday already seemed a long way away, although coming here had been such an adventure. She felt a tiny bit choky when she remembered saying good-bye to Mummy and Daddy at the station, but the other people in the carriage had been kind and the lady in the corner had shared some chocolate with her and an elderly gentleman with a white moustache had told her some stories about the country through which the train was rushing — stories about the men who fought and tried to keep the Romans out of Britain and made their camps on the hilltops which she could see from the window.

She remembered how tired she had felt after a time and how the train wheels had sung her a lullaby until her head had slipped on the old gentleman's shoulder and she had slept. When he had roused her after a while and told her that the next station was hers she looked out and saw that the short day was nearly over. The sky was heavy and grey and through the steamy window she noticed that the lights were lit already in the cottage windows near the line. Then, almost before they were able to get her case down from the rack and she could tie the lovely scarf Mummy had given her for Christmas, the train had stopped and she was being helped out on to the platform. Her nice friends all waved to her and she was glad they did, because she felt suddenly very lonely and unhappy standing there with her case by her side while everybody else seemed to be saying 'Hullo' or 'Good-bye'. The flickering lamps on the platform did not shed much light and she was not sure who was going to meet her and she had swallowed a nasty lump in her throat when an arm was slipped round her shoulders and a slow, kind voice had said:

'Why, m'dear, I reckon you must be little Jane coming to stay along of us … Have you got a kiss for your Uncle William?' and before she could say a word she was lifted off her feet and given a good hug. Then she had laughed — and it would have been just as easy to cry — and looked up at him when he set her down again and felt much happier at once because he looked so nice and brown and friendly. He smelt nice too and his face was rough and prickly and his eyes crinkled at the corners.

Then he took the suitcase in one hand and her own hand in the other and set off down the platform to where the guard was helping an old porter to get some luggage out of his van. Her trunk was already on the platform so her uncle had said something to the porter and then led her out into the station yard.

As she lay now in her warm nest she recalled how very cold it had been when Uncle William had helped her into the battered-looking little car and wrapped a rug round her.

She could not remember much more of the journey, which was not very comfortable because her head ached and her feet got cold and the car smelt of petrol which was horrid. Once or twice Uncle William looked down at her and smiled his crinkly smile but he didn't bother her with questions much and by the end of their journey she was too tired to notice anything. She did realize though that the car had stopped in a farmyard, for when her uncle helped her out she could see the shapes of barns and ricks and big buildings all round her against a darkening sky.

Then a door had opened to let out a great gushing stream of golden light and she had been caught up again in strong arms and pressed to a warm, soft bosom.

After that everything was hazy although she seemed to remember being undressed before a kitchen range in which a fierce fire was glowing and noticing a rug made of scraps of gaily coloured rags. Next there was bread and milk — very sweet and hot — in a bowl and then this lovely soft bed which was already warm when she snuggled down into it.

And now it was morning again and here she was in her new home and it was exciting to think that everything she could see now and everything she would see to-day would be new. This was really the most exciting thing that had ever happened to her. Nothing would be the same and she would have time to explore everything for the first time, and everything this morning included Uncle William and Aunt Kate because she had not had time or opportunity to get to know them very well last night.

She sat up in bed and shivered as the cold struck through her thin pyjamas. The room was filled with a cold, clear light that was certainly not sunlight and Jane guessed that it must be very early. She wondered if she ought to get up and dress but felt rather shy about this. And she was sure that she would not know her way about the house which had seemed to be full of dark, winding passages when her aunt had led her upstairs last night.

But there was something very curious about the light so she plucked up her courage and jumped out of bed. The linoleum was icy to her bare feet but she forgot socks or slippers when she reached the window and looked out on to a strange, white world.

While she had slept the snow had fallen and although it had been too dark for her to see her new home when she had arrived, anything which she might have recognized was now smothered under a blanket of snow.

Directly outside her window was a sloping roof and it was the reflection from the snow on these tiles that filled her room with the curious, clear light. Jane had seen snow before of course but it had never seemed as white and clean as this. At home in the streets it had turned brown and slushy almost as quickly as it had fallen and even in their narrow little garden it had seemed reluctant to stay for long.

But here it was very different. This snow was thick and white like the icing Jane had been lucky enough to have on her tenth birthday cake. There were no marks on it anywhere. Nothing yet had touched it. Nothing had spoiled its crystal beauty and, as she watched with chattering teeth, the sky over beyond the tree tops in front of her blushed a delicate pink and the flat, white snow blushed too in sympathy as the sun — red, fiery and enormous — slipped up over the edge of the world and began a new day.

Jane ran back to the chair by her bed and put on some clothes as quickly as she could. It was almost certainly too early to go downstairs to breakfast but it was too exciting to stay in bed. This was the first sunrise she had seen and, as her window faced the east, she was soon able to feel the warmth and comfort of its rays. She leaned her elbows on the narrow sill and watched the cold, white world waken into life. First she noticed how the clouds above the rising sun were flushed with lovely pink and then she looked down and wondered what the snow was hiding. Below her gabled window and the sloping roof on which the snow lay so thickly was a garden — but a garden very different from the one at home. This garden, even under its winter covering, looked to be rather a muddle for there were many fruit trees in it and some bushes and a broken archway with an overgrown rose tree straggling over it. A wall made of rough grey stones divided the garden from the road which Jane imagined must cross the snow-covered waste in front of her. Then she remembered that this farm was called 'Moor End' and that last night her uncle had made some remark about 'crossing the common'. Jane had never been in such a lonely place before, for as far as she could see there was no living thing.

She opened the window, pulled her suitcase nearer and stood on it so that she could lean out and put her fingers in the snow on the roof. It was crisp on the top and soft and powdery underneath and quite dry. She let it run through her fingers and it sparkled in the sun. Then she leaned out a little farther and looked over to her left, where at the corner of the garden a gigantic elm tree stretched its delicate, bare branches to the sky. Right at the top of the tree she saw some big black blobs and wondered if they were old nests and how they could stay so securely so high up. Beyond the tree and the hedge she caught a glimpse of some white walls, and a dark roof. Then, as she watched, a plume of blue smoke rose slowly into the still air from a squat chimney.

The sun crept up the glowing sky and warmed Jane's cheek. Quite near a cock crowed a proud challenge to the morning and from somewhere below her in the garden a bird burst into song — a clear, sweet trill that sounded doubly sweet in the quiet of the morning. Then she saw the singer perched on the swaying branch of a fruit bush and as he turned to greet the sun she saw the splash of orange on his breast and knew him to be a robin.

Next came the sharp click of the latch on a gate and the sound of someone whistling. Jane slid back into the room and rubbed her tummy where the window-ledge had pressed into it and watched a man come round into the road. She could only see his head and shoulders because the rest of him was hidden by the garden wall but he looked so rough and wild that she wondered if he was a tramp. He was wearing a very old and battered soft felt hat with the brim turned down and had a sack over his shoulders. He was not near enough for her to see his face clearly but he looked very brown and quite old because he walked with a stoop. Jane wasn't sure what he was whistling but it sounded rather sad. He walked steadily through the snow and then, when he was quite near, looked up and saw her watching him from the open window. Jane felt herself blush scarlet as he stared at her but suddenly he pushed his hat back from his forehead to show a thatch of grey hair and smiled at her.

Perhaps he wasn't a tramp after all? He seemed nice and friendly so Jane rather shyly waved and the old man pulled his hat forward again and shuffled on.

Just as she was wondering what to do next her bedroom door opened and she turned round to see her aunt's surprised face.

'Good-morning, my dear, and how are you this morning?' she began almost before she had seen her at the window. Then — 'Goodness gracious me, child, and what are you doing out of your nice warm bed? And got your clothes on too! And the window open! And snow all down your skirt! Upon my soul but you gave me a shock I can tell you. Have you been walking in your sleep, child? Or couldn't you sleep in a strange bed? Are you all right, my dear? Not queer? And you haven't been coughing have you? You'll tell your auntie if you're not well won't you? … Well! Well! Come here and give me a kiss … and your face as cold as charity.'

Nobody would have said that Aunt Kate was as cold as charity for although it was a cold morning she was as warm as toast. Her hands were warm and her cheeks were glowing and she smelled of soap and something which Jane later knew to be wood smoke.

'May I come down now, Auntie? I haven't been up very long really but I think the snow woke me and then it was cold so I put my clothes on but I didn't know where to wash so I thought I'd wait till you came … And you didn't mind me opening the window did you? And I saw a little house over by the big tree and a tramp came out of it and I heard a robin and then I saw him and may I go and play in the snow?'

Her aunt held her at arm's length.

'A tramp, m'dear?'

Jane nodded. 'Um! Old and brown and with a very old hat and a sack over his shoulders. Almost like Rip Van Winkle but he hadn't got a long beard … And I'll tell you another thing. He was whistling!'

Aunt Kate laughed.

'Why that was old George! He's no tramp, m'dear. He works here and lives next door in the cottage. He's a lazy old rascal and don't you get talking to him too much for there's nothing he enjoys like a gossip … Now I'll show you the bathroom and then downstairs you come and sit by the fire and keep me company while I get the breakfast.'

When Jane came down the narrow little winding stair which led directly to the kitchen she felt that she had never been in a friendlier room. It had been lovely last night when she had been tired, but this morning everything was so clean and bright with the brass gleaming and the flickering light of the fire throwing quaint shadows round the walls and over the table with its gay, checked cloth that Jane fell in love with it at once. There was a luscious smell of frying bacon too and quite suddenly she realized that she had never felt so hungry before. She couldn't remember really *wanting* a meal for so long that this sudden hunger made her feel quite shaky. All the time she had been ill everybody had tried to make her eat when she didn't really want to, but now the smell of the bacon and the sight of a big crusty loaf on the dresser made her mouth water.

'Now you'll be having a cup o' tea with me, my dear,' her aunt said as she bustled to and fro. 'There's nothing like a cup o' tea in the morning and this will warm you up … You can be drinking the milk that they say is so good for you for the rest of the day but hot tea is just what you need now … Sit down by the fire on that little stool and make your uncle a bit o' toast and drink this … My! But you're a thin little thing, aren't you?'

And before Jane could answer she found herself on a wooden stool in front of the fire with a toasting fork in one hand and a mug of tea in the other. Then her aunt cut some bread and when she wasn't looking Jane popped some of the crusty crumbs in her mouth. The tea was hot and strong and bitter. The firelight glowed brightly between the bars and was comfortingly warm on her face. She felt that her cheeks must be toasting in lines just as the bread at the end of the fork was doing. Rather like a tiger with his stripes, she thought, as she burned her fingers turning the toast!

'When's Uncle coming down?' she asked shyly as her aunt came in from the scullery.

'Coming down? Why, he's been down these two hours or more, m'dear. He'll be in soon for his breakfast … On a farm we're all up afore the light in the winter … Your uncle's been seeing the cows be properly milked and it'll be hard for him getting the milk to town this morning with the snow.'

'When can I go out and play in it, please?' Jane asked with one hand to her burning face.

'Plenty of time for that,' Aunt Kate replied. 'I'll be showing you the chickens and ducks after breakfast and you can be learning how to feed them ... How many pieces of toast have you done? Only three? ... Your uncle will eat six but maybe he'll be so surprised to get any that he'll think it a Sunday, for as a rule we only have toast o' Sundays. We don't like the snow on a farm except that it fills the wells and starts the springs breaking again for it makes more work than usual what with fetching hay from the barns for the stock ...'

'What's stock, Auntie?'

'Stock? Why bless the child! Livestock, o' course. All the animals and the like. Now here's your uncle I'll be bound for I can hear him knocking his boots on the wall outside.'

So Jane hurried with the last piece of toast and stood up for a kiss when her uncle came in blowing on his hands and stamping his feet.

'My word!' he said, as he lifted her up, 'I can see I'm going to be a lucky chap while young Janey is with us! Toast on a week-day! Why the week'll be going backwards next!' but before Jane could answer he had sat himself down and was half-way through his bacon and eggs. And when she sat down herself that hungry feeling came back and she had nothing more to say until she had cleared her plate and started on some toast and marmalade. Long before she had finished her uncle had tossed down two mugs of scalding tea, tickled her neck as he passed behind her chair and gone out again. By this time Jane felt that so much had happened to her since she first woke that her first day at Moor End was ending rather than just beginning.

When she had finished her breakfast she helped Aunt Kate carry out the dirty crockery into the stone-floored scullery, where she was puzzled by the sight of a big brick copper and a rainwater pump, and then she was told to run for her coat and rubber boots. When she came downstairs again her aunt was ladling a smelly mess out of a big iron saucepan into a pail and when Jane wrinkled her nose in disgust she said, 'You may not like it, my dear, but the fowls do and if you like eggs you must look after the chickens. Just behind the scullery door you'll find a big box of meal. There's an old bowl on the top and I want two bowlfuls of the meal in here ... Make yourself useful, my dear, and you'll be saving your auntie's legs miles a day afore long.'

Jane found the meal and watched it being mixed into the pail with the mess and then followed her aunt out of the back door. The snow was as nice as it had looked from her window and outside the back door — which was really at the side — was the farmyard through which they had driven last night in the dusk. On the left was an enormous shed open at the front where the farm carts and some other weird-looking machines were stored. Opposite the back door was an old barn with black wooden walls and a roof which sloped unevenly down towards the road. To the right Jane caught an exciting glimpse of another barn with what looked like half a door and guessed correctly that this was the stable. Beyond the big barn was a farm gate leading to the rick-yard where the great stacks were now covered with roofs of snow and looked rather like the birthday cakes of giants! But Jane had no time to stop and look around because her aunt, in an extraordinary old coat and with a man's hat on her head, was plodding through the snow towards the farm gate. She was followed by several agitated hens who emerged from underneath the shelter of some farm carts and tried to run through the snow after her and the steaming pail. Jane ran ahead and tried to open the gate but her aunt had to show her how to lift it slightly up and towards her before it swung open easily enough. She danced through and saw that there were big double doors to the barn on this side also and another long shed which could not be seen from the house. Then her aunt called her back and told her to shut the gate.

'That's your first farming lesson, my dear. Always close a gate after you because that's what they're for. If you leave 'em open the cattle will get out and no end o' harm done and trouble to be taken.'

By the time Jane was at her side again a crowd of chickens — white and black and golden-brown — and some proud cocks too were all dashing towards them to another gate at the far side of the rickyard. The four hens who had somehow got out of this field into the barns were still following them as best they could and squawking excitedly, as they fluttered and scrambled over the snow. Then Aunt Kate unlatched this smaller gate and Jane followed her through snow and chickens to the feeding troughs near some little black huts

Jane ran ahead to open the gate for her aunt.

on wheels. The mess was poured into the troughs and then Jane was shown how the nesting boxes at the back of each of the huts were opened and she was allowed to put her hand into each nest and see if there were any eggs. She found a few which she placed carefully into the empty pail, but broke one of them by pressing it too hard when she picked it out of the nest. She was shown how the huts had to be cleaned and how the special water containers must be kept full of fresh water. Aunt Kate explained that a man called Alfie usually did the cleaning and feeding but that he had been ill since Christmas and that she had been meaning to go down to the village one day to see how he was getting on. She told Jane also that there were never many eggs first thing in the morning.

After a few days Jane got used to her aunt's way of talking and realized that although her tongue was rarely still she never said an unkind word about anybody or anything. She was never idle for even when she had time to sit down her fingers were busy with knitting needles and on the very first day Jane was promised a new jersey in any colour she fancied. But this first day was such a thrill that she was tired by dinner-time and fell asleep afterwards in her uncle's rocking chair by the kitchen fire. She couldn't remember a morning in which so many things had happened, for after the chickens had been fed, Uncle William had met them and led her away to new delights. First he had taken her into a big yard which was roofed at one end and under which twenty or thirty cows were sheltering. Jane did not think she cared for cows at all for these were very large and they all stared at her with big brown eyes while their jaws moved sideways with a peculiar crunching sound. She held tight to her uncle's hand as he led her across the yard, where the snow was already dirty where the cattle had trampled it into the thick straw.

The old man whom Jane had seen from her window was carrying a big bundle of hay on a pitchfork and filling the racks so that the cows could eat it without getting it dirty. As he went back to the barns for more his master stopped him.

'George,' he said, 'this is Miss Jane come along to live with us. She's been sick and we be going to make her well at Moor End. Take care of her, George, but don't spend all day gossiping — and, Jane my dear, you mind what George says and don't get in his way and interfere with his work and remember he's been on this farm as long as I have.'

Old George pushed his hat back from his forehead and grinned at Jane. It was a nice friendly smile but she did wish that he had more teeth. He would have looked so much nicer! Then Uncle William took her close up to the cows and she gripped his fingers hard because she wouldn't show him that she was scared and said suddenly, 'I think they're lovely, Uncle, but haven't they grown any horns yet? How do they toss people?'

'This sort never grow horns. They're called Red Polls and that's easy to remember. There's another sort called Shorthorns and they're easy to know too but we haven't got any of those at Moor End now. 'll take you to the market one day … No need ever to be afraid of cows, m'dear. They won't hurt you. They're hungry now and they hate the snow but George keeps 'em snug in here!'

And from there he took her to see the milking sheds where a cheerful red-faced girl in rubber boots was cleaning out the stalls and swilling the concrete floor. It was very cold here but Jane made up her mind to come back later and watch the cows being milked.

The great barn into which they went next seemed as lofty as a cathedral and indeed the wooden roof was crossed with beams and supported by pillars just like a church. Her uncle showed her the big bins where the grain was stored and the sacks of potatoes that were covered with straw to keep them safe from frost. On the floor was an ugly-looking machine with a large circular knife and this he explained was for cutting up swedes and mangolds. 'George is my stockman, and it be part of his work to keep the stock fed. Cattle must have roots in winter and he cuts 'em up in here every day ... Don't play with it, my dear, else you'll cut your finger off.'

Next he led the way through the great barn to the stable and Jane was introduced to three enormous horses called Short, Charlie and Primrose. Uncle William had a word and a pat for each of them in their stalls and promised his niece a ride one day.

The next excitement was Sally who came bounding up to her master when they went out into the snow and sunshine again. Sally was a golden cocker spaniel with soft brown eyes and great, flopping, silken ears. Jane squealed with joy and flung her arms round her and Sally licked her face as if she'd known her all her life.

Her uncle laughed. 'She's not much of a farm dog really but she was given us two years past Easter and your aunt's taken to her. You'd better take Sally round with you while you're with us, Janey. She'll be company for you and the exercise won't do her any harm ... Now you'd better trot round on your own for a bit, my dear, but don't get too tired or cold. Your aunt'll be in the kitchen if you want her.'

Jane's eyes had filled with tears at the mention of Sally but she felt too shy to thank her uncle properly. Fancy saying 'take Sally round with you' just as if it was possible to lend a lovely dog to anyone as easily as that! And perhaps Sally wouldn't want to come with her? That was a terrible thought! She looked up at her uncle who was closing the stable door and then down at the dog who was watching him and wagging her stump of a tail.

'I can't say thank-you enough, Uncle. It's the most wonderful thing that has ever happened to me ... But do you think she'll come with me?'

'Sally!' her uncle said sharply and the dog jumped up at him and dirtied his jacket with her paws. 'Sally! This is Janey. Take care of her.' And he walked off whistling softly between his teeth.

Jane rested her hand on the dog's head and then knelt down beside her again on the snow. 'Sally darling,' she whispered, 'I do want a special friend here so badly. I'm lonely really. Will you stay with me?' From that moment Sally and Jane went nearly everywhere together.

The snow was still on the ground next morning and at breakfast Uncle William remarked that there was more on the way.

'Wind's getting up,' he said, between gulps of hot tea, 'but sun's out now and if you want to explore, Janey, you'd better go out now. Alfie's back this morning so he'll do the fowls for you, Mother.'

So Jane, wrapped up warmly, ran out into the sunshine and called for Sally, who came bounding and yelping round the corner of the house. Yesterday Jane had stayed round the farm but this morning she was going to explore. She wanted to be the first to run over the fresh snow on the common but more than anything she wanted to go up to the wood that crowned the hill opposite the house.

The road now was marked with the tracks of the cars and lorries which had passed since the snow fell, but no footsteps showed on the grass when Jane and Sally ran on to it. They ran uphill towards the field that separated the common from the wood and after a little, Jane noticed some strange markings on the snow and realized that they must be the tracks made by birds as they hopped over the frozen surface searching for food. There were other odd marks too — parallel rounded dents about four inches long looking as if a short, thick pencil had been gently pressed into the snow. At dinner time Uncle

William told her that these were the tracks made by the rabbits' strong hind legs.

Sally seemed to know that they were going to the wood, for she found a hole in the hedge by the gate and waited while Jane climbed over before trotting up a track at the side of the field. Jane stopped and looked back at Moor End Farm and its barns glowing in the sunshine. The buildings were far enough away to look rather like a doll's house or a model farm and she could actually see old George crossing the farmyard and her aunt shaking a duster out of an upstairs window. She shouted and waved but they could not hear her and all that happened was that some birds cluttered up out of the trees above her. When she turned Sally was waiting for her at the edge of the wood.

Now that she had actually arrived Jane was not quite sure that she wanted to go in, for it looked very dark and lonely. She went a little way up the path with Sally at her side but all was quiet and still and what she described later as 'ghosty'. Then it got darker and the wind rose and whispered through the close-set trees and shook down the snow from their branches with horrid little thuds. Sally meanwhile was whining excitedly in some bushes and when Jane stopped under some low branches she saw her scratching madly at a mound of freshly-turned brown earth. She was puzzled for a minute and then remembered that this mound must be a molehill — something she had been told about but had never seen before. She supposed that the mole must have his home under the little hill and was afraid that Sally might catch him and kill him so she dragged at the dog's collar and pulled her back to the path.

Jane was wrong about the mole living under the hillock for although he does live underground his home, or fortress as it is sometimes called, is under a much bigger hill which is usually hidden beneath a bush. The smaller hillocks of fresh earth are thrown up by the mole as he burrows just under the surface of the ground in his search for worms.

There was not much snow under the brambles and bushes and in one sheltered spot Jane found some tiny, golden flowers nestling close to the ground among rich, dark green leaves.

'They're like gold stars that never go out,' she told Sally as she went down on her knees. 'They're the only flowers alive in the snow. I must take them home.' She picked a few, ran out of the wood into the sunshine and down the hill to Moor End.

Aunt Kate was busy with the dinner so Jane rummaged about in a cupboard under the stairs and found a little blue jar into which she put the golden stars. She hoped her uncle would notice them in front of his plate at dinner-time but he seemed to be too hungry and in too much of a hurry to notice anything when he did come in and she felt too shy to show him. When she was helping her aunt clear away later though she asked her what they were and why they grew in the snow.

'They're so brave, Auntie. They were all alone and nearly hidden and it's such a cold time for flowers.'

'Why, child, they're naught but celandines. They're common as weeds everywhere!'

'Well I don't think they're common anyway and I've got a better name for them. I'm going to call them Gold Stars.'

✕

Two days later the weather changed. When Jane went out into the garden after breakfast with scraps for the birds, patches of grass were showing on the lawn. The branches of the trees were dripping and the ground felt wet and squelchy under her rubber boots.

'I'll be able to see what the country is like to-day,' she thought. 'All I've seen so far is snow … I hope I like it when it comes to life.' And all through that day the wind blew warm from the south-west and, as the sun cleared away the clouds, a green world broke through the crust of white. The road gleamed and tinkled with running water; great slabs of melting snow slithered from the roofs and thudded on to the ground beneath. The robin, which Jane had seen on her first morning, sang lustily from the bare branches of the fruit trees and followed her cheekily as she explored the garden. She saw the melting snow fall from the strange shapes which now revealed themselves as brussels sprouts and cabbages; she saw the remains of old nests hidden in the thickness of the hawthorn hedge and, in a sheltered corner by the old stone wall, she found the first snowdrops of the year. There were only four — so frail and delicate in their fragile beauty that she almost feared to touch them.

'They're as white as the snow,' she whispered as she put her hands round them to warm them, 'and I know now why they are called snowdrops … but I wonder why they always hang their heads?'

At dinner-time Uncle William came in splashed with mud. She heard him struggling out of his great rubber boots by the back door and ran to meet him.

'Well, my Janey,' he said as he lifted her up on to the copper in the scullery, 'it's a good thing the weather's broken. Now we can get on a bit in the fields.' But later, when he had finished his first helping of meat, he looked across at his wife and said as he nodded towards Jane, 'She's not lonely is she? Maybe we ought to get some youngsters out here for her!'

Aunt Kate laughed. 'She'll make friends soon enough I'll be bound. She's happy enough running around with Sally, aren't you, Jane?' Jane nodded. There was so much to see and to do in this strange new life that she hadn't had time to miss someone of her own age. Besides she had Sally now and secretly she rather enjoyed being by herself. She had spent so long in bed when she was ill and made up so many adventures for herself then, that she was still quite happy making her own fun. But it was rather strange that she should meet two new friends for the first time, that very afternoon.

'Can I go out exploring?' she asked her aunt when she had helped to clear away the dinner things. 'I'd like to go up the lane and see where it leads now the snow has gone. I'll take Sally and be back to tea.'

'Don't get lost then because we'd be missing you now if you don't come back to us. And don't go too far and get tired else we'll be getting into trouble from your mother.'

The sun was still shining when Jane and Sally set out up the lane that led to the top of the hill. She had never been this way before and she knew now that, on that first evening when her uncle had brought her from the station in the dusk, they had come from the opposite direction and crossed the common before arriving at the farm. She was still on the same road but it seemed more exciting as it left the open country behind and wound uphill between deep banks crowned with thick hedges. She knew that on the other side of the left-hand hedge was a field, beyond which was the wood where she had found the gold-starred celandine. But there had always been something exciting about the top of a hill to Jane because you never knew what you were going to see when you got to the top, and this lane was particular fun because she couldn't see over the hedges and every one of its many corners was a surprise.

The water from the melting snow was rushing down each side of the lane and several times Jane had to stop and clear away some rubbish with the toe of her boot to help it on its way. Great white and grey clouds sailed across the blue sky and when Jane stopped to look over a gate she could see

Jane found a lovely place to sit, and felt rather King-of-the-Castle.

the shadows chasing each other across the patchwork of her uncle's fields.

At last she reached the brow of the hill and it was as exciting as she had hoped, for now the country opened out below her and she looked down into a wide and lovely valley. Far away, so that it looked like a collection of toy models, a village clustered round a grey church. As she watched, the sun rushed out from behind a woolly cloud and touched, with a magic golden finger, the weathercock on the top of the church spire, so that it flamed for a second like fire. Still patched with snow the little fields spread like a carpet below her and here and there a farmhouse with barns and golden ricks was clearly seen. Across the plain ran, straight as a ruler, a railway line and she saw a toy train puffing and crawling across the picture.

On her left there was a break in the high hedge where a rough cart-track joined the lane. A little way along this path on the left three mighty trees crowned a little knoll.

'If I could get up there,' Jane thought, 'I'd be on the top of the world. I could see more than I can see from here … Come on, Sally darling. Let's make that our secret place.'

Chalk showed white through the sides of the little hill and when Jane began to scramble up she noticed that the roots of the trees pushed through the soil so that they seemed to be clutching and clawing into the earth. She used the roots to pull herself up and then, rather out of breath, sat down on a flat tree-stump at the edge of the hill. She could not really see very much more than from the road but it was a lovely place she had found and she did feel rather 'King-of-the-Castle'. Sally came back panting and sat, with lolling tongue, with her head against Jane's knee, while the little girl stroked her silky ear.

Under the trees, whose branches spread wide and low, the ground was covered with twigs and a carpet of black husks and little brown, triangular nuts. Jane was wondering if these were good to eat and what the trees with their smooth grey trunks were called, when Sally growled softly and she turned round to see a boy, of about her own age, coming along the track from the road. He was bare-headed and very fair and was wearing a blue jersey with a polo collar and light corduroy shorts into the pockets of which his hands were thrust. He looked surprised when he saw her but came on steadily enough with a smile on his face. Jane got up, smiled shyly in return, and they both waited for the other to speak first.

'Hullo,' said the boy at last. 'Who are you? Have you come to see the bramblings too?'

Jane didn't know who the bramblings might be but wondered whether they were some friends whom the boy was going to meet here, so she just shook her head and said, 'Not specially I haven't, thank you. I just thought it looked a jolly place to be in. I like looking at things from high up.'

'So do I,' said the boy. 'What's your name? Mine's Richard Herrick and I live at the rectory and here's my father coming. The bramblings was his idea but we're both keen.'

'Oh!' said Jane as if she understood, but still feeling rather shy. 'That's fun too isn't it? My name's Jane and this is my dog — or truthfully she belongs to my Aunt Kate, I s'pose — and her name is Sally.'

Then a tall, jolly-looking man dressed in a long, black garment with a leather belt round his waist came along the path and Jane could see at once that he was Richard's father because his eyes were blue too and although he had not got very much hair left what he had got was just as fair. So Jane stood on the tree-stump while the tall man and the small boy smiled up at her and somehow Jane knew that they all liked each other very much and that they were going to be friends.

'Her name's Jane, Father, and her dog is called Sally.'

'I know Sally,' the parson said. 'She lives at Moor End ... and I know who you must be too, young lady, for I heard you were coming to stay with our good friends the Watsons ... Stay where you are, Jane, and we'll come up. We must get to know each other and you must come to the rectory and see the rest of the family whenever you want to.'

Then the man and the boy climbed up the chalky slope and shook hands very solemnly with Jane and Sally wagged her tail and fawned over Mr Herrick in a shameless way.

'If we make too much noise they won't come,' Richard said after a little. 'I would like to see them again, wouldn't you, Jane?'

Jane took a deep breath, went very red, and said bravely, 'If you mean the bramblings I expect I'd like to see them, but I don't know what they are. You see I've never really been in the country before and I don't know anything about trees and flowers and birds — 'cept I know a robin of course! I don't even know what these big trees are called.'

Mr Herrick put an arm round her shoulders and pulled her down on the stump beside him.

'Well spoken Jane,' he said, 'and don't you worry about not knowing. The stupid people are those who don't know and are afraid to confess it ... If you'll be friends with us we'll try and tell you all sorts of things about the country ... We came here to-day, Jane, to see some birds called bramblings ... We're both keen on birds and in the holidays and on Saturdays in term-time Richard comes visiting with me and we see who can spot the most birds ... Now if you'll give me time to light my pipe I'll risk Mrs Smithson's anger and tell you about bramblings and beech trees.'

'Who's Mrs Smithson?' Jane asked wondering who would ever be so stupid as to be angry with this nice man.

'Mrs Smithson is very old and has been in bed for eight years. She lives in Jasmine Cottage, the other side of Moor End Common, and I go and have tea with her every Thursday. I'm supposed to cheer her up but generally it's the other way round.'

'I think she's an old witch,' Richard said suddenly. 'She looks like one anyway.'

Jane wanted to giggle at this but Mr Herrick was rather cross and told Richard not to speak about other people like that again even in fun. Then he got his pipe alight, asked Jane if she was cold, twisted round on the stump so that they all faced the trees with their backs to the path and started to talk quietly.

'These trees are beech trees and you will know them by their smooth, grey bark and by the way the branches spread wide and very low over the ground. In summer the small leaves of the beech are so thick that not much sunshine can reach through. The fruit of the beech is in those hard, bristly balls of which you see the husks now on the ground. Not every year — I think it's every fifth year — two little brown triangular "nuts" which are inside each of the little balls are filled and very nice to eat. Other years these "nuts" are nothing but empty shells. Last autumn the beech harvest was good and both squirrels and badgers and some children from the rectory came here to collect the nuts. And there is a lovely bird, called the brambling, which likes beech nuts — which are generally called beech mast by the way — more than anything else, and we came here to-day hoping to see some. If we're quiet I think they'll come. You won't see the brambling in the summer-time because he lives somewhere else then. I expect you know that many of our birds like the swallows, the martins and the cuckoos come to us for the summer and fly home again in the autumn. The brambling is a winter visitor although he belongs to the same family as the finches … Now I'll keep quiet for five minutes and we'll see whether he comes.'

'Can I ask something first, please?' Jane said. 'Why are the roots of these trees sticking out of the ground? Won't they fall over in a storm?'

'I don't really know why some roots are so near the surface,' Mr Herrick replied, 'but perhaps it's something to do with the chalk. Beech trees love chalk and you will always see them at their grandest on chalky soil. Now keep still and we'll look for the bramblings.'

They heard a car roaring up the road behind them; they heard the wind sighing in the high branches of the beech trees and the drip of melting snow, and then Mr Herrick suddenly took his pipe from his mouth and pointed with the stem as, with a flash of white, a small bird flew under the low branches of the nearest tree. Richard gripped Jane's arm and whispered, 'And there's his mate! Look!'

Jane could see them clearly now that they had both settled and were eagerly picking and pecking among the mast. The nearer bird had a glossy head with a short, hard little beak. His tail was brown and when he spread his wings to flutter to the next tree they saw that they were barred with white and chestnut. Underneath he was white and altogether was a very a handsome little fellow. His mate was browner.

For five minutes they watched the bramblings and then Jane shivered and Mr Herrick got up and knocked the ashes out of his pipe against the tree-stump.

'Come on,' he said. 'It's getting cold. I've got the car in the road and we'll soon have you home, Jane. I'm afraid Mrs Smithson will be very angry with me and she'll probably have drunk all my tea.'

'Then you'd better come and have some with us,' Jane said bravely but Mr Herrick only laughed and shook his head as they slithered down the side of the knoll.

Sally jumped into the back of the car with the children but almost before they could exchange a word they were back at Moor End and Uncle William had come out of the farmyard to see what visitors were coming in a car. He shook hands with Mr Herrick and asked Richard to come in and have tea with Jane.

'You can pick him up in half-an-hour on your way back, Rector. We'll be glad of his company and so will Jane, I'll be bound.'

Later that evening when the shutters were up and the rising wind howled round the old house and the tea things had been put away and Richard had gone, Jane sat on the stool at her aunt's feet and watched the fireglow between the bars and was quite, quite sure that this had been the happiest day of her life.

'And I'm to go and see them all whenever I like,' she said to herself, 'and Mr Herrick says I can go visiting with him and Richard and look for birds too ... An' Richard says there's lots more to see in the spring and summer ...' and here she fell asleep with her head against Mrs Watson's knee.

February

Jane woke to hear the rain rattling on the roof outside her window and gurgling happily down the gutters. It made little splashing noises on the window-sill too and occasionally there was a louder thud as a big drop came down the chimney and plopped on to the stone hearth.

Although she was only half awake Jane was particularly disappointed about the rain because she had an idea that there was something special happening to-day and when you were going to do something exciting, nice weather always helped. She snuggled down into the feather bed and then remembered that she was going to the rectory to tea. Mr Herrick and Richard were coming to fetch her in the car and she was to meet Susan and Peter Herrick for the first time. She wondered whether Susan and Peter were nicer than Richard but didn't think they could be because Richard was the best thing that had happened to her since she had come to Moor End. Since she had met him by the beech trees at the top of the hill she had discovered that he was nearly twelve and cycled every day to the station for a train journey to school. Susan went to the school in Townsend where Jane herself was going after Easter. Peter was only four and Richard didn't say much about him.

When she came down to breakfast Aunt Kate was vigorously scrambling eggs.

'Well, Janey,' she said, 'Do you know what they call to-day? Second of February be Candlemas and I allus remember my mother telling me:

If Candlemas day be fair and bright,
Winter will have another flight.
If Candlemas day be cloud and rain,
Then winter will not come again.

So by the look o' the morning the winter is over but that I *won't* believe … Now my dear just pass up your plate and we won't wait for your uncle.'

Later in the morning the rain stopped and fog crept down the valley from the wood on the hill and smothered the farm with a dingy, dripping blanket. Jane ran out to the barn to see if she could find a friend and discovered old George moodily slicing mangolds in the dangerous-looking machine. She still found it difficult to understand his slow speech and, as she hated to hurt his feelings by repeating 'I beg your pardon' it seemed safer to do all the talking herself. She sat down on a lumpy sack and chattered on while the machine whirred and the chips of yellow mangold fell on a pile by George's feet. Just outside the big open doors a trickle of water fell from a broken gutter above and Jane noticed how the falling drops had washed the soil away leaving a pattern of clean, gleaming pebbles. She watched the big drops fall and then ran out, raised her face and opened her mouth to taste the water. The first drop fell on her nose and was unexpectedly warm so she moved slightly as her uncle came round the corner of the stable and laughed at her.

'First lambs arrived last night, Janey. Three so far and one set o' twins. If it's fine tomorrow I'll take you up but it's too mucky now for you'd get stuck in the mud. Lambs allus seem to come at awkward times as Frank, my shepherd, says, but there ought to be more to-morrow.'

Then there was another excitement as a big lorry lurched and splashed into the farm yard and George had to stop cutting up mangolds and help the two men to load up with sacks of potatoes which he wheeled on a trolley from the back of the barn. There was not much Jane could do to help but she made them all laugh with her questions and was allowed to climb into the driver's seat and examine the picture of a beautiful film actress which was pinned up above the windscreen. So the morning slipped by and almost before she realized what had happened it was dinner time.

Mr Herrick and Richard arrived just after three o'clock when the sun was doing his best to chase the last of the fog away.

'Gosh!' Richard said when he saw Jane in her best blue coat and hat. 'Why are you dressed up like that? You're coming to see us — not going to church.'

'Thank you for looking so nice, Jane,' his father added. 'Don't take any notice of Richard. He's always untidy and is always getting into trouble for it at school. He doesn't know any better ... Boys are like that! Come and sit in front with me.'

After he had turned the car in the lane and they had waved to Aunt Kate he went on:

'The catkins are out, Jane. We saw them just now. I'll stop at the top of the hill and show you.' By the track that led to the beech trees he stopped and pointed to the high hedge where the fluffy 'lamb's tails' were dangling from the bare branches of the hazel.

'January is not too early to see them,' he said, 'but there were not many a fortnight ago. I love them because they mean that spring is on the way. Look Jane! When I shake them the pollen falls and you can catch it on the back of your hand.'

'Golden star dust,' Jane said. 'Lovely!'

Mr Herrick pulled the branch lower.

'Can you see some bright red threads on the tips of those little green buds? Those are the female flowers which are fertilized by the golden pollen from the male catkins and that is how we get our nuts in the autumn.'

Richard reached up and pulled off a twig with three fluffy tails.

'Put it in your smart new coat, Janey,' he smiled, 'but be careful you don't spoil it.'

Although Richard laughed at her she pulled the catkins through her button-hole, where they dusted the blue cloth with gold, and sat back defiantly as the car rushed down the hill and over the bridge into the village of Townsend. The rectory was hidden behind a row of elm trees by the old grey church and Jane felt her heart banging hard against her ribs as the car crunched up the drive. But she needn't have been shy because Mrs Herrick was as nice as her husband and Susan was plump and rather stolid and Peter, who never left his sister's side, was just as friendly.

By now the sun was shining weakly, but because the grass was damp and water was still dripping from the trees Mrs Herrick lent Jane some rubber boots so that they could all stay out of doors until tea time. Richard showed her a secret camp he had made in an elm tree and allowed her to pull herself up to it by means of a hanging rope. From the little platform twelve feet from the ground they looked over the garden to the old stables where, he told her, there was an owl's nest. After tea they showed her a big room called the nursery at the top of the house. Here there were more old toys and books than Jane had ever seen in one room before and all of them in a most glorious muddle. Susan proudly produced her collection of wild flowers and Jane was fascinated to see how she had pressed each bloom with its stalk and leaves and then, when dry, fixed it into a big book.

'I'd like to make a collection too,' she said. 'Will you help me, Susan? It would be wonderful to take home flowers from Moor End that will last me all my life.'

Susan was delighted to be asked to help her new friend. Richard looked rather surprised at the idea of Jane wanting to keep flowers all her life but was too polite to say so. He thought Jane rather a baby in lots of ways but secretly he liked her very much, although it would never do to let her know. So while Susan and Peter ran downstairs to tell their mother about the flower collection Jane was going to make when the flowers were ready, Richard got out the old nursery gramophone and gave Jane a concert.

It was nearly dark when Uncle William called for her in the car on his way back from delivering some fowls to the butcher in Townsend and while she was putting her coat on in the hall he said:

'Why don't you youngsters come over to Moor End to tea to-morrow as 'tis Sunday and come up and see my new lambs with Janey first … And they'd best come in their old clothes, Mrs Herrick, and with their rubber boots too, but they'll be welcome however they come!'

And so it was agreed that if it was fine the rectory children — including Peter — should walk over after dinner and Jane should come to meet them and Mr Watson promised to bring them home in the car. Then Mrs Herrick kissed Jane and told her to come again soon and Peter hugged her round the knees and Susan said 'Good-bye till to-morrow Jane' so solemnly that everyone laughed, and that was the end of another very happy afternoon.

Next day the sun came up rather pale and watery again but the rain kept off and directly dinner was over Jane put on her boots and started off to meet her friends. At the top of the hill she ran along to the beech trees and climbed up just in time to see the Herricks toiling up the road towards her. She called to them and Richard saw her and shouted back.

'Stay there Jane, we'll come along ... Peter ought not to have come 'cos he's tired already!'

But when they did arrive and Peter was helped up the steep bank he was muttering fiercely.

'I'm not tired. Peter's *not* tired. Peter can walk nundred miles.'

'Uncle isn't coming,' Jane explained. 'He goes to sleep on Sunday afternoons but he told me how to get there and he told Frank this morning that we were coming so it will be all right! ... Are you rested now Peter or shall we wait a little longer?'

At the top of the hill Jane turned and saw the Herricks toiling up the road.

At this insult Peter went scarlet in the face with rage and started to scramble down the bank himself with the result that he missed his footing and rolled down the last few yards. Susan patted him clean, and dried his tears and nothing more was said about being tired as they turned into the first field gate and Jane led them along the hedge towards some higher ground three fields away.

The sun, though low in the pale sky, was shining fitfully and the brown field by which they were walking was tinged with a delicate green.

'It's like thick grass coming up,' Jane said but Richard explained that it was winter-sown wheat. Then he stopped suddenly and grabbed Jane's arm ... 'Look Janey! See that bird swooping and diving and almost tumbling in the air as he flies. That's a lapwing. Father told me that they do their courting at this time of the year and that's the male bird showing off. Here he comes! Look!'

Jane saw him clearly as he fluttered and twisted nearer to them. At first he seemed to be quite an ordinary black and white bird with rather a heavy, ponderous flight but when he was close she saw that he had an odd little crest on his head and that the feathers on his back and wings gleamed with blue and green and red. As he swooped over their heads and then back again he cried mournfully, 'Pee-wit! Pee-wit!'

'Some people call them peewits,' Richard went on, 'and another name for them is green plover. I like them ... I found a nest once but it isn't a nest really as they just lay their eggs in a little saucer place the mother scoops out of the soil or in the furrow of a ploughed field. They always lay four eggs all point inwards.... I read in one of my bird books that if the mother lapwing thinks you're going to find her nest she pretends to be hurt and flutters and limps and cries out to make you notice her and then leads you away from the nest.

I've never tried it though ... The eggs will be laid next month and it would be fun to find a nest ... We'll come.'

They climbed a stile and crossed another field and then Susan said:

'I can hear the lambs. Keep still everybody and you'll hear them too.'

And sure enough the sound of a plaintive baaing came to them on the breeze from over the hill and when they crossed another field Richard said, 'Sniff! I can smell sheep.'

They hurried on over the brow of the next hill and looked down into an enormous field which sloped down to a little stream. A hundred yards down the hedge was a black hut on wheels with a wisp of smoke coming from the little chimney. Lower down the hill was a square enclosure fenced with wooden hurdles. The children were standing high enough to look down into the big pen and could see that the ground was thick with straw on which sheep were lying and lambs were staggering about. On one side of the enclosure where the hurdles were interlaced with straw it looked as if there were a number of separate compartments or pens and the enclosure itself was divided by another wall of hurdles. The lambs and their mothers were on one side of this wall but on the other side the ewes were lying in the straw and there were no lambs to be seen.

'I wonder why?' Jane said when they had noticed this.

'Those are waiting to have their lambs, silly,' Richard replied. 'Look! That must be your uncle's shepherd just coming out of one of those little pens now ... Let's go and see him. Is he nice?'

'I don't know,' Jane replied, 'I've never seen him before but I'm sure he'll be nice because they're all so friendly round here.'

Then a dog barked and came bounding up towards them. He was an untidy looking dog with a shaggy grey coat and a sharp muzzle and Peter was just heard to remark:

'Take him away. I don't like him,' when there came a shrill whistle from the lambing pen and the dog stopped short, turned, and trotted back to the hut with his tail between his legs. The children walked down the hill and the shepherd came out of the pen and waited for them. He was short and stocky and wearing a cloth cap, corduroy trousers strapped below the knees and some sort of an apron with pockets in it round his waist. His face was brown and wrinkled and when Jane said, 'Good afternoon, Shepherd,' he smiled slowly and said,

'Master said you'd be coming oop. You be welcome … all of ye.'

After a little they became used to his broad speech and could understand nearly everything he said. He told them he had not taken his clothes off for four days and nights and that because the days were so short most of the lambs were born at night.

'Ten last night,' he said as he bent to light his pipe. 'Wind was a blowin' fierce round about midnight and 'tis allus the wind as brings the lambs.'

'What's the matter with that lamb,' Jane said suddenly. 'It's horrid. It's got two skins on.'

The shepherd laughed and explained that yesterday one weakly lamb had died and that last night he had lost a ewe. As he must find a mother to feed the motherless lamb he had taken the skin from the body of the dead lamb and tied it over the back of the orphan. After one or two doubtful sniffs the sorrowing ewe had accepted the frantic and hungry newcomer as her own.

At the foot of the hill the shepherd was waiting for them.

'Ewes be mighty particular mothers,' Frank explained, 'and they knows their lambs by smell. This un will take the little un now and I'll have that old skin off his back to-morrow.'

He went on to tell them that as soon as the lambs were two days old they were turned out into the field with their mothers and only fed in the outer enclosure of the lambing yard.

'Why don't you have all this business nearer the farm?' Richard asked.

Frank didn't find this quite so easy to explain although he seemed to know the answer but they gathered that this particular field was chosen because it faced south, caught all the winter sunshine that there was and was sheltered by the slope and the hedges from the north and the east. He told them too, much to Jane's disgust, that at the beginning of June, which was 'marking-time', all these jolly little lambs would be herded together and 'ear-marked' because every farmer marks his own lambs as his own by making a 'lug mark' on the right ear.

'How do you do it?' Susan asked solemnly.

'I cuts the edge of his yer and then cuts a slit in from the straight edge.'

'Well I think it's absolutely vile,' Jane said. 'And I'm going to talk to Uncle about it at tea time. Why can't you just write the name of each lamb on a label and tie it round its neck! If Uncle used that purple pencil which doesn't rub out they could wear their names round their necks for ever and you wouldn't have to torture them ... I think its beastly and I don't want to look at the lambs any more. May we look in your hut please?'

But there were so many things in the hut that it was difficult to see them all and it was very hot and smelly inside. A little fire was burning and a kettle was hissing gently on the top of the stove. There was a calendar for 1938 pinned on one wall and on the floor and on a shelf opposite the window were stacks of bottles — some empty and some full — and all sorts of metal cases with large labels on them. There was no bed but there was a large, low, wicker chair with some old cushions and a little folding table. From the roof hung a hurricane lamp.

Jane didn't care for the smell at all and was the first to back out into the open air; but Richard seemed fascinated by the bottles and jars and asked so many questions that Frank laughed and pushed him outside.

'Come oop and see me again, young genulmen ... I'll learn you to be a shepherd maybe ... Now you'd best all be away home for your tea. Quickest way is down by brook yonder and then follow her along till you be cum to edge o' wood by Moor End and if you be smart you'll be finding a liddle path through the wood ... but go through wood and don't follow brook ... Good day to ye all ...' and he ambled off down to the enclosure again.

'I love him very much,' Susan said unexpectedly but Peter sat down suddenly on the grass and rubbed his eyes.

'I shall have to take him on my back,' Richard said sadly. 'We were stupid to bring him ... All right, ALL RIGHT, Peter! Don't fuss ... We all know you can walk "nundred" miles but I'll give you a ride now!'

They went down to the gate in the corner of the field and walked along by the brook where the water was brown and muddy and tearing at the soft banks as it rushed along. Susan took Jane's hand as they squelched through the mud and said, 'My boots are too heavy. I hate them.'

Susan's life seemed to be made up of loves and hates and nothing in between, but Jane was rather glad that the little girl liked her because she loved them all and every minute of this exciting new life.

Richard, who was in front, stopped for a moment to put Peter down, and waited for the two girls.

'We'll come to this place in the hols and dam the stream here. It's nice and narrow and runs deep … I say, Janey! Does Mrs Watson make toast for tea? This is one of the days I want toast for tea and I'm jolly hungry this minute … I'm glad we came … Come on, Samson!'

'Samson,' asked Jane. 'Who's Samson?'

'Peter, of course. We call him Samson 'cos he's so small and not very strong yet.'

'Oh!' Jane said. 'I see.'

But she didn't.

Now they were near the wood. The sun was going down behind the hill and the trees at the top were outlined, hard and black, against the fiery, stormy sky. Lower down, the tree tops were merged into shadow and, just for a moment, Jane caught her breath in fear because the wood looked almost as if it was waiting to pounce or to slip down the hillside and smother them.

'If you're smart you'll find the way through the wood,' Richard said quietly. 'That's what he said and I think there's a bit of a track up the hill here … He told us to leave the stream, didn't he? Come on.'

But as they got nearer to the edge of the wood the track disappeared and Susan said that they were all bewitched and that the wood was magic. Jane had thought this the very first time she had been in it and if she had dared she would have liked to have held Richard's hand. But she didn't dare and she didn't think of it when he stooped low under some hazel bushes and called triumphantly:

'Here it is. Here's the path. Now we shan't be long.'

It was not much of a path and they had to walk in single file and once or twice crawl under trailing brambles. It was gloomy too and rather eerie and Jane noticed that even the fearless Richard was whistling loudly as he led the way. He stopped once and pointed to an untidy muddle of sticks in the fork of a high tree.

'Do you know what that is?' he asked Jane.

'Of course I do. It's a nest.'

'What sort of a nest?'

'A bird's nest of course!'

'It isn't a bird's nest. It's a squirrel's drey.'

'A dray is a thing horses pull ... A big cart.'

'P'raps it is but this is a squirrel's drey anyway and if you all stay still he'll come back ... The squirrels must have woken up from their winter sleep and they're busy building their house ... Be quiet, Peter! Don't sniff like a baby!'

Peter gulped, stood first on one leg then on the other, and held fast to Susan while they all waited at Richard's command. Then the squirrel came back like a flash of red lightning in the tree tops with a stick in his mouth. Jane saw his great bushy tail curled over his back as he jumped from a swaying branch into the top of the tree under which they were standing. In the fading light she glimpsed a flash of little black beady eyes staring down at them and then, with a flick of the glorious tail, he had gone again.

'There you are,' Richard said complacently. 'I told you it wasn't a bird's nest ... Come on!... Let's hurry!'

When they came out of the wood they saw the lights in the windows of Moor End and always after this Jane remembered to look for the little warm, comforting squares of light that welcomed her home when she was out in the dusk or the dark.

'We saw your light when we came out of the wood, Auntie,' Jane said as she took off her boots in the porch.

'We all of us be needing something to guide us along the road to home!' Mrs Watson smiled. 'There's some say a lighted farmhouse window means as much to a countryman as does a lighthouse to a sailor … But come along in all of you for you must be tired out … I've made some toast for your tea.'

March

Jane woke to sunshine — the first bright sunshine for many days — and to an unfamiliar throbbing. Since she had come to live in the country she had taken a much greater interest in the weather and every morning, as soon as she woke, she sat up in bed so that she could look out of the window.

This morning the curtains were rustling and blowing. A strong, cold breeze ruffled her hair and made her shiver as she reached for the eiderdown and pulled it round her. She could see that the sky was blue and clear and while she was still puzzling over the mysterious throbbing it was drowned by the lovely liquid song of a bird. Clear and strong, a pure whistle swept up to welcome the sun as Jane jumped out of bed and ran to the window.

'I know what it is,' she said to herself. 'Richard told me. It's a blackbird. I'm beginning to know the birds.'

He was swaying on a branch of the apple tree just a few yards from her. His black-as-jet plumage gleamed as if it had been polished; his bill was a vivid yellow and his bright and cheeky eye was ringed with orange. And how he sang!

Jane pursed her lips ready to whistle with him when she saw one of the farm cats slinking over the frost-powdered grass towards the apple tree.

'Fly away home, Blackie darling,' she called and the blackbird cocked his head at her and flew off down the hedge-side crying his wild alarm of 'chook chook' followed by that odd rattle which he always makes when he is frightened and that warns every other bird in hearing. The cat made off in disgust and Jane went to her bedroom door and whistled softly. There was a scrambling and scratching noise from below and Sally came bounding up to say 'Good morning'. Aunt Kate did not like dogs upstairs at Moor End and she said so more than once, but there was something so pathetic and appealing about Sally waiting in the hall for Jane's morning whistle that she pretended not to know of these early visits. After Sally had leaped upon the bed and licked her new mistress's face Jane washed and dressed and ran down to breakfast.

'Keep the door closed if you're going out, Jane,' her aunt called from the scullery. 'They've started threshing and the chaff blows in everywhere ... Seems to me your uncle always picks a windy day for threshing though it seems cold enough this morning for wind to be from east ... and that reminds me, young lady, to hope you've got your warm knickers on and no nonsense ... and you're not to go out in the yard after without a coat else I'll be dosing you up with something in bed and *that* I've no time for ... And here's your porridge and you'll come to no harm if you eat that up ...'

Then Uncle William came in rubbing his hands and scattering chaff on the spotless floor. He dropped a kiss on Jane's head as he always did, and when she asked him if she could come and help he nodded, because his mouth was full and then said:

'O' course you can, Janey. And bring a big stick to kill the rats!'

Jane shuddered. 'I don't have to do that, do I? You're teasing me, Uncle.'

'If you don't someone else will,' he twinkled. 'So you'd better come and see how it's done.'

When Jane went over later with Sally the rickyard seemed full of men. All the farm hands were there except Frank the shepherd and there were one or two faces she had never seen before. Between the stacks stood the threshing-machine which, until to-day, Jane had not seen outside the big, open barn where the carts were kept. It had always looked complicated but harmless, but now it was rumbling and shaking with life as it was tended and fed by its servants working around it. It must have had a big appetite because it needed ten servants to feed it! Some were on the top of the big rick tossing the sheaves from their pitchforks to others waiting below who, in turn, flung them on to the moving band which carried them to the thresher's hungry mouth. Uncle William was over by the tractor which, as usual, was making a hideous noise in supplying the power to the thresher. When he saw Jane he smiled and strolled over towards her, but stopped on the way to speak to two more men who were loading full sacks of grain on to a farm truck. Jane was beginning to realize that however much work there was to do on a farm nobody seemed to hurry. She had never seen her uncle or old George run anywhere, but the work was done just the same. Jane was not old enough to realize that those who work on the land know that you cannot hurry nature and that animals who are fussed and flustered and shouted at become suspicious and irritable and are not therefore the good servants of man that they are intended to be.

She looked up at the strange bareheaded young man on the top of the rick. He was wearing an old blue jersey over a khaki shirt and grinned cheekily at her. His arms moved slowly as he flung down the sheaves but although he never seemed to hurry he was working steadily and fast. George was like that too for he was always slow and gentle with his

Jane and Sally went over to the rickyard. The threshing machine was rumbling and shaking.

horses and although he was an old man Jane realized now how much work he could do in a day. And Uncle William only seemed to be in a hurry at meal times, which was rather silly of him but even now, on one of his busiest days, he had time to explain things to a little girl.

Jane smiled up at him and slipped her hand into his hard brown one. He was a very nice uncle and Sally jumped up too and licked his other hand. Then he took Jane round to the other side of the shaking, roaring monster and showed her the little chutes from which the golden grain was pouring into sacks fixed to receive it. Jane dabbled her hands in the glittering stream and then plunged them into the sack and let the corn run through her fingers. Each tiny, individual grain was smooth and hard and golden and she remembered how she had been told at school that life was waiting in every grain, and how the corn went to the miller for grinding into flour and then on to the baker to be made into our daily bread.

From the next chute came a stream of smaller grains mixed with some chaff and from the next a stream of dust and dirt and the seeds of weeds which had been harvested with the wheat. Uncle William explained how the thresher first beat out the grains from the ears and then shook and sifted them through revolving drums and eventually separated the good from the bad and flung out the straw on the other side.

'What happens to the straw?' Jane asked.

'It all goes back to the soil sometime m'dear. We'll make this lot into stacks again and autumn time when there's no more grass in the fields for cattle, George'll bring 'em in here and use the straw for bedding 'em down just like he's doing now ... And while they're in here the cows tread their own muck into the straw and that makes the manure we spread on the fields to make the grain or the roots grow again ... That's how it goes, Janey ... My father used to call it good husbandry and I reckon he's right for every good farmer ought to leave his land better than when he took it over, and I'll find that right difficult … You can stay and watch if you like but keep away from the tractor and that belt … Go up on the rick if you like with young Joe.'

So she climbed the ladder until she was higher than the threshing-machine and could see the sheaves of corn disappear into its hungry mouth.

'Young Joe' smiled a welcome and dropped his pitchfork to help her up and then told her to keep out of their way as he and his mate speared the sheaves and swung them down to the men waiting below. The wind was cold on the top of the stack but the sun shone brightly in the clear, blue sky and Jane could see the big elm tree towering above the roof of the house. To-day the delicate branches seemed tinged with red.

At eleven o'clock, when the stack was much lower, Aunt Kate came to the back door and held up a steaming mug. Jane knew that this was for her and scrambled down the ladder. She asked her aunt about the colour of the elm tree while she warmed her hands round the mug of hot cocoa.

'Never mind about the tree my child but just take your coat off *outside* if you please and shake it before you come in my clean kitchen … Just look at the mess you're making! You're smothered in chaff and it's in your hair as well. I do declare that you're as bad as your uncle!'

But Jane wanted to know why the tree looked red so she went out into the garden and looked again. It *was* red!

She walked over the grass with her mug between her hands and looked up through the branches to the rooks' nests high overhead. Now she could see that the tree was bearing buds of two different kinds. Some were quite small and rather pointed and others were larger and rounder and some of these were bursting into clusters of tiny red flowers. Higher up in the tree there seemed to be more of these flowers and Jane saw now why the branches had looked red in the sunlight. Later, when she asked Mr Herrick, he told her that the small buds were the leaves which did not burst until *after* the little red flowers had bloomed.

When she wandered back to the rickyard the stack on which they were working was very much smaller. The thresher was still roaring and shaking and belching out straw on one side and filling the sacks with golden grain on the other. Now Jane noticed for the first time that a low fence of wire netting had been fixed on stakes right round the stack and that two farm cats were inside the fence playing with half dead mice. Three strange terriers were trembling and yelping with excitement outside and two lads were standing near armed with heavy sticks.

Jane did not like the look of these preparations and went to find her uncle. He was weighing a sack of grain which one of his men had wheeled over from the thresher and did not look up until she tugged at his sleeve.

'What are the boys doing with those sticks?' she shouted above the din.

Her uncle looked surprised. 'Doing? Why waitin' for the rats to be sure. I told you about them.'

'Rats?'

'Aye! Rats! Rats and rabbits be greatest nuisance on a farm, Janey. Rats live under the stacks and eat grain that should be made into bread. Wire be there to keep them from escaping like … Where you be going, Jane?'

'I don't want to see them killed however beastly they are, thank you, Uncle. I'm going into the garden.'

A little later she heard some excited shouting and yelping and when she went back after tea the bodies of scores of horrid-looking rats were piled by the remains of the threshed stacks.

At five o'clock, the machine was stilled, and the men smiled good-night to Jane and Mr Watson after they had covered the half-finished stack and the thresher with tarpaulins. Old George had been carting the filled sacks and storing them in the barn and he was locking the padlock on the big doors when Jane went indoors with her uncle.

'Ninety sacks I reckon,' he said to Aunt Kate, as he took off his boots. 'Not too bad, the lads have worked well to-day and you needn't tell me your kitchen is full of chaff because we can see 'tis as clean as usual.'

Mrs Watson tossed her head as she poured out his tea.

They threshed for the next two days as well and then as soon as they had finished the cold wind dropped and Jane left her coat at home when she went out into the fields with her uncle.

'Come and see how George handles his horses,' he said. 'He's no good with a tractor but there's no man round here runs a straighter furrow for the taters than old George.'

There was one very big field close to the farm which was divided by a rough and muddy track and George was working on the side that ran uphill to the road. The horses drawing the plough plodded slowly down towards the path while George with his old hat over his eyes and his pipe between his teeth guided the plough which was cutting a deep furrow and throwing up the rich brown soil on each side.

'He's done eight this morning so far,' Mr Watson said. 'He's slow but no tractor could cut surer, straighter nor cleaner. If you want good work you've got to be patient, Janey.'

And sure enough the rich, dark, freshly turned furrows ran straight as rulers up the hill, getting smaller and narrower until they vanished. When the horses reached the edge of the field, old George clucked at them and swung hard on the handles of the great plough as they turned and started up hill again. Jane watched the soil curl over the edges of the pointed blade and was reminded of a big boat cutting through the water.

Suddenly Sally, at her side, yelped and Jane looked up to see something brown bounding in great leaps across the turned earth to the next field.

'Is that a rabbit, Uncle?'

'No, my dear. 'Tis a hare and I dare say if you watch carefully in these fields for a while you'll see the hares standing up and fighting each other. Mad as a March hare, they say, and 'tis true. This month, which is hares' courting time, the bucks often stand up and box each other.'

'Have you ever seen them, Uncle?'

'Surely I have. But it's only this time o' year they act so crazy so you keep a good look out for yourself.'

No man ran a straighter furrow for potatoes than old George.

On another ploughed field the soil had been broken up finely and now the tractor was drawing over it what looked like a long red box on wheels.

'Oats!' Mr Watson explained. 'Drilling we call it though I reckon you'd call it sowing. The seed is in the box and runs down the tubes into the liddle furrows made by the driller ... See how many rows we can drill at a time ... Like to get up tractor with Sidney, Jane?'

The tractor was uncomfortable and extremely noisy and Jane was just thinking that she would make a polite excuse to go back to her uncle when a familiar bird few up from the ground a few yards ahead of the tractor and with a piteous cry fluttered round their heads. Jane shouted and tugged at the driver's arm and with a cough and a splutter the tractor stopped.

'Look! We nearly ran over it. It's a nest with one egg in it. It's a lapwing isn't it?'

Over their heads the mother bird twisted and dipped, crying mournfully as Sidney jumped off and lifted Jane down beside him. Just six feet in front of them in a slight hollow in the soil lay a sharply pointed egg. It was olive in colour and heavily blotched with dark brown. As Jane went down on her knees beside it and cupped it, for a second, in her hands she almost cried for joy.

'It's the first I've ever found! Isn't it wonderful? I found it by myself, didn't I? You won't touch it, will you? You'll take care and drive the tractor round and leave her alone to lay some more eggs, *won't* you?'

The man smiled indulgently but he marked the place with a stick and when the tractor had roared into life and Jane was up beside him again he swung it clear and left the lapwing her new home.

'First egg, I reckon,' was all he said. ''Tis full early to see 'em much afore Easter time.'

'Thank you *so* much,' Jane said with such fervour that Sidney looked at her in astonishment.

'I'll leave stick there,' he said, 'an' you can cum back next week when she's sitting on her four.'

But it was more than a week before Jane came that way again. That evening after supper the telephone bell rang just as she was going up to bed.

''Tis for you Janey,' her uncle called from the hall. ''Tis a young man to speak to you.'

Now Jane was not at all used to the telephone and secretly was rather scared of it. And like all people who are nervous on the telephone she shouted.

'Is that you, Jane? Don't *yell* like that. You don't have to scream! Is it Jane speaking?'

Jane gulped.

'Yes,' she said. 'I'm Jane. Who are you please?'

'It's Richard you chump! Listen, Janey. What do you think has happened? Young Susan has got scarlet fever and they won't let me go to school ... I haven't had it. Have you?'

'It's no use Richard. I can't hear you.'

Richard repeated himself patiently.

'Don't be silly Jane. Of course you can hear if you listen. Have you had scarlet fever?'

'Yes, Richard, I have.'

'Well I haven't and its jolly lucky that I haven't 'cos I've got a holiday now. And if you've had it we can meet and I thought I'd come over to-morrow and we might make a birds' nest map.'

'A *what*, Richard?'

'Don't shout. A BIRDS' NEST MAP, I said ... Anyway I'll be over about ten in the morning and show you ... Bye Janey.'

Jane put the receiver down and found that her hands were shaking and sticky. When she explained what had happened and her aunt said, 'And how's the poor little lamb herself?' she realized that she had not even enquired about poor Susan!

Next morning, when Richard arrived at Moor End on his bicycle, she did ask him and he said:

'Oh! She's not too bad Mother says but she's a shocking colour! Won't it be a lark if I get it?'

Jane remembered her own scarlet fever and was quite certain that she had never thought of it as a lark. But boys were silly like that and she supposed it wiser to say nothing because he couldn't really mean it.

'I found this drawing book in the nursery,' Richard went on as he fumbled in his knapsack, 'and the pages are big enough for us to make a start. The idea is to choose a district and make a map of it and then mark on the map where we find nests. I've got some coloured inks at home somewhere and it might be a good idea to use a different coloured ink for each kind of nest ... We might have red for robin, and black for blackbird and blue for a thrush like her egg. What do you think?'

'I think it's a wonderful idea. Let's start right away ... Start the map *now!*'

Later they were sitting on the top bar of the farmyard gate. The sun was warm again to-day and the bitter wind of the threshing days had gone. Richard licked his pencil when he thought Jane wasn't looking — but she was — and started to draw a plan of the farm buildings, the garden and part of the lane where the hedges were high.

'... An' we'll make a log-book too ... You know, Jane? A book where we can keep a record of the date and kind of nest and where we found it and how many eggs and when they hatch. All that sort of thing...! Would you like to keep the log book if I start it off for you?'

Just then George came across the yard leading Primrose, and Richard jumped down and opened the gate for him.

'An' what be you two up to this marnin'?'

'We're going to look for birds' nests, George.'

'Ave a look just behind stable door then,' he said with a chuckle, 'an' see if you sees what I see just now.'

They ran across the yard and a little bird flashed past them as they fumbled with the catch on the bottom half of the stable door. Short, the oldest of the cart horses, was stamping and fidgeting in his stall and it was rather dark but Jane was the first to notice something moving between the wall and an old horse collar hanging just inside the door. She grabbed Richard's arm just as another bird flew out into the sunshine.

'That was a robin,' Richard said. 'I believe they're building now … Let's stay and watch.'

Richard was right. A pair of robins was building a nest within four feet of the horses and within a very few minutes each bird had visited the site seven times. One of them had only to go a few inches to find scraps of stuffing from the old, broken collar and not very much farther to find lengths of horse hair. It was probably the male bird who went farther afield and returned with moss and once with a length of wool. Many times during the day the children came back to the stable but the two robins were quite fearless and by five o'clock had finished their new home.

So the robin's was the first nest to be marked on the map, although quite early in the morning Jane reminded Richard of the rooks' in the elm tree so these were marked in as well as he could. He did not find the map as easy as he had imagined. He had seen it all so clearly in his mind but when he tried to get it down in the drawing book he found that the page was not big enough and it was difficult to sketch in the lane as well as the farm buildings. After several attempts he decided to put the farm and the garden on one page and the lane on another.

After they had watched the robins for a little they searched the thick hedge in the garden and Richard soon found a blackbird's nest with three eggs in it.

'That must be the blackbird that sings in the morning,' Jane said. 'Find me something to stand on, Richard, so that I can look in.'

They fetched a box from the wood-shed and Richard parted the prickly twigs of the hawthorn so that Jane could see down into the nest.

'It looks like a thrush's nest from the outside,' he explained, 'but you can always tell the difference because although both birds line their nests with mud the blackie adds a final layer of grass ... Can you see it, Jane? Put your finger in gently and feel it ... The thrush's nest is always plastered inside with *smooth* mud ... Now take out an egg gently and we'll look at it.'

'I'm afraid to, Richard. I might break it. And will the baby bird inside the egg die if the mother doesn't come back soon and warm it?'

Richard laughed, reached for an egg and dropped it into Jane's hand. It was warm and so light that she could hardly feel it on her palm.

'You'll remember the blackie's egg now won't you, Jane? It's nothing like the thrush's, which is a lovely bright blue spotted with black. This is greenish-blue and you can see that the speckles are brown.'

Although they searched the rest of the garden before dinner they did not find a thrush's nest; but they did find a starling's in a hole in the old apple tree outside Jane's bedroom window. They could not see the actual nest because the hole was too small but they did watch the pair of starlings carrying in fragments of straw.

'I don't think much of this bird,' Jane whispered as they stood quietly by the hedge. 'He's not a beauty, is he?'

'I suppose he's not as smart as the blackbird,' Richard replied. 'He's different isn't he? See how he's waddling and running over the grass now. The blackie hops. This chap's feathers have got purple and green in them ... There he goes again ... He's got another bit of straw.'

'What are the eggs like?'

'Pale blue. No spots. I'll find one for you one day, Jane ... Let's add this one to the map.'

Richard stayed to dinner and afterwards they searched the lane and part of the common. Jane found a thrush's nest at last in the fork of a holly tree in the hedge and Richard clasped her round the knees and lifted her up so that she could see the sky-blue eggs.

Higher up the road towards the beech trees and low in the hedge they found a nest with four tiny eggs the same colour as the thrush's but without the black spots.

'Hedge-sparrow,' Richard said. 'Father told me that it isn't really a sparrow at all and no relation to the house-sparrow you see round the farm yard and in towns. You don't often see this chap flying around. He seems to creep along on the ground under hedges and bushes looking for insects.'

'I shall remember the hedge-sparrow anyway,' Jane said, 'because of her lovely eggs ... I wonder, Richard, why it is that a dull little bird like this should lay such bright coloured eggs while I could hardly see that lapwing's egg I told you about 'cos it was the same colour as the ground.'

'That's why, I suppose,' Richard said. 'I mean that the lapwing's egg is camouflaged so that people and other big birds and animals like stoats shan't see them on the ground and steal them.'

'That doesn't explain why the hedge-sparrow's eggs which nobody can see are such a lovely blue and why the blackie's are different again. I can't understand ...'

And neither could Richard and after a little he said that he thought he would go home and look out his coloured inks and start to mark the map.

'And you write up the log book Jane. You can remember everything we've found to-day … If it's a lovely day to-morrow let's go and explore the wood and see what we can find there. I can't very well make a map of it but we'll keep a record of the nests and eggs we find and I'll bring some sandwiches and perhaps we could camp up there on our own … Now we'll go back for my bike and see if the robins have finished their nest in the stable.'

So they turned back towards Moor End until Jane stopped half-way down the hill and reached up for a spray of vivid white blossom on the hedge.

'I didn't see it when we came up. What is it, Richard? It's like a white star and it's got no leaves.'

'I can't remember,' Richard confessed. 'But it always comes first in the hedges and if it's out here I expect we shall see lots in the wood to-morrow. It's got sharp spikes so don't prick yourself… Here! Come down Jane. Something is moving in the ditch … Under those leaves. Look!'

Jane scrambled down and watched as he moved some rubbish aside.

'Gosh!' he said. 'It's a hedgehog! Watch, Janey! He's curling up into a ball.'

This was the first real hedgehog that Jane had ever seen although Mrs Tiggywinkle had been one of her earliest friends in a book. She couldn't help thinking now how funny this one would look dressed up in a lace cap and apron! But it was wonderful to see how the little animal protected itself because when Richard first uncovered it Jane could see its funny little face and snout and the prickles covering its back. Then, when it realized that it had been discovered, it tucked its head sideways and under and rolled itself into a tight ball with all the prickles erect. Jane put out a finger and touched one. It was very sharp!

Then Sally, who had been exploring higher up the lane, came rushing up and began to bark furiously when she had sniffed at the hedgehog in the ditch. But the least excited of them all was the hedgehog and although Sally tried to move it with her paw she only hurt herself.

'Let's leave it alone,' Jane pleaded. 'Sally! You're very naughty! Come here at once.'

Strangely enough they never saw the hedgehog again although Jane looked for it many times throughout the summer.

※

The next morning was as lovely as Jane had hoped it would be. Aunt Kate, although she looked suspiciously at the bright sunshine on the barn roof, agreed that Jane could take her lunch to the wood if she liked.

'Though why you should want to do so, my dear, is more than I can guess seeing that you could come back here and have a nice hot meal in comfort. But there! I never was one for these picnics but I've often noticed that it's those who come from the towns that want to go sitting all over the country ... But I must say Janey dear that you're looking as if you've never had a day's sickness in your life for you've filled out and you've some colour in your cheeks at last and your mother and your dad'll never know you when they see you at Easter ...'

'Auntie!' Jane shouted. 'What did you say? Are Mummy and Daddy coming to see me here?'

'There now! And I've let it slip out for we didn't mean to tell you yet and to make it more of a surprise like ... There, there, my darling child! What are you crying for? Of course they're coming to see you for your uncle thought they should and

Easter is in a fortnight and you and I will polish up the spare room a bit for them ... And after Easter if Dr Marshall says yes then it's school in Townsend for you, my Janey ... Isn't that a bicycle bell I can hear? And there's Master Richard himself! Be off with you and I'll have your sandwiches ready in ten minutes.'

Jane never forgot that day in the Round Wood by Moor End. There is always one day in the year when it seems that you can say 'Yesterday was winter but to-day spring has come' and often that day comes in March. In the streets of the town it is difficult to recognize that day although forsythia in a sunny corner and the gallant challenge of the frail and pink almond blossom are among the first signs of the year's awakening. Daffodils, of course, herald the spring happily and when Jane ran out to tell Richard of this morning's news the daffodils in the garden that yesterday had been yellow tinged sheaths of green were now nodding their lovely, frilled heads to welcome the sun.

'Father says that if we don't spoil the trees we can cut some pussy-willow for the church next Sunday. It's Palm Sunday, Janey. Will you come? We have a procession all round the church and go up to get our own palms.'

Jane thought she would. It was a long time since she had been to church.

When the sandwiches were ready they set off up the track by the hedge leading to the wood. It was only a week or so ago since they had come to it from the other side after watching the lambs and Jane remembered how, on that dark, wintry afternoon, she had felt afraid of it as it had loomed above her in the dusk. But this morning it was very different for the sun was shining brightly and a few fleecy, white clouds were sailing like blobs of cotton wool across the clear blue of the sky. Already some of the trees in the wood ahead of them showed a delicate green and, at their side, the tiny white star-like flowers that they had seen the previous evening hung about the thick hedge.

'I asked Father the name of this,' Richard said. 'It's blackthorn and the flowers come out before the leaves and that's why you can see the blackthorns so clearly. He said that they are the flowers of the sloe which is a little purple fruit but I can't remember what it is like.'

'What are these little green leaves on the other branches?'

'We used to call them 'bread and cheese' but I don't know why. They're the leaves of the hawthorn and they come before the flowers — not like the blackthorn. We had an old Nanny once who told us we were never to bring either blackthorn or hawthorn into the house 'cos both were unlucky. Seems silly, doesn't it?'

Then they reached the wood itself and this morning the sun was strong enough to filter through the branches of the trees and dapple the undergrowth with golden pools. And all around them the wood was full of bird song. At once they heard the blackbird's urgent warning and a clatter in the tree tops as some wood pigeons flew out into the open. Then a thrush sang in its lovely contralto and when they stood still the wood seemed to be full of little movements and rustlings and of chirrupings and whisperings.

'They're all so busy! That's what it is,' Jane whispered. 'The wood is waking up to-day and all the birds and animals are making their new homes ... Oh! Richard! Who's that? Someone is laughing at us.'

Even as she spoke there came again an eerie, harsh cackle of laughter from somewhere near.

'Stand quite still and we'll see him. It's a jay,' Richard whispered. 'I've seen them before in this wood.'

They were leaning against an oak tree just off the track and, after a little, the cackle came again and then Richard grabbed her arm and pointed ahead. She followed the pointing finger and saw the jay swaying at the top of a hawthorn bush — a very handsome gentleman indeed! His plumage was pinkish-brown and there was black and white on his head.

'He's got a crest on his head like the peewit,' Jane whispered under her breath and Richard nodded. Then, 'Watch him when he flies,' he said and clapped his hands sharply.

Up flew the jay with a harsh cry of alarm and Jane saw then that the wings were black and white and beautifully marked with bars or checks of a bright blue.

'I've got one of those blue feathers at home, Janey. I'll give it to you and you can wear it in your Sunday hat! Father says the jay is a bully and little birds are afraid of him. He eats baby birds and eggs too and destroys fruits in the gardens. Gamekeepers kill them same as they do rats and stoats and owls.'

Although they searched hard they could not find the jay's nest and after a little there were so many other things to see that they gave up looking for nests.

Jane and Sally discovered the secret glade on the south side of the wood. Richard was following a track uphill and they were keeping in touch with each other by whistling and calling when Jane crawled under a low hazel bush and found herself in fairyland. The sun was streaming straight down into a lovely little dell which was carpeted with a host of creamy white flowers all nodding and swaying as if they were whispering to each other. Jane bent to pick one and saw that the stalk was very slender and carried three delicately cut, dark-green leaves about half-way down. When she looked more closely she saw that some of the six-petalled starlike flowers were tinged with purple. They were the daintiest and prettiest wild flowers she had ever seen growing. Richard came crashing down through the wood at her call and broke into the dell where some larch trees made a feathery green screen at the farther end. Sally barked a welcome and then ran back and jumped up at Jane when she called her.

'Oh! You're dirty, Sally. Your feet are wet. Where have you been? … Look, Richard! … Look, Richard! I believe there must be a stream here too and that she's found it … Isn't it a marvellous place? Did you know it before?'

Richard shook his head. 'I thought I knew this wood, Jane, but I've never been before. It's grand. Let's keep it a secret. There *is* a stream down there. This is marvellous. Wait, and I'll come down to you.'

'Be careful Richard. You're treading on the lovely flowers … What are they?'

'I can't remember flower names,' he said. 'Young Susan is the flower expert but I think these are windflowers. And you don't want to worry about treading on them. There are plenty anyway.'

High up the dell, on a sheltered bank they found a host of tiny sweet violets.

'I thought they were always blue,' Jane said. 'Some of these are white and others are purple.'

'I believe somebody told me that the blue ones don't smell like these. P'raps they're a different sort.'

Next they found primroses gleaming in the shadow under the hazel bushes on the bank of the stream. Richard deigned to help Jane pick a bunch for Susan.

'It's no use picking the windflowers,' he said. 'I remember that they always die quickly after they're picked … And the violets are too small and the stalks are too short and so these primroses are about all we can take her … and we musn't forget the pussy-willow either. It's Father's day for seeing Mrs Smithson and he told me that he'd call at the farm for any we can get. I expect if I ask him he'll fix my bike on the back of the car.'

After they had enjoyed their picnic they found another clearing, higher up the wood, which was dominated by a great wild cherry tree smothered in white blossom.

'Do you think it would mind if we took some branches home for Auntie Kate?' Jane said as she held up her hands to catch a few softly falling petals. 'There's so much blossom that it looks as if it ought to smell, but I can't smell it.'

After a struggle Richard managed to reach the lowest branch. With his big knife he cut off some sprays of blossom which Jane clasped to her as they continued their search for the pussy-willow. At last, down by the little stream at the bottom edge of the wood, they found some. The shrubs, still without leaves, were bursting into flower. The shining brown cases of the buds had been pushed aside by the soft, fluffy 'palm', some of which was tinged with tiny yellow flowers. There was plenty of it so Richard cut two large bunches and was careful to cut cleanly and not to spoil any one bush but to take some from all.

They followed the little stream which led them into the meadow with the big brook through which they had come a few Sundays ago.

'What shall we do, Janey? Shall we go home now? Something tells me that it's nearly tea time and I don't want to keep Father waiting too long else he'll be mad with me ... Let's go down to the brook first and then we can go back the hidden way through the wood. Look! There are some wild daffodils. Father always calls them Lent lilies ... I shouldn't pick them ... You can't carry any more flowers anyway and there are plenty at home.'

Down by the brook they found some bright golden flowers like giant buttercups.

'I remember them,' Richard said. 'They're called kingcups. See how thick the stalks are. I s'pose that's because they have to suck up so much water ... Come on Janey! We've found enough for one day and I'm getting hungry.'

When they got home with their arms full of blossom Mr Herrick had just arrived.

'Palm for us on Sunday,' he said, 'Thank you, Richard.'

'And these primroses are for Susan,' Jane said, 'and will you give her my love and tell her I'm beginning to collect some flowers but I can't do much without her.'

'That's kind of you, Jane,' the rector said. 'When are you coming to see us again? I hope Richard isn't being a nuisance.'

'Not at all, thank you,' she said seriously and then blushed when she realized he was teasing her. 'Did you know my mummy and daddy are coming to see me? They're coming at Easter.'

'Then I hope I shall see you all at Easter,' he smiled. 'Are you cycling or coming with me, Richard, and how's the map getting on?'

'I'll come with you and tell you all about it, Father. Do you mind helping to fix the bike on the back? Good-bye, Jane! See you on Palm Sunday I hope. I'm in the choir but you'll never recognize me!'

April

April came in with a roar and a bluster on the Thursday before Good Friday. Jane was wakened early by the wind threshing through the branches of the big elm tree and by the cawing of the agitated rooks. As she sat up in bed as usual the sun was only just showing a faint tinge of red above the horizon so she knew that it must be very early.

Then she remembered.

This was the most important day of the year because Mummy and Daddy were coming this evening and she was going to Crossmarket in the car with Uncle William to meet them. She slid down into bed again and wondered how she was going to pass the time until they came. She felt excited and rather empty inside but after a little she drew her knees up to her chin and dozed until the rooster in the field beyond the rickyard greeted another day. The rooks were still making a lot of noise too but she wouldn't get up until she heard old George click his garden gate and come stumping down the road past her window.

She supposed Mummy would look the same but she did hope that she would not look as worried as she had last winter. And she hoped Daddy would like Moor End. It would be terrible if he didn't, but surely everybody who saw it would love it!

Now that Jane had been here for three months the remembrance of real home was not very clear. Except for Mummy and Daddy, Moor End seemed to be home now and this Easter everything was going to be wonderful because she was going to have the best of everything. She was wondering whether she dared to whistle for Sally when she dozed off again and was wakened by the dog scratching at the door. By now the sun was up and shining fitfully between the racing storm clouds and when she leaned over the banisters to look out at the time the solemnly ticking grandfather clock in the hall struck eight.

'I hadn't the heart to wake you my dear,' her aunt said as she whisked a plate out of the oven, 'for you're to look your best when your mother comes to-night. I shall pack you off to bed this afternoon if you get too excited ... Now, my dear! Just eat that up and no nonsense ... And what are you going to do this morning? We did your mother's room yesterday all but one thing I'm thinking.'

'What's that, Auntie?' Jane asked with her mouth full of bacon and egg.

'We didn't get any flowers and a guest room must have flowers. You go out after you've finished your breakfast and see how many you can pick and show your mother and dad what flowers we grow down here ... If you can't get enough on the common and in the wood there's plenty o' daffodils in the garden although I promised rector he could have the best o' those for church on Sunday.'

So Jane found a basket and with Sally went straight up to the wood as soon as she could. The primroses were bigger than those she had found in the dell with Richard over a week ago and she picked some violets too. She did not pick any windflowers because she remembered what Richard had told her, and after breaking off a few twigs of cherry blossom she wandered out into the meadow above the brook. Just where the tiny stream trickled out of the wood she found a creeping plant with rich green leaves and many little yellowish-green flowers, making a gay golden patch in the shadow of the trees. The stalks were too short to fit into her posy but she picked a few for her flower collection and was told later by Mr Herrick that it was called golden saxifrage. At the top of the meadow where the soil was dry she found some cowslips. Jane knew these flowers because she had often seen them sold by hawkers in the streets at home but she had never seen them growing before. As she began to pick them she saw that the leaves were rather dark, like those of a primrose, and grew close to the ground. The stalks were nearly eight inches high carrying clusters of the lovely little blooms which hung like dainty, golden bells. Lower down the field the grass was thick with buttercups but she soon tired of picking these. By the stream, where the ground was soft, she found a new flower — a flower with a stalk about twelve inches high crowned with eight or ten four-petalled blooms of delicate lilac. She picked some of these but left the big marsh-marigolds alone thinking that these would be happier in the mud by the stream.

Then a sudden hailstorm sent her running back into the wood for shelter. She found the hidden way under the hazel bushes and crept under the trees and listened to the rattle of the hail stones on the leaves above her. At her feet were many bunches of pointed dark green leaves and because there were not any flowers with them Jane did not know that these were bluebells getting ready to spread a misty, purple carpet through the wood.

When the hail stopped and the sun came out again she thought she would try the common, and the lane. Most of the flowers in her basket were yellow so she hoped to find some reds and blues before she went home to dinner.

As she crossed the common on her way from the wood she passed a gorse bush ablaze with colour but the twigs were too prickly to pick. The hawthorn trees were all in leaf now but the blossom was not ready yet and not until she reached the lane did she find any more flowers. The first was the tiny bright blue speedwell in the hedge above the ditch but these were too small to pick. Next in a sheltered place she found a lovely rosy pink flower. The blooms grew in twos and threes on longish, forked and jointed stalks and she picked all she could find although there were not many. Each bloom had five petals but each petal was divided so that, at first, she thought there were ten. These were red campions.

There were celandines in plenty too but she did not want these so she climbed the bank and squeezed through the hedge into one of her uncle's fields. Sally was out of sight farther up the lane and Jane forgot her as she glanced down the hedgeside and saw something strange coming towards her. Her first instinct was to call and whistle Sally but instead she stood quite still and watched. A small animal with short ears and a blunt head rather like that of a cat was coming towards her carrying in its mouth a baby rabbit. At first it was difficult to see the hunter for the size of its prey but suddenly it saw Jane and dropped its dinner. She saw then that the strange animal was about twelve inches long, with a reddish brown coat and a bushy black-tipped tail. Its legs were very short and its little black eyes glared at her fearlessly. Jane remained quite still and the stoat sat down and watched her over the body of the rabbit. Jane shivered and wondered what to do. It seemed ridiculous, but this bloodthirsty little hunter made her feel afraid for a moment and she wondered who would move first. Then she shouted and called for Sally. In a flash the stoat grabbed at his meal and disappeared into the hedge, before the dog had time to raise her nose from the engaging scent she had just discovered.

After that adventure Jane went home and after dinner was allowed to arrange the flowers in her mother's room. Then, because she was pale with excitement, Aunt Kate sent her to her bed with a book.

'And there you will stay, my child, until your uncle is ready! I was to tell you that he has to go to town on some business earlier than he thought so you're to go with him, if you please, and have tea out. Maybe he'll ask you to pour out for him so be sure to remember that he likes his tea strong.'

How could Jane rest after that exciting news? But she did do her best not to fidget about on the bed and she read a few pages of her book without knowing what she had read and at last Aunt Kate came back and helped her to dress. She wore her blue skirt and her red jersey and two smart red bows to match on her short plaits.

'*Need* I wear a hat, Auntie?' she pleaded. 'You know how I hate hats since I've lived with you and it's not a Sunday and it's not raining and it's not very cold.'

Mrs Watson looked at the little girl staring up at her with wide, dark eyes. Her cheeks, now flushed with excitement, were rounder and her lips were redder than they had been on that January evening when she had first come to Moor End. Her mother would hardly know her for the doctor had only last week confirmed that she had gained nine pounds in the country air and could start school in three weeks' time.

'*Please Auntie*! I promise I won't feel the cold and I love to feel the wind in my hair. You've done it so beautifully that it just couldn't get untidy.'

Suddenly Mrs Watson felt the tears rise to her eyes. Who would have thought that little Jane could mean so much to her in three short months? She turned towards the window and said gruffly:

'Do as you like, my child, but don't catch cold. If I say it as shouldn't you look bonny enough without your Sunday hat.'

They went out into the farmyard together and found Uncle William and George lifting some machinery into the back of the car.

'We're calling at the blacksmith's first, Janey,' he smiled. And then, 'I hear I'm to take you out to tea. Is that right?'

Jane nodded happily but her aunt said, 'And just see that she eats a good tea William, and don't let her get her hands dirty at the forge and don't leave her on her own while you go off wasting your time with your friends in the town and you'd better go in and tidy yourself up a bit I'm thinking.'

Jane saw George smile behind his hand as Mr Watson went indoors obediently.

Jane got into the car and waited impatiently for her uncle who had not seemed pleased with the suggestion that as he was going to meet his relations he should change his suit.

At last they started and did not stop until they got to the forge on the outskirts of the town. Mr Watson pressed the button of the electric horn until a lad came out and helped him in with the machinery. Jane hoped that she would have the opportunity of exploring this exciting-looking place which was rather like a dark cave with some witches dancing round a fire in the background.

She need not have worried because Uncle William came back and opened the door of the car for her.

'Come and see how a horse is fitted with two new pairs of shoes,' he smiled. 'We bring ours here.'

The blacksmith's shop was even dirtier than it looked from outside. It was paved with bricks which had worn very unevenly and the floor and walls were covered with oddments of rusty iron. The smith was in the far corner, with a great horse beside him, and Jane edged a little nearer so that she could see what was happening. He grinned a welcome to her and she watched, fascinated, as he pressed a handle up and down with his left hand. As he worked the bellows the fire, spread on some raised brickwork, hissed and roared as the air rushed through the glowing coals. A train of sparks flew upwards into the wide funnel of an overhanging chimney and, in a few moments, the fire was white hot. Then Jane saw an iron bar glowing in the midst of the fire and suddenly the smith grabbed a long pair of pincers and pulled it out. He worked so fast that it was difficult to see exactly what he was at but she did see him place the bar over the pointed end of the anvil and, with mighty blows of a heavy hammer, beat it into the shape of a horseshoe. The clanging of the hammer on the hot iron made a sweet music that Jane never forgot.

Soon the hot shoe was ready to be fitted and the smith lifted the horse's great hoof between his own knees and pressed on the shoe. Jane cried out as a cloud of acrid-smelling smoke rose up but the horse did not flinch and Uncle William reassured her.

'He can't feel it, m'dear! There's no feeling in his hoof! Now watch.'

After marking and trimming the hoof a little the smith put the shoe back into the fire and heated it again. Another hammering and then it was flung with a hiss into a trough of water at his side until it was cool enough to nail on. Before Jane could count the number of times the smith had to put his hand to his mouth to get a fresh nail the shoe was firmly fixed and he had straightened his back and come over to speak to Mr Watson. It was arranged that they should come back for the machinery on their way home and then they said good-bye, and went in search of tea.

The blacksmith welcomed Jane with a grin, and she watched, fascinated, as he worked the bellows.

Mr Watson seemed rather undecided as to where he should take his small niece but after a little he pulled up outside a baker's shop.

'Reckon this will do for us, Janey … Come along in and see if they can find us some toast.'

He stumped through the shop into a little room at the back where there were five small bamboo tables. Uncle William did not seem to be very used to tea-shops for he stumbled against a chair and banged against an old lady before they reached a table in a corner.

Jane felt very proud of herself when the waitress put the tea-pot in front of her and she poured out for her uncle. She remembered that he liked his tea strong and when he smiled at her over the rim of the cup and told her that this was the best cup he had had for months she blushed with pleasure. They had toast and cakes — as many cakes as they wanted — and then they left the car at the station and went back to the town. It was a long time since Jane had looked at shop windows but these were very different from those at home. This street was narrow and the shops were older and she had never seen a shop like the ironmonger's they visited. There was hardly room for both of them inside for there were barrels and boxes on the floor and all sorts of cards and articles hanging from the ceiling and only a little space above the counter where the proprietor's head suddenly appeared like a picture in a frame.

Uncle William bought a lot of things here and said he would call for them later when he had the car. Then Jane wanted to buy something for Aunt Kate and persuaded her uncle to come into the draper's and help her to choose some leather flowers to wear in a button-hole. Mr Watson was too polite to say that he did not think that these would ever be worn and Jane was too excited to listen to him if he had.

At last it was time to go to the station.

Dusk was falling now. The porters were lighting the gas-lamps on the platforms and the signal lights glowed red and green against the sky. An express thundered through on its way to London and then the yellow light on 'their' train came into sight round the curve. Jane, nearly sick with excitement, grabbed her uncle's hand as the carriage doors swung open.

Perhaps they hadn't come!

Perhaps Mummy had been taken ill or Daddy couldn't get away from business.

'Let them come, God,' Jane prayed. 'I can't bear it if they don't.'

And, at once, her prayer was answered for Mummy's arms were round her and Daddy lifted her up and they were all talking and laughing and hugging each other.

'But you've *grown*, my darling. Hasn't she, Daddy? ... Let's look at you under this lamp ... And you've put on weight and you've got some roses in your cheeks again ... No, Will! I won't be hurried and I can't help it if we are in the way for I haven't seen my Jane for three months and now she's grown up.'

But they got into the car at last and Jane and her mother had to sit in the back and make room for the parcels from the shop and the machinery from the forge. The moon was up now and when they turned off the main road to the lane which led across the common Jane grabbed her mother's hand.

'Look Mummy. There's Moor End right ahead! See how the white walls show up in the moonlight.'

Then there were more welcomes and the thrill of watching Mummy's face when she was led into her room and saw the flowers. And Daddy, who was rather tall, only laughed when he banged his head on a low beam in the corridor, so Jane was sure at once that he was going to like Moor End. Then there was Sally to introduce and a tremendous supper which

Jane couldn't eat and although she would have liked to stay up until the news she was too tired and didn't complain much when bed was suggested. And to-night her own mother came up and helped her to undress and brushed her hair and was there by her when she said her prayers. Daddy came too when she was tucked up and puffed clouds of smoke all round her tiny room and made her sneeze.

She fell asleep before her mother left her.

※

They had hot cross buns for breakfast and Uncle William hurried his as usual after explaining that the cows had to be milked and the work of the farm go on even if it was Good Friday.

But Jane had a lovely day. She took her father out after breakfast and introduced him very proudly to George. She showed him the milking sheds and the barns and the mangold cutter and she showed him where they threshed.

In the garden she was finding some of the nests for him when she heard an odd tapping sound from the other side of some fruit bushes. She listened carefully and put her fingers to her lips as she crept round the bush. Then she beckoned to her father and together they watched a speckled thrush with a snail in its bill which it was battering against a big stone lying at the edge of the garden path. When the bird had flown off they looked closer and saw that this stone must have been used as an anvil for the thrushes for years because the moss and grass around was littered with fragments of shell.

Strangely enough Jane heard another odd tapping that day. After dinner she took her parents to the wood and, just inside, they stopped in surprise at the sound of a stick being drawn quickly across iron palings. At least Jane could not think of any other comparison although she knew there was no such fence for many miles. Then came a steady tapping almost as if someone was hitting the trunk of a tree with something hard. And this was exactly what was happening because the noise was made by the long, strong bill of the green woodpecker, as he tested the trees to see if they were hollow in his search for grubs. Jane's mother did not seem to be very interested in the wood and suggested several times that they should go for a walk where it wasn't so muddy and messy but Jane whispered, '*Please* be quiet Mummy. We must see what makes that noise.'

Then a bird flew across the path and, in the sunlight, they saw that he was green above and greenish yellow underneath with a blaze of red on the top of his head and neck. As he passed over he gave a loud, echoing cry which was rather like a laugh but Jane put her finger to her lips when her father started to laugh too. The bird landed on to the trunk and tapped the bark with his strong, sharp beak and Jane knew that this was the noise she had heard before. She looked forward to telling Richard about this discovery to-morrow when they went to tea at the rectory. It was always satisfactory to tell Richard anything because he seemed to know such a lot already.

When the woodpecker flew away Jane looked up at her mother's glum face and laughed.

'You can speak now, Mummy! I'm so sorry you don't like the wood but I thought you would be as excited as I am.'

'It isn't that I don't like it, darling. I'm not used to woods and it's so muddy and I haven't got wellingtons on like you … If you and Daddy would like to go on exploring on your own I'll wait for you outside.'

Then Daddy laughed too and Jane whistled for Sally and they all went back down by the hedge to the common and the lane. The sun was bright and quite hot and Jane thought that Moor End had never looked lovelier. The elm tree by George's cottage had lost its blossom now and was bursting into green leaf; buds on the chestnut tree before the house were shedding their brown sticky covers and showing their curled, pale green leaves. In the orchard two pear trees were a foam of white blossom.

And so this Good Friday slipped by and Easter Saturday was just as lovely. In the morning Mrs Watson told Jane that she could pick all the best daffodils in the garden together with some sprays of pear blossom.

'For years now I've taken flowers and helped decorate church for Easter,' she said. 'Maybe I'm not much of a one for church these days but right is right and I know how I was brought up and Easter for sure and Christmas and Harvest Festival too William and I goes off to do our duty.'

Mr Watson was too busy to stay at the rectory but he drove the others over in the car and promised to call for them before six.

Richard and Peter were waiting for them on the rectory gate. Poor Susan, who was not feeling ill now, was still in her room but banged on her window and waved to them when they got out of the car. Mrs Herrick came bustling out into the porch with her arms full of flowers and shook hands with them all and kissed Jane and apologized for the muddle in the hall.

'The rector's in church,' she said, 'and perhaps you would all like to come across and help us make it beautiful … Oh, Mrs Watson! What beautiful daffodils! We couldn't do without your daffs at Easter and I'm sure these are the best you've ever brought.'

She turned to Jane's parents.

'I *do* so hope you don't think it rude of us to be so busy. But we did want to see you and we're so fond of Jane and yesterday of course the rector was in church most of the day and so that only left to-day …'

And she smiled at them sweetly and dropped a ball of string and some pruning shears and they all trooped out of the house and across the garden and through a little gate into the churchyard.

'There's a jackdaw's nest in the belfry, Jane,' Richard said. 'One day I'll get Dad to let us go up there.'

'I'd like to go up when the bells are ringing,' Jane said.

'You wouldn't! If you *heard* them from inside the belfry you would be deafened and old Marston the sexton told me once that the row would kill you. Nobody could stand that amount of noise, he said. They'd just go mad and blood would come out of their ears and they'd die … that's what he says.'

Jane accepted these horrors with wide-open eyes. She was never really quite sure when Richard was serious but although she would have liked some more details she did not feel that they should continue to discuss corpses inside the church.

It was beautiful little church — very old and with a glorious window behind the altar glowing with reds and blues and purples. The floor was of stone, worn uneven by the feet of thousands of worshippers who down the ages had made this place the very centre of their lives.

Mr Herrick, in his long black cassock with the black leather belt, came down and spoke to them, and then Mrs Watson and Jane's mother went to help the other three ladies who were busy tying bunches of spring flowers to the pulpit and to the graceful oak screen that divided the choir from the rest of the church. Meanwhile the rector took Jane and her father round and showed them some traces of ancient paintings on the south wall and explained that hundreds of years ago when nobody could read or write the Church sometimes taught her people the story of the Gospel in pictures. He showed them the font with its carved stonework and then led them to the tiny chapel at the end of the north aisle where there was another altar dressed in royal blue with a tiny silver lamp hanging on a chain from a beam in the roof.

Soon the dim church began to gleam with colour as daffodils, primroses and cowslips were spread about the ancient walls and pillars; and it all looked very lovely when they went back to tea.

Afterwards Jane wrote a little letter to Susan telling her about the flowers she had already found and asking her to get well soon so that she could come to Moor End and help her to mount the wild-flower collection properly. Then it was time to get ready to go home because Uncle William would be in a hurry and must not be kept waiting.

That evening after supper, Jane and her daddy went out into the farmyard. The moon was up and the roofs of the old barns were bathed in silver. In some places the shadows looked like great dark pools and the only sound was the funny gurgling noise made by her father's pipe.

'You like it here, Janey?'

'If it wasn't for you and Mummy I'd like to live here for ever.'

'School soon you know.'

'I don't mind, Daddy. I'd like to go now. I wish I could go with Richard but I can't. Susan will be there but she's rather small for me.'

Her father laughed and knocked his pipe against his heel.

'As long as you're happy Jane and getting better all the time we're happy too ... There's a present coming for you next week ... Something you'll like I think and something that will help you on your way.'

But he wouldn't say any more than that and when an owl drifted over the yard, perched on the barn and hooted at them, they went indoors.

✕

Jane never forgot her first Easter day at Moor End. Many times later in her life she came back to the place she had learned to love but the memory of this one day never faded. Everything about the day was right. The weather was perfect. Sun, cloud, wind and blue skies. An April day. Everything was fresh and clean. Everything was growing again and even Jane could sense something of the message of Easter as Mr Watson — in the best suit she had ever seen him wear — drove them up the hill, past the glory of the beech trees and then down into Townsend. Birds were singing for joy of the day and, out from the old grey tower of the church, the bells sang too as Jane had never heard them sing before — 'Ding, Dang! Ding, Dang! Din Dan, Bin Bam, Bam Bom Bo!' But inside the church they could hardly be heard and Jane gazed entranced at the beauty before her. She had seen the flowers last evening and she had been to church a week ago; but now the sun was pouring through the great east window and the altar stood in a pool of golden light. The organ was playing something triumphant that made her feel trembly inside and when she looked again she saw candles blazing and the biggest candle she had ever seen in her life was burning in a great candlestick at the foot of the altar steps.

The church was nearly full when the choir came in. Then two boys carrying more candles — one of them was Richard with shining face and parted hair above his white surplice — and then Mr Herrick in a magnificent coloured cloak.

There was a wonderful hymn which they all sang as the choir and Mr Herrick walked round the church. 'Hail thee Festival Day!' Jane sang with the others so loudly that her voice cracked as Richard passed her with his candle. But he didn't even look at her and when they all came out in the sunshine again and everybody was wishing everybody else a 'Happy Easter' he came tearing out of a side door and said, 'Hello everybody' so that it was difficult to believe he had ever looked as angelic as he had ten minutes ago.

'Will you walk home with me, Daddy? I don't expect dinner will be ready yet and it's such a lovely day. I want to show you the beech trees. Do you mind, Auntie?'

Mrs Watson, who was secretly very worried about the dinner, welcomed the idea and told Jane that there would be no need for her to hurry. When the car had gone Richard persuaded them to go with him into the rectory garden.

'Do you know anything about bees, sir?' he asked Jane's father. 'I've never seen so many before round one tree. Come and look,' and he led them through the garden to the orchard where a crab-apple tree was smothered in pink and white blossom. Long before they reached it they heard the hum of tens of thousands of bees and when they stood under the laden branches they were able to watch them burrowing into the centre of each rosy bloom now opening wide in the sunshine.

'We ought to have hives,' Richard said. 'I've often told Father about it but nobody seems to have the time in this place to do anything.'

Jane was surprised at this remark because she had never known anyone do as much in the time available as Richard. But all she said was: 'Come over on Tuesday, Richard. I shall be lonely without Mummy and Daddy.'

At the top of the hill Jane turned off the road and showed her father where she had first met the Herricks, and seen the bramblings. She made him climb to the top of the mound and look out over the valley. She showed him the weathercock on the church tower and the rectory garden and the school, where she was going soon, at the end of the village street.

When they saw Moor End Farm waiting for them in its sheltered valley Jane's daddy stopped for a minute to light his pipe. Then he put an arm round her shoulders and held her close.

'You love it all, don't you, Janey?'

There was something in his voice that checked her answer and she looked up at him in surprise.

'I think you love your new life so much that you'll never want to come back to us.'

'Daddy, darling!' and she buried her face against his coat. 'However much I love Moor End I only want to be with you and Mummy … Let me come back with you to-morrow 'cos I'll always have this to remember.'

And neither of them said anything else until they opened the kitchen door and sniffed the dinner.

※

Jane hated the next day. Thursday now seemed a year ago and instead of being able to look forward to something wonderful she was now dreading the good-bye.

The morning dragged and she didn't want her dinner and there was a lump in her throat that wouldn't get out of the way and when she looked at her mother she wanted to cry.

When Uncle William brought the car round to the door later and the luggage had been strapped on the back Jane was not to be found.

Mrs Watson was worried.

'And I told her this morning that you'd be wanting her to go to the station with you … She's not herself to-day poor child and right sorry I am … Maybe she's in the garden …'

But as soon as Aunt Kate had disappeared Jane came out into the road from the farmyard. Her eyes were big and black in her white face but she walked steadily up to the car with Sally at her side.

'I don't want to come to the station,' she said. 'I want to say good-bye to you here,' and while mother and father looked at her in astonishment she hugged and kissed them both and without another word turned and ran up over the common towards the wood.

Now that they couldn't see her it was easier to cry but she would not even turn round when she heard the car start. With thumping heart she pounded on up the hill while Sally ran along by her side. The trees at the edge of the wood wavered indistinctly through her tears.

When she reached the dell she flung herself down among the primroses. The leaves were cool and refreshing to her hot little face and the pale blooms smelt of the earth. After a while Sally bent and licked her ear and Jane sat up and blew her nose. She looked up at the patch of blue sky between the treetops and, as she sat with her hands round her bare knees, a little bird with a long forked tail and a white breast with chestnut brown and blue at the neck flashed across the clearing, turned gracefully, swooped towards Jane and then skimmed away over the tree tops. Another and yet another followed.

Later, when she felt better and had run down to Moor End again she saw Uncle William in the farmyard. He was standing with his back to her and looking at the stable door.

Jane went up and slipped her hand into his.

'Hullo, our Janey,' he said just as if nothing had happened. 'The swallows are home again and I've never known 'em so early ... Look!'

As he spoke two little birds with forked tails and a blue sheen on their wings twisted and glided round the yard and then disappeared into the darkness of the stable.

'They were coming home,' Jane whispered to herself. 'I shall go home too when it's time.'

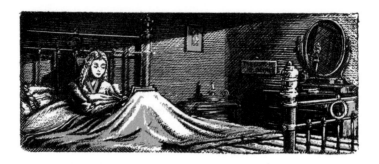

May

Moor End Farm,
May Day

Darling Daddy and Mummy,*

I made up my mind yesterday when I was coming home from seeing the witch with Richard that I would try and write special letters like this one to you. I shall still write my Sunday letter of course but if I wake up early like I generally do and now it is so light before I get up I shall have time to write about what I did the day before. I hope you will like what I write darling Mummy and Daddy but if I write quickly while I remember and if I have time it is rather like sharing with you all the things that happened.

This morning the cuckoo woke me up shouting at the top of his voice. He was so loud and close that he must have been in the garden and I think he was in the elm tree over by the cottages. Do you remember the big elm tree?

---

* *I have corrected Jane's spelling in these letters because it wouldn't be fair to show you her mistakes. You must remember that she missed a lot of school when she was ill. MS.*

Now I must tell you about the witch. Of course she wasn't REALLY a witch but Richard teased me about her and took me to see her and although she looked about a million years old she wasn't as old as that really and was very nice and gave us some cake.

We couldn't have seen her if you hadn't given me the bicycle. I keep on saying thank you for the bicycle. It was the loveliest present I have ever had. Just as lovely as Sally who isn't really mine yet but I hope she will be one day. Now that I go to school which is such fun it is lovely to go for a ride in the evening with Richard. Susan will come with us too when she comes back so you see what a lovely present it is.

Thank you again very much for the bicycle. Sometimes I pretend that he is a war horse and sometimes when I whiz down the hill to Townsend I am flying like a swallow.

Now I must tell you about the witch. Richard said that he knew one and that because to-day is May Day she would tell me to go and bathe my face in the dew. But I haven't because I am writing to you instead. Yesterday after school I had tea at the rectory and then we started and all the way he said she was a real witch and that she lived by herself in a lonely cottage because everybody else was afraid of her. Of course I knew that there aren't *really* any witches and I laughed at him but presently we came to a very dark wood — not like our wood here by the house — but a wood of pine trees all growing very close together and very straight up. The wood came down to the road on each side and it was like going into a tunnel. Then Richard got off his bike by a little gate and said we must leave our bikes in the hedge and was I afraid to go any farther because this path led to the witch's cottage. I said I wasn't but I was a bit and we walked through the wood and I thought we were like Hansel and Gretel and that perhaps the witch's house would be made of ginger-bread. The cottage was just outside the wood on a steep slope so that the top of the chimney was only as high as we were standing. Richard said that he read a book called *Bevis* which I would like for my birthday please and that the boys in that book found a witch's cottage like this one and that was what had put him on the track. He said that if we a threw a stone down the chimney and it was a witch then the stone would explode and burst out of the chimney like bullets out of a gun. So we didn't try that and crept round the side of the cottage and there was the old witch in her little garden with an enormous black cat. The garden was full of wallflowers but the awful thing was that we could see her broomstick in the porch standing up ready for her to fly off with her horrible cat at night when the moon was up.

Richard said could I think of anything I wanted charmed away and I could only think of the wart on Aunt Kate's little finger and I didn't think she would like me to say anything about that. Then Richard sneezed and the old witch looked up and though I don't think she could see very well she called out in a squeaky voice, 'Who be there?' so we thought we'd better go down though I would have gone home. Her face was all lines and very brown and old. She was very bent and used a black stick and when we came close she could see us and she mumbled at us with her lips and asked us what we wanted. The big black cat pushed my legs and purred and as it didn't turn into anything I stroked it and it was a nice cat. After that it was funny because the witch seemed pleased we had come and Richard said could we have a drink of water and she hobbled in and knocked the broomstick over but nothing happened except that she brought some cake as well. We sat in the porch in the sun and Richard kept nudging me so I asked her straight out what would happen if I went out and bathed my face in the dew on May morning. I had to shout it twice because she was deaf and then she cackled and laughed and said it would make me specially beautiful and I thought she was rather silly and Richard very stupid too because he kept on giggling.

When we had finished the cake and we had told her who we were she asked us to come again 'cos she was old and lonely.

Perhaps we will one day but now I'm tired of writing and it's time to get up so that is the story of the witch who looked like one but wasn't.

Wednesday

Do you remember the apple tree on the lawn that reached almost to my bedroom window? (You see how I am keeping on with this letter like I said I would. When I have enough I will send it to you and start another). About the apple tree. Richard showed me where the starlings were building a nest in a hole in the trunk and last night when I came home I borrowed a chair from the kitchen and climbed up to look into the hole. I couldn't see far but there was a tiny chirping so I expect the babies are there now. But that isn't what I wanted to tell you about. I just looked up in the tree where the flowers are out now all white and pink and saw something that looked as if a branch had been sawn off and the stump had grown grey bark on it. While I was looking a little bird flew off and I saw it was a nest made to look like the tree. I told you about our bird's nest map when you came at Easter so you see I had to know what this nest was but couldn't see in.

Now in one of the barns they keep some ladders so I went round and George was just ready to stop work and I asked him if he would mind carrying round a short ladder for me. He said, 'Pleasure be mine, miss,' and the other men laughed but he brought the ladder and held it for me while I climbed up and looked in. It was the most wonderful nest, very small and round and neat. Outside it was just like the trunk of the tree and was made of pieces of bark and grey moss and all stuck together with pieces of cobweb. I put in my hand and the sides were warm and smooth and lined with hair and wool and feathers and then I felt five tiny eggs and picked one out. It was grey with some pink on it and blotched with brown. I asked George to let the ladder stay there but he wouldn't do that. I waited to see if I knew the bird when it came back and I did. It was a chaffinch with blue on his head and a pink chest and with white bars on his wings.

I rang up Richard to tell him. Mr Herrick answered the telephone and he seemed rather busy so I said not to bother Richard. It would really be better if Richard could always be the one to answer the telephone at the rectory. I asked him once if he could because although Mr Herrick is nice he muddles me up. Richard said he hadn't got the time and that the telephone belonged to his father anyway which was a silly thing to say. When I see Richard next I think he will be pleased about the chaffinch's nest because I have found it by myself.

Later

He was pleased. I went in to the rectory after school and he was home early and I told him. When I got home I went to talk to Uncle because if he is not too busy he always wants me to tell him about school and this is jolly difficult sometimes. I can't think why he should want to know what they tell me but he is always asking. He was in the farmyard talking to George and while Sally and I were waiting for him to finish I saw some birds whizzing round the yard very fast and then some of them went into the stable and I remembered that these were the swallows that I saw come back the night you went home. Uncle took me into the stable and showed me the nest built on one of the beams. He lifted me on to Primrose's back and when I stood up I could see into the nest and the mother swallow stayed there for a minute and then flew off with a squeak. There were five eggs, rather long and narrow and they were white with brown spots and Uncle said that the swallow eats flies and insects and that the father swallow was

It was a chaffinch's nest, with five tiny eggs in it.

perhaps bringing food to the mother on the nest. He told me that the swallows can fly so fast that they catch the insects in the air as they fly and that soon these eggs would be hatched and then the mother and father work all day to feed the babies. When we came out he showed me another swallow which disappeared under the gutter of the roof nearer the house. There is a mysterious hidden room I think at the top of this barn by the house. There is a black door which is always locked 'cos I've tried it lots of times and a little dirty bit of a window up by the gutter where the swallows went. When I ask Uncle what is up there he laughs and says that it's an old granary which he doesn't use now and that it's full of rubbish and I can't go there because it isn't safe. But all the same there is no other place I want to explore more than this especially as there must be another swallow's nest there. So I asked Uncle again if he would unlock the door for me to see it but all he said was, 'Wait for a rainy day when George hasn't anything to do and then he can clear some of the rubbish out o' way,' and the funny thing is that George heard him and went away grumbling to himself but he doesn't mean it really. George often asks me, 'How is your ma and pa?' Now I think I shall post this special letter to you and hope you like it. I will write some more next week.

With lots of love,

from

JANE

I shall call these the Moor End letters and the Sunday ones the Janey letters because those are more about me and these are what happen here.

✖

Moor End Farm,

Darling Mummy and Daddy,

I am so glad you liked the first Moor End letter. Here is another though I seem to be getting lots of things to do and I am never indoors as it is so light in the evenings but I shall keep on trying. Now I want to tell you about Saturday because I was with Uncle nearly all the time and he told me lots of new things about the farm. It is fun to be on a farm because things are never the same. Don't think I am silly to say that but something is always happening and it is always different. Uncle and George don't do the same things here that they did when I first came and that is why I love it very much because there is always something fresh to see.

After breakfast Uncle took me out to the fields. We went up the lane and the sun was very hot and there was a most luscious smell. I was sniffing it very hard and Uncle said had I got a cold and I said, 'No but what was the smell.' Then he showed me all the hawthorn trees in the hedge and on the common and how they were now smothered in white flowers. He pulled some down for me to smell but wouldn't pick any because he said it was unlucky. The bees were thick on the blossom and when the breeze came the lovely scent blew down the lane to us. Uncle said that some people called the hawthorn May because it bloomed in that month. He said that in autumn all these trees would be covered in red berries called haws.

Then we went into the potato field and there was George with Short and Charlie pulling the plough up and down between the ridges he had made in March. Uncle showed me that it wasn't a real plough but what he called a hoe which slid along just under the earth. Where George had not been the soil was green with weeds and Uncle said that the hoe loosened their roots and then the hot sun killed them. George smiled at me but he looked very hot and a bit grumpy. But the men in the next field looked grumpier and I didn't blame them because they were hoeing too but they hadn't got a horse to help them — just hoes with long handles. They kept prodding and scraping the weeds out between some tiny green plants which Uncle said was kale. I thought it was a beastly job for them and I don't think they liked it either. Uncle said the kale was for the cows to eat in winter. Half this field was turnips which you know I hate and I do hope Auntie won't make me eat them when they are ripe. Uncle said that sometimes he has to sow turnips three times because a fly comes and eats them up just when the seeds start to grow. It seems silly that a fly should like turnips.

We went along the path between the fields and opposite the potatoes was a field quite green with what looked like grass about a foot tall and I remembered this was wheat. It looked lovely because when the wind came it made it like little waves on a pond. Uncle stood quite still and just stared at it and grunted and then Sally whined and he said, 'It'll do,' and we went on till we came to the field where once, when they were sowing the oats, I had seen a peewit's nest with an egg in it. The man on the tractor had put a stick in the earth to mark the nest and I could see the stick so I asked Uncle if I could go and look and he said I could and he held Sally because she gets excited on the fields. The oats were just coming up but I went as quietly as I could to the stick and quite suddenly a peewit flew up and made a great noise and fuss and fluttered round. The nearer I got to the stick the more sorry I felt for him 'cos he was so worried but I nearly trod on the mother before she moved. I would never have found her but for the stick and do you know when she moved there were four of the most WONDERFUL baby peewits. They were little balls of speckled yellow fluff and they were all crowded together and panting with their little beaks wide open. I picked one up and it made a tiny chirp and was so light that I could hardly feel it in my hand. When I put it down it scuttled back to its brothers. All the while the mother and father peewits were flying round and crying so hard that I went back to Uncle and Sally.

Then we went to see Frank and the sheep. I told you about the lambs a long time ago and now they are growing up. Frank's hut is still there and the lambs and their mothers are eating something on the ground and out of troughs. Uncle won't let them go where they want and they are crowded into squares made of hurdles.

After that we went home.

Monday

I wrote you a Janey letter yesterday and didn't tell you about the horses because I wanted to save it for a Moor End letter.

Because the horses are in the stable every day I had forgotten that they do not stay there all the summer. Yesterday after breakfast Uncle said that to-day was going to be the one day in the year that the horses liked best and that however old they were they always behaved like ponies when they went out to the fields in May.

So we went out into the yard and George came round in his best suit and a hard black hat and Auntie told me this is to show that it was Sunday and he isn't really working but just helping us by coming. Uncle led Short out of the stable and George took Primrose and Charlie and gave them a drink at the trough like they always do before they go out to work. Then, Uncle led the way up the track past George's cottage and told me to run on and unlock a padlock and open a gate to a big field on the left. It was a lovely field covered in buttercups. I was just opening the gate when I heard one of the horses whinny like they do when they are excited and come galloping up behind me and there was Short dragging Uncle along. Uncle laughed and let him go and the other two horses followed him into the field. We shut the gate and watched them go quite mad and fling up their heels and whinny and dash round the field with their great hooves thudding. Primrose came close to Charlie and kicked out at him but Uncle said it was only in fun. Then they started rolling in the grass with their feet in the air and Uncle and George said it was a good thing but I don't know why.

I stayed and watched them for a long time after the others had gone in.

One thing happened yesterday which was fun. Auntie has got some hens which she calls broody because they don't lay eggs but only want to sit on their own and hatch them out. In the morning a friend came to see her and brought her nine duck's eggs and when she had gone Auntie gave them to me for my own and said I could borrow the broody to hatch them out. She showed me what to do. In the orchard we dug a little hollow place and poured a little water into it and then some hay to make a nest. We put the eggs in the nest and fetched the broody, who fluffed her feathers out and looked very fat, and put her on the eggs. Then we got a little wooden house with bars in front and put it over her and she sat down on the eggs and there she was a prisoner. Auntie says I must put water in a dish outside the bars so that Broody can reach it because she gets very thirsty and that I can let her out each day just for a few minutes to eat. In a month's time I'll have nine ducklings of my own and it is very exciting to think about.

Auntie and Uncle are darlings.

With much love,

from

JANE

XXXXXX

Saturday evening

Darling Mummy and Daddy,

I am starting this to you to-night instead of putting it in my Sunday letter because it is not the sort of news that ought to go into a Janey letter.

It hasn't been a very nice day because it rained this morning but Mrs Herrick asked me to go and have dinner and tea at the rectory and play with them there all day. I did tell you I'm sure that Susan is quite better now and the funny thing is that maybe she never did have scarlet fever — Richard and the others there all call it 'SF' — because nobody else has caught it from her. Susan says she has read every book they would let her have three times over and that now she hates jig-saws too. I have pressed all my wild flowers but 'cos I wanted Susan to see them I put them inside a big drawing book in my bicycle basket and took them with me.

I never knew I would enjoy my new bicycle so much. It goes nearly everywhere with me and although I have to push it up the hill to the beech trees coming home it is thrilling to rush down going to school. Sometimes when it is dry I come home a different way and ride over the rough path between the peewit field and the potatoes. It is longer this way but I like it very much because I can see how much everything has grown since last time.

I wanted to tell you about the swift.

When I got to the rectory I saw Richard and Peter and Susan and Mr Herrick all watching something on the lawn in front of the house. I rang my bell just to show that I was there and Richard turned round and glared at me and then beckoned so I left my bike and ran over.

They were all looking at a bird struggling on the grass. It was a black bird with very long wings and short legs. I thought it

97

was hurt because it kept on trying to fly but couldn't get off the ground. Richard said that it was a swift and that he had seen three blackbirds attacking it while it was on the grass. Mr Herrick picked it up and put it on the palm of his hand and held it high over his head. Then the swift dived off his hand and suddenly it was flying. It twisted and turned and made a sort of screaming cry like 'chee-ree-eee' and then flew very fast high over the house. When it was flying I saw that its wings were VERY LONG and curved and narrow.

Then Mr Herrick told us all about the swift and I will tell you because I don't think you know much about birds.

He said that no other British bird can fly faster and that it hardly ever lands on the ground because its proper home is the air where it catches insects. Its wings are too long to get it into the air easily from the ground. Sometimes perhaps it falls because it has smashed into something when flying so fast. When it is down it is nearly helpless and that is why other birds attack it, which I think is beastly of them.

He said too that the swifts, with swallows and house-martins, come to us every summer from Africa. I asked Richard whether he had ever found a swift's nest and he hadn't but he said you can sometimes see the swifts clinging on the wall of the house. That is the only way they rest except when they are in their nesting place under the roof.

I never thought I could be so keen on birds and flowers but they are both fun and if you come here for the summer holidays like we said then I can show you my flower collection.

I will write another letter to-morrow and answer yours but I did want to tell you about the swift.

When I got home after tea I went to see my Broody and give her some food. I lift up the bar of the coop and put her dish just outside and she gets off the eggs for a minute or two. She is very good about going back and you would laugh to see the way she moves the eggs a little and then sits down on them. Auntie says that she will sit on them until they are hatched which will be at the beginning of next month. I don't know what I shall do with all the ducklings but they are the brown sort which don't need a pond to swim in.

Now I must stop because it is bed-time but I must tell you about the bluebells. I went up to the wood last evening after I got home with Sally. Our side is *COVERED* with bluebells. I have never seen them like this before and when you look at them all growing it looks like a purple carpet. I took some home to Auntie but she said that they won't last long and it's better to leave them to grow in the wood which I s'pose is always the best.

That's all for now.

With love,
from
JANE

June

Jane woke before the day. She woke when the night was very still and when the moon was high in the sky. She shifted on her pillow as the barn owl screamed outside and then looked out through the bars at the end of the bed to the apple tree bathed in silver.

Her room high up under the roof was hot and for a few minutes she tossed and turned wondering why she had wakened. The owl cried again and his shadow darkened the room as he drifted silently over the garden.

Jane flung back the single blanket and jumped out of bed. She leaned from the window as she had so often done since this had been her room and looked out on to a black and silver world. It was as light as day but not like daylight. The garden, which in to-morrow's sunlight would glow with colour, was now still and cold. The road over the common was a silver ribbon. Like a magic road leading to fairyland, she thought, as she leaned farther out of the window and looked up the hill where the wood loomed like a shapeless monster over the valley.

Just before she had gone to sleep last night Jane had thought that when she woke up it would really be summer because it would be the first day of June. Perhaps it was the first of June already but she had not imagined that it would be like this. This was her birthday month and last night Aunt Kate had reminded her that it would probably come in the middle of haymaking which would be fun.

'We'll make you a grand party, Janey,' she had said. 'Your birthday is on a Saturday and you can have the Herricks for the day in the hay-field … We'll tell your uncle to keep one field for Janey's party.'

Jane sighed. They were very sweet to her. She was never lonely but it would not be a proper birthday without Mummy and Daddy and she did not suppose that either of them would be able to come. What a long time it seemed since she had arrived at Moor End in the dark and wakened to find a world deep in snow. How lovely it was here and how marvellous to feel well and strong again.

Her head slipped sideways and suddenly she was sleepy. She yawned and ran back to bed and the next thing she knew was the sun on her pillow and June was really here.

As she got out her bicycle after breakfast a slight mist was still lying in the hollows so she knew that it was going to be a hot day. She cycled up the lane and sang a little song to herself because she was so happy. Halfway up the hill on the right was a gate leading into the root field. She got off and climbed up two rungs and waved to George who was rather moodily hoeing a few yards away.

'Hullo, George!' she called. 'Isn't it a lovely day …? I've got history this morning and it's my favourite lesson … George! I've always wanted to ask you but do you like hoeing?'

George straightened his back and regarded her gloomily. He pushed his hat to the back of his head and wiped his face with his bare arm.

'Be off with you young Miss,' he said after a little. 'Be off to your schooling.'

'But do you *like* it, George? I should hate it.'

He laughed at her then and bent his back again as she climbed down and picked up her bicycle. The sun was stronger and the air was heavy with a sweet, clinging scent. It would not take long to whiz down the hill when she had passed the beech trees so she thought she would push her cycle to the top.

The hedges were high here and there was a ditch on one side where, in the spring, she had seen a hedgehog with Richard. On the opposite side of the lane was the big hay-field which her uncle had shown her the other day. When she found a gap in the hedge she put her cycle down again and climbed the bank to look at it. As she watched the standing grass gleaming in the sunshine a gentle breeze sprang up and changed its colour as the ripples passed over it. Perhaps this was her birthday field?

The sweet scent, although not very strong, was more fragrant here. It seemed to come from a strangely shaped flower growing in clusters at the end of a long, smooth stalk which wound its way through the dense hedge. Each bloom was made up of little pink trumpets and the leaves grew in pairs just below the flower. She remembered that this must be honeysuckle and tried to pick a few blooms but found the stalk too tough.

Besides the honeysuckle both hedges here were splashed with the pink of the lovely dog rose with its five delicate petals. On some of the bushes which the sun had not yet touched the buds had not opened. Jane thought they looked like dainty little pink cups.

At the top of the hill she wasted a few more minutes and ran up the mound to the beech trees which now were in full leaf. She stooped under the low, sweeping branches into a cool green tent and wondered why such a big tree had such small leaves. She picked a twig now and went out with it into the sunlight to look at it. Each tiny leaf of the most delicate green was fringed with a silky down.

Jane put the twig in her satchel and looked down into the valley. The air was still too hazy for her to see far but she loved this view because the country was laid out before her like a picture map. Townsend looked a toy village at her feet and suddenly she heard the first stroke of nine from the church tower. She tore down the track, jumped on her cycle and rushed down the hill. Flying must be like this, she thought, as the air roared past her and her two little plaits stood straight out behind her head! Then the road flattened and the hedges were lower so that she could see into the fields. A cow looked at her over a gate as she flashed past before slowing down for the crossroads and passing the church.

But the clock was no longer striking and she was late for school.

✕

Next Saturday it rained.

Jane did not seem to mind rain in the country as much as she had at home but it was rather a nuisance when it came on a Saturday which was the jolliest day of the week.

'Will it rain all day, Uncle?' she asked at breakfast time. 'Richard and Susan are coming. We were going to take sandwiches and follow the brook up past the sheep field and see where it goes.'

The farmer looked up from his plate and smiled but his wife spoke first as she usually did.

'Well you can't go gallivanting about the fields in this weather,' she said. 'And what you can do here with those youngsters I don't know.'

'Would you like me to telephone Richard and tell him not to come?' Jane asked innocently.

'Certainly not, my child … And what makes you think we can't give the rectory children a meal I should like to know? … Of course they're to come as arranged … Maybe you could all have a picnic in the big barn.'

'I've got a better notion,' Uncle William said as he set down his cup. 'I reckon, Janey, this is just the day I've been waitin' for … You come along with me,' and here he looked across at his wife and closed one eye in a most meaning wink.

'Where are we going, Uncle darling? Shall I want a coat?'

He nodded and waited for her at the back door. Outside the rain was still slanting down gently and all the gutters were singing. There was a lovely smell of warm, wet earth and green things growing. Mr Watson looked up at the grey sky and then down at Jane as she joined him with a coat over her head.

'Won't rain for more'n hour or two,' he said. 'Now Janey! What did I say about the old granary and a rainy day? Come along and we'll see what it looks like.'

He led the way to the barn which adjoined the house and unlocked the padlock of the mysterious black door. As it creaked open a swallow fluttered over their heads with a plaintive cry and as Jane looked up another flew out from under the eaves and the two circled the farmyard together.

'They've nested here for many a year,' Mr Watson said. 'A pair in the stable and a pair here come every spring. You'll find their nest on the rafters I'll be bound … Can you get up that ladder first, my lass?'

Jane saw that although the slope was steep the ladder was fixed and the steps were broad. She climbed up carefully, one step at a time, and when she reached the floor above called back.

'I've got my eyes closed, Uncle. I'll wait for you before I look properly. Hurry up!'

While she waited she heard the murmur of the rain beating on the roof and smelt the dust of ages and dry wood round her.

'Now look, Janey,' Mr Watson said as he pulled her away from the hole in the floor through which they had both just climbed. 'I've been thinking I'll hand this place over to you youngsters to do what you like in ... What do you think of it?'

Jane didn't know what to think for all that she could see when she opened her eyes were cobwebs in the grey light of a filthy window and a most glorious muddle of rubbish on the floor.

Mr Watson picked up an old sack and rubbed it across the window and let in a little more light. Then he undid a catch in the wall and pushed open a wooden door that swung outwards over the farmyard.

'Don't come too near, Jane,' he warned. 'I'll have a proper bolt fixed for 'tis a nasty drop from here ... Was a time when we hauled sacks of grain up through this door and stored it behind you.'

Then Jane saw that the floor space opposite the window was divided into separate compartments with a low, sliding door to each and she guessed how the great piles of golden grain would look when stored between the partitions.

'We'll soon get this rubbish cleared,' her uncle continued. 'George hasn't much to do this morning and he'll soon get this done. Hi! George!'

George came out of the big barn and looked up at his master with suspicion.

'Come up here George ... I've got a job for ye.'

George crossed the yard reluctantly and slowly climbed the ladder.

'Seven year ago was the first toime I sez this place should be cleared out,' he began, 'but reckon I be too busy to start on 'er to-day.'

'But you will, George. You'll start on her now and get her clear in an hour. 'Tis to be Miss Jane's own place and you'd best throw everything out of doors here into yard and get it under cover as soon as you can … And give the floor a good sweeping too.'

George looked at his master reproachfully, hesitated, and then decided to say no more. Jane would have liked to have stayed with him while he worked but Mr Watson told her that she must keep out of the way until the rubbish had been cleared.

'Like it, my dear?' he asked as they crossed the yard to the big barn.

'Like it! … I'm so excited I don't know what to say to you. How do you know so well what we like to do when you haven't any children of your own, Uncle William? … You always seem to know.'

Mr Watson did not answer for a moment and then loudly cleared his throat.

'Hrrmph! … You can have that place for your own, Janey. Somewhere about upstairs — in attic most likely — there'll be some bits of furniture you can have. Make it your own house and save it for wet days … Ask your aunt to give you a picnic up there to-day with those youngsters from the rectory.'

Then came a terrific crash as George began to fling rubbish out of the open door of the granary into the farmyard. For a few minutes Jane watched the pile grow.

'Better keep out of his way, Janey,' Mr Watson said. 'Come back presently and you won't know the place.'

It was still raining when Richard and Susan arrived on their bicycles an hour later, and Jane, who had been watching the road from the shelter of the big barn, ran out to meet them.

'We've brought our sandwiches just the same, Jane,' Richard said as he shook the water from his oilskin cape. 'Isn't this rain a beastly nuisance? What shall we do?'

'It's going to clear after lunch. Uncle said so ... And I've got a surprise for you both now so put your bikes in the barn and come and see.'

By now George had made a splendid clearance and was sweeping clouds of dust out into the rain. When the children climbed up to see him he leaned his hands on his broom and rested for a minute.

'And why be oi wastin' my time a'doin' this I would loike to know? ... Just fur the loikes o' you young rascals, I reckon ... I'm not a'goin' to do no more now ... You can get down them cobwebs yerselfs ...'

But he gave them a broad grin as he went carefully down the steep ladder and pointed to the beam overhead.

Jane looked up and saw a swallow's nest right above them. A faint 'cheep ... cheep' told them that the eggs were hatched, and at that moment the mother fluttered through the narrow space under the eaves and flew to her nest.

'The father is outside,' Richard said as he rubbed a spy-hole in the dirty glass of the window. 'He's in a state.'

'Let's not take any notice of them,' Susan said in her deep little voice, 'and p'raps they'll get used to us and we can watch the babies grow up.'

Next they went to find Aunt Kate who had already been warned by her husband and told that he had been foolish enough to mention the attic.

'Wet boots off and left on the mat IF you please,' were her first words. 'I've wasted half the morning in the attic already but you'll find some odds and ends just inside the door and you can take what I've put out for you ... Susan, my pet, you'd better stay down here with me for you're not big enough to be lifting chairs and tables and cupboards about ... You and I will be having a cup of something warming maybe while those two do the work.'

So Susan sat on the kitchen table and tried to slice beans while the others staggered down the stairs and out into the yard with some pieces of furniture. Richard managed to haul most of these up the ladder with a rope while Jane pushed from below and by lunch time they had made the old granary into a little secret home of their own which they were sharing with six swallows. Mrs Watson insisted that they should each have a mug of hot soup with their sandwiches and while they were sipping this and watching the swallows the rain stopped and the sun came out. In ten minutes the roofs were steaming, sparrows were splashing in the puddles in the yard and the sky was blue.

Richard crammed the last half of the last bun into his mouth, stood up and flung back the door so that the sunshine streamed into the granary. When the bun was under control — 'Buck up!' he said. 'What are we waiting for? If we hurry we shall find the brook in flood … Are you coming too, young Susan? You won't slip in and get drowned will you? You're very small.'

His sister gave him an indignant look. 'Jane and me will be getting flowers so you can go where you like,' she said solemnly.

They left some crumbs on the floor for the swallows although Richard thought they would rather have flies, locked up the granary and put on their rubber boots and set off through the wet grass to the wood. The sun was hot now and the air was sweet with bird song and the scent of flowers. Just at the entrance of the wood in a shady place Susan found the first slender spikes of foxglove standing higher than herself. Jane gently touched the handsome, bell-shaped flowers and saw that although they were a lovely rose-pink outside, the inside of the blooms was spotted like a leopard's skin. She picked the best spike carefully and put it in her satchel to add to the collection.

In the wood where now there was more leaf than flower, the water was still dripping from the trees and the only other sound was a soft, purring note which Richard said was a turtle dove. They stood still for a moment to listen and the soothing song went on and on and on … and on … until Jane felt that if she stayed much longer she would go to sleep.

'I'd like to see them,' Richard said. 'But I suppose we can't wait. Come on!' Out in the open again the sun was hotter than ever as they went down the meadow to the brook. Some cowslips were yet in bloom and the buttercups still made a golden carpet for their feet. Down by the water they found a new flower on reddish stems quite three feet high, massed in dense clumps of creamy white fragrance.

'I've never smelt anything so sweet,' Jane said. 'Unless p'raps it was the honeysuckle in the hedge the other day. What's it called?'

'Queen of the Meadows,' Richard replied promptly. 'That old Nanny we had told me that and I've never forgotten it.'

'It's meadowsweet,' Susan said stubbornly. 'Anybody knows that. It's a common flower and it's called meadowsweet and we'll pick some for Jane … and here's some forget-me-nots down by the water if you want some.'

They wandered up the side of the stream and after they had crossed the big sheep field reached another little wood. Here the elder trees were white with blossom and in the shallows of the brook they found the water black with wriggling, squiggly tadpoles.

A little higher where the stream broadened, and where they were away from the shadow of the trees, something bright and coloured flashed by them in the sunshine.

Richard clutched Jane's arm.

'Gosh, Janey! Did you see him? I believe that was a kingfisher. Let's squat down on our macs and keep jolly quiet and maybe he'll come back. Father told me they always hunt the same part of the river. Can you stay still, young Susan? If you make a movement or a sound I don't like to think what I'll do to you.'

After a little the kingfisher came back with a tiny silver fish in his long beak but he flew so fast that Jane saw little more than a streak of vivid, royal blue.

'He makes a nest of fishbones at the end of a tunnel in the bank,' Richard whispered. 'Wasn't he grand, Jane? He looks royal doesn't he? No wonder they call him *king*fisher.'

While they waited again in silence there came a plop and a splash from the brook and they saw a ring of ripples spreading towards the bank.

'I see him,' Susan gasped. 'Look! Under the water ... A brown rat swimming like mad ... Now he's disappeared under the bank.'

They wandered up the stream and followed it first on one bank and then on the other through strange fields and by farms and lanes which only Richard had seen before. Susan slipped in the water twice so before they turned back they took off their shoes and socks and paddled properly. In one sheltered place five or six gorgeously coloured dragonflies hovered and Richard said they were like fairy bombers which Jane said was horrid of him.

On the way back they stopped at a farm where they saw some cows going in and begged a glass of milk. There was a lorry in the farmyard and the driver asked them where they were going. When Jane said, 'My uncle is Mr Watson of Moor End,' he said, 'Jump in beside me then. I be going there.'

So they went home a different way and although Susan was tired they had all had a lovely afternoon and found several new flowers for the collection.

Next morning, before breakfast, Jane ran out to see the Broody. To-day was the important day according to her aunt's reckoning and sure enough she was right. When Jane peeped between the bars of the coop old Broody fluffed herself out and uttered several warning clucks. Then she saw two tiny balls of yellow and brown fluff moving under the hen's body and with a shout of excitement ran back to the house.

'They're out, Auntie! The ducklings are out! I can see two of them already ... What shall we give them to eat and must they have something to swim in?'

Aunt Kate explained that Broody could safely be left to hatch out the ducklings by herself and that the babies needed no food yet and must not be given enough water in which to swim.

'Leave her till after tea my dear and then we can take away any eggs not hatched out if she hasn't pushed them out o' the nest herself. To-morrow you can give the babies a little damp biscuit meal on a bit o' flat board.'

Jane went up to the coop several times during the day but could not see how many were out of the eggs. In the evening Mrs Watson came with her and they gave Broody some food. After a little persuasion the hen came off the nest to show seven little cheeping, trembling ducklings huddled together. Two eggs had been pushed to the back of the coop and these Aunt Kate picked up.

'They won't hatch now,' she said. 'They be no good. The hen knows.'

Jane went down on her knees in the grass and looked at the ducklings' tiny webbed feet and little baby bills which opened wide as they squeaked in surprise at being deserted by their mother.

'There's always one weakly one,' Mrs Watson went on. 'Always one that is born small and somehow never seems to thrive. The others will push him out of the way and grab the food first ... There he is, Janey ... I told you there'd be one ... To-morrow you'll have to give him his food separately else he'll get nothing … Come on, old lady … Back to your babies,' she said as the Broody fluffed out her feathers, shook herself and then settled back on the nest.

Next morning, before school, Jane was shown how to mix the biscuit meal and put a little on a flat board so that the ducklings' tiny bills could pick up the damp crumbs easily. She gave them a dish of water too and laughed to see how they dabbled and drank after every morsel of food. Aunt Kate told her that they must be fed 'little and often' until they were bigger and that she would look after them until Jane came home from school.

A week later, as the weather was so lovely, the ducklings were allowed to run free on the lawn and were only put into the coop at night. They grew quickly — all except the weakling, which did not seem to want to live and which George disposed of when Jane was not there — and she loved

The ducklings were allowed to run free on the lawn. They grew quickly.

them all. Aunt Kate said that of the six survivors two might be drakes because they had a slight upward curl to their tails but that really it was too early to tell. So Jane pretended that they did know and named the drakes George and Gerald and the ducks she called Clarissa, Camilla, Caroline and Cicely and although Richard teased her she maintained that she knew them all apart.

Every morning now the sun rose high into a clear, blue sky and by the time Jane rode up the hill to the beech trees it was already hot. Her uncle's cornfields blazed with scarlet poppies and a handsome lime tree in the rectory garden sang with the music of myriads of bees seeking the honey of the little flowers. There was something very odd about the lime tree because, during these hot days, Jane could smell its sweet, honey-like fragrance quite thirty yards away in the road but when she went into the garden and under the tree the scent was not so strong. When she asked Mr Herrick why this should be so he picked a twig and showed her the tiny, greenish flowers. It was strange that these hardly smelled at all but the scent of the tree was stronger farther away.

In the lane where the tall wild parsley towered above the nettles in the ditch, the butterflies danced in the sunshine and all day long over the common and above the fields the larks sang and sang. Jane never tired of watching the larks soaring into the blue sky but neither Richard nor she ever found a nest, although they often searched.

One evening Mr Herrick walked over to see the Watsons with Richard and when it was time for them to go back Jane and her aunt walked to the top of the hill with them. A few swifts flashed by screaming their eerie cry and then a host of small birds came sweeping rather like leaves in an autumn wind down the lane towards them. The rector said that these were young starlings, who had now left the parent birds and were joining together in great flocks.

Halfway up the hill Mrs Watson stopped at a field gate.

'This is Janey's birthday field,' she said, 'and Willum says he cuts on Saturday which is Midsummer Day and Janey's birthday too … We'll be expecting you, Richard, and Susan for the day and to tea in the hayfield.'

They said good-night at the beech trees and Jane and her aunt turned back. It was not often that Mrs Watson left Moor End and never before had Jane known her to volunteer to come for a walk so she felt a little shy of her to-night.

'Where's Uncle?' Jane asked after a little as the bats fluttered crazily overhead.

'Busy as usual my dear … Always something to be done farming but I had a feeling I'd like some air to-night for it's been that hot in the kitchen to-day … I remember, Janey, walking down this lane midsummer time when I was no older than you. 'Twas much the same but rougher to the feet … Seems to me the hedges were higher then but the honeysuckle smelled as sweet as it does now … and never then did I think the time would come when I'd be mistress of Moor End …! And who would have thought we'd have a little girl to come and live with us this year when we've no child of our own … Now your uncle has lit the lamp for I can see the light through the trees … He'll be wondering whether I've run away and left him …'

The fine weather held and Midsummer Day dawned with a mist in the hollows that heralded heat. The postman's van came at breakfast. Jane rushed out to meet him for although there were parcels on her plate she wanted to open her parents' present first.

It was a small square parcel and when she had torn off the paper she found a camera with love from them both on her eleventh birthday. Then there were cards from old school friends at home, a beautiful card from the rectory friends with an extra message from Richard that read 'Don't worry we are bringing your present!'

From Aunt Kate — who must have been let into the secret of the camera — came an album in which the new photographs could be stuck. Uncle William's present was a book with many brightly coloured pictures of birds and their eggs and he seemed as excited as his niece as she turned the pages and then flung her arms round him.

'There, there, my dear,' he said gruffly, 'I'm right glad you like it ... They told me in the shop at Crossmarket that it was a good 'un and if it's not what you like they'll change it ... Now I must be off for George has started cutting ... Come up when you like ... Come now with me.'

When they reached the field the horse-drawn mowing machine was already clacking its way round. The edges had been cut and the grass was falling in flat swathes at one side. Uncle William leaned on the gate and for a long minute said nothing. Jane, happy and excited, looked up at his brown, wrinkled face and then followed his glance to the wide expanse of flower-flecked hay waiting for the reaper. As she watched, the surface rippled in the warm wind that came in puffs from the south. Tall, white marguerites, golden buttercups, pink and white campions and spears of red sorrel swayed gently in the breeze.

Then Uncle William told her how the grass did not become hay until it was dried by the sun and the wind and that soon Sidney, with a big wooden rake in front of the tractor, would push the cut grass into bigger and wider rows called 'windrows'.

'This afternoon if weather holds — which it will — you and the others can turn it to dry t'other side and then if there's time, start making haycocks ... When we're sure the haycocks are dry we make haste to put it all in a rick afore it rains which would spoil it. Wet hay is no good to farmer or to his stock.'

Jane waved to George as he drove past and then went down to the common for a change to wait for Richard and Susan. Here the grass was long and sweet too and she lay down at full length in it and closed her eyes. The sun beat down comfortingly on her brown cheeks and showed pink through her eyelids. In the grasses waving above her head the grasshoppers chirped and leaped and the air was full of a strange and mysterious humming. 'It would be easy to believe in fairies now,' Jane thought. 'It's as if they're all singing. It's only when you're really still that you can hear them.'

The breeze rustled the grasses again and when she turned her head a little she could see the tiny bell-like flowers of some heather a few inches from her face. She was reminded of a poem by a man called Stevenson which they had learned at school. It was called 'My Kingdom' and suddenly she realized how well the poet understood just how a little girl felt when she was lying in the grass on a summer day. She couldn't remember it all — just three lines which kept jingling in her mind —

'This was the world and I was king;
For me the bees came by to sing,
For me the swallows flew.'

'What a lovely birthday I'm having already,' she thought, 'and there's still so much of it to happen.'

Then she heard the tinkle of bicycle bells and straightway forgot her little kingdom and ran over to greet Richard and Susan as they rode into the farmyard of Moor End.

'Happy birthday, Janey,' Richard said as he came to meet her. 'But what have you been doing to yourself? You've got hay in your hair ... Come over here and open your parcels.'

The first was a big book about flowers with beautiful coloured pictures. This was from Mr and Mrs Herrick. Susan's parcel contained what she called 'a lot of useful things'. And they were most certainly useful, for there was a notebook with a shiny cover, two pencils with point-protectors, a piece of rubber, a pair of very second-hand scissors 'for cutting flowers' and a bundle of green gardening twine.

'I do hope you'll like my birthday present, Janey,' Susan said as she stood on one leg with excitement. 'I chose them all myself and I wouldn't let Mummy come into the shop even. The string is to do up flowers with if you hadn't thought of it.'

After Jane had hugged her, Richard said, quite shyly for him, 'I've got a book for you too Janey and I do hope you won't be sick of books but I told you about this and I did want you to have one of your own … It's my favourite book.'

When the paper had been ripped off she found *Bevis*, by Richard Jeffries. Almost before she had looked at it Richard snatched it himself and began to turn the pages.

'D'you remember the old witch on May Day, Jane? There's a lot in here about Bevis and Mark finding a witch like we did and I'm sure that's where I got the idea of ours … But you'll love the book … You'll just have to!'

Then they went in to show the new presents to Mrs Watson who, after duly admiring them, said, 'And you're all just in time to take your own dinner up to the field with you … Your uncle has promised to take the birthday tea up in the car but you'd best be out all day to-day in the sunshine … It's not all sandwiches to-day for there's a salad in a bowl and plenty of lemonade and some fruit and cake so you should manage … Now be off with you and let me get on with my work … Never did I think I'd be bothered with a great girl of eleven round Moor End …!'

When they reached the field nearly half the grass was down and Sidney with his tractor had pushed the cut hay into long windrows.

'After dinner you three can help to turn it,' Mr Watson said. 'It'll be dry enough in this heat. Now put your food in the shade else it will spoil ... Let's give young Susan a ride with George on the mower.'

George was only too pleased to stop for a minute and while Jane had a pat each for Short and Charlie, he lit up his dirty old pipe. Then, with Susan on his knee, he clucked to the horses and the 'clack, clack, clack' of the mower started up again.

By noon it was too hot to stay in the sun so they moved into the shade of two big elms by the gate. George unharnessed the horses and gave them their nosebags and clumped off down the lane to his cottage. Sidney stopped the tractor and sat down under the hedge and lit a cigarette. Uncle William stayed with the children and shared their lunch and then lay back and went to sleep for twenty minutes. Jane felt sleepy too and even Richard was quiet as he leaned against the trunk of the tree and looked up through the leaves to the sky. Susan wandered off to speak to the horses.

In the afternoon they worked by turning the windrows with long wooden rakes. The air was sweet with the smell of the hay and the sun was still so hot that Richard took off his shirt and Susan put on a pink sunbonnet which made Jane rather envious. Presently Uncle William told them to rest again while he went down for the car. He was soon back with the tea and Aunt Kate, who looked very nice in a new flowered dress.

'And I've got a sunbonnet for you too, my dear,' she said to Jane, 'and right sorry I am I didn't think of it this morning ... It'll be a bit on the big side but it'll keep the sun off your neck.'

They were spreading the cloth under the tree when there

came several loud 'coo-ees' and calls of '*Janey*! Happy Birthday, Janey!'

Five girls and two boys were standing on the bottom rung of the gate and they all waved furiously when Jane stood up.

'Auntie! What *shall* we do?… They're friends from school … Shall I tell them to go home, though it is nice of them to come isn't it?'

'Not a bit of it. Bring them over and make them stay to tea … Richard! If I tell you where the buns and cakes are kept at Moor End could you borrow one of those bicycles and bring some more up for us … Now let me get the candles on the cake before they come over.'

Jane's eyes filled with tears as she ran over to welcome her friends. Everyone here was so kind to her and it was such a shame that Mummy and Daddy couldn't be here too. But the tears had dried by the time she reached the gate.

'You're all to come in here to tea,' she called. 'Aunt Kate says so and so do I … And thank you very much for coming.'

The children opened the gate and put their bicycles in the shade and came over to the elm trees chattering like sparrows. Richard was soon back with more food and for a few minutes was rather disdainful of 'all those kids'. Eleven candles were lit on the cake and they all sang 'Happy birthday to you'.

There was a slice of cake for everybody including George and Sidney, who were taking their tea cold from lemonade bottles.

The Townsend children had healthy appetites in spite of the heat and Mrs Watson began to get very worried as the pile of sandwiches diminished; but in the end everybody had plenty. When they had all finished and there was not a crumb of birthday cake left one of the boys from the village got up and called for three cheers for Mrs Watson, which was a very nice way of saying 'Thank you'.

Then Jane took some photographs of them with her new

*Five girls and two boys were standing on the bottom rung of the gate.
'Happy birthday Janey!' they called.*

camera and before they went home they all helped to turn the hay and build some haycocks. Mr Watson told Jane that as soon as the hay was absolutely dry it could be carted to the corner of the field near the gate and built into a rick. The tractor would drive the elevator which lifted the hay tossed on to it up to the men building the rick.

Soon the shadows began to lengthen and George harnessed the horses to the mower, sat sideways on Short's back and lumbered off down the hill to the farm. Sidney left the tractor in the field but covered it with a tarpaulin.

The Townsend children said good-bye shyly to Mr and Mrs Watson and boisterously to Jane.

'See you Monday, Janey!' they called. 'Thank you for a lovely party.'

Then Richard said, 'I s'pose we ought to be going too. We have had a grand day and thank you all very much ... Look at young Susan! She's asleep already.'

'I'm not,' his sister replied indignantly, 'but I'm glad it's not so hot now. I think I like this part of the day best.'

'You Herricks will come along home with us,' Mrs Watson said, 'and help us finish up Janey's party properly ... We'll telephone your mother, Richard, and Mr Watson will run you home in the car after supper ... Can you stay awake for supper, Susan?' Susan slipped her hand into Mrs Watson's and smiled her thank you and so they all got into the car and went down the hill to the farm.

Later, when her uncle took the rectory children home, Jane went too. As they rushed through the night, which was warm and very still, she watched the flies and moths flicker in the glare of the headlights. Once the lights picked out a rabbit crouching with terror in the road and when they were nearly home again, a big bird rushed towards the car as if it was going to attack them and Jane instinctively ducked her head.

Uncle William laughed. 'The owl, I reckon!'

Jane waited in the farmyard while her uncle put the car away. The sky blazed with stars and the longer she gazed the more stars seemed to appear. When Mr Watson had locked the barn in which the car was kept he joined his niece and slipped an arm round her shoulders.

'Stars be too bright to-night,' he said. 'Reckon there be wind and rain on the way … Maybe we'll have to cart the hay to-morrow.'

A huge beetle droned over their heads and was followed by a big bird a flying clumsily with mottled wings.

'That wasn't an owl, Uncle. What was it?… Oh look! I think it's caught the beetle.'

'Reckon it was a nightjar,' Uncle William said, 'You'll hear him soon making a noise like your aunt's sewing machine … Come along in, Janey, for it's time you were in bed even if you are eleven years old to-day.'

July

The Granary,
Moor End Farm.
July 1st

Darling Mummy and Daddy,

I am sorry that it is such a long time since I wrote you a Moor End letter but I don't seem to have had much time for writing letters lately because I am out of doors nearly all the time when I come home from school. Of course you have had my Janey letters every Sunday but I do want you to know some of the other things that are happening on the farm.

I am starting this now in the granary that Uncle William gave me one wet Saturday just before my birthday. I will really try and write something every day this month and then next month you will both be here for the holidays and when I think of that I am so excited I can hardly write at all.

First of all I had better tell you that the ducklings are growing up beautifully but maybe George and Gerald aren't going to be drakes like Aunt Kate said because they don't seem to be having curls to their tails after all. It is a good thing to have ducks to lay eggs but Uncle says I had better call these two Georgina and Geraldine and maybe the one I call Clarissa will have to be Charlie. Sometimes he is very funny and I love him very much just the same. Auntie says that Broody will p'raps lay an egg soon and get tired of the ducklings and forget all about them. I shall have to feed them and then in October they ought to start laying eggs.

Now I want to tell you about the sheep shearing. I expect you remember Frank the shepherd 'cos I think I told you how we went to see him when the lambs were coming soon after I came here. Last Friday two other men who are shepherds on other farms came to help Frank shear our sheep. I saw them doing it when I came home from school and I didn't like it much because the sheep were baaing all the time and looking hot and frightened before they were done and white and thin and silly after. It is rather difficult to explain how it is done and I hated watching them because it looked cruel but Frank says it isn't and that God put sheep in the world to give us wool and mutton. The men who did the clipping sat on one end of a form and another man brought a sheep which they dragged on to the form on its back. Then the man with the clippers started clipping at the wool very quickly until the wool, which is called a fleece, was pulled off like an overcoat. Then another man took the fleece and rolled it up and the poor, thin-looking sheep which looked quite naked was pushed off into another corner of the rickyard where they had put some hurdles. I don't think this shearing is much fun and although Uncle says the sheep are much more comfortable in the hot weather without their wool I feel jolly sorry for them when it is being done.

They did it on Saturday again and now all the sheep are back again in their fields and I am glad I can't hear their baaing any more. The other men have gone too.

I have been helping Aunt Kate pick the raspberries in the garden. I never knew they grew quite like they do here. I like raspberries very much and we are going to send you some in a big tin with green leaves inside to help keep them fresh. They grow so fast that every evening after tea there is another basketful ready and we have made lots of jam and bottled them too. In the morning when we look at the bottles the fruit is a most lovely red colour. We have raspberries and cream for breakfast too.

The most exciting thing I am looking forward to is Sally's puppies. Uncle says they will be born in about a week and that I can choose for my own whichever one I like. Sally is so sweet that I am sure her puppies will be wonderful.

I don't think I have much to tell you about birds like I did before when I wrote you Moor End letters. Richard has been rather busy with butterflies lately and I am not so good at them. But he says the birds don't sing much now and even the cuckoo makes quite a different sort of noise as if he has forgotten how to 'cuckoo'. He just says 'cuck-cuck' and sounds very tired. When he first came to Moor End I thought I liked the cuckoo but now I think he is a beastly bird. Sometimes, on the way up to the wood we used to see a tiny naked baby bird dead on the ground and then we knew the baby cuckoo had pushed it out of its nest to die. Richard says the cuckoos 'cuck' like this now because they are almost ready to fly back to Africa and that later on the young cuckoos will go too. I can't think how they can find their way without their mothers and fathers. But when we walk carefully in the wood and along by the hedges the baby birds flying are everywhere but it is difficult to know them because they haven't got their coloured feathers yet.

Now I must go and pick some raspberries but I won't post it yet until I have written some more.

※

Saturday

I am sorry I haven't written any more since Tuesday but I am so busy. I am writing this on my window ledge in my pyjamas because it is *terrifically* hot still and we have had a marvellous day. What do you think Uncle William did? He took us in the car for a picnic and we went miles and miles. He isn't so busy on the farm now. This morning he said it would do us all good to get away for a change and when I said Richard and Susan were coming over he said, 'Ask them to come along — the more the better.' So when we rang up Mr Herrick he said they all needed a holiday too and they would all come and bring their car. When they came there was Mr and Mrs Herrick and Richard, Susan and Peter and two others called Judith and Jimmy. They are twins and their mother is in hospital and they haven't got much money I don't think, so the rector brought them for a treat. They are nine and were great fun. Some of the time they came in our car.

I don't know the way we went but it was through Crossmarket and over the railway and then a long way along some lovely lanes till we came to some hills which were covered at the bottom with very green ferns called bracken. We had our picnic in a shady place and then left the cars and climbed up the tallest hill till the bracken stopped and there was heather.

On the way there was a little wood of pine trees — rather like the one that led to the witch's house I told you about. There was a path through the wood and I was going first with Susan when I saw a big, dusty heap of pine needles and when we looked carefully it was almost moving. It was an ant's nest and Uncle says there must have been *millions* of wood ants in the pile which is a sort of a city they make for themselves. We poked a little hole in it and at once thousands of little ants came scurrying out carrying bits of rubbish. Some carried white eggs bigger than themselves and Mr Herrick said that if we came back this evening the hole would probably be mended. I thought the ants were like soldiers because they all seemed to know what to do. Sometimes when one ant wasn't strong enough to carry a pine needle another one would come along just as if the first one had called him and then they would both carry it back to the hole in the nest.

Then we walked up to the top of the hill where the grass was very short. It wasn't so hot up here because there was a wind and we could all see a very long way. Richard said he was glad he hadn't brought our food up here because it was a hard climb and Uncle said we *had* brought it with us and everybody laughed especially Judith and Jimmy who laughed long after everyone else had stopped. Somehow I don't think they are very used to laughing and I am rather unhappy for them because although you are away nearly all the time their mother is ill in hospital which is far worse.

We came home a different way and had tea out in the garden of a tea-shop place in a village. While we were waiting for tea Mr Herrick took us to look at the church which was *very old indeed* and stood on a little hill with the houses round it. Mr Herrick said that the men who built old churches like this hundreds of years ago always built on a hill if they could because the church was God's house which must stand above everything else in the village. I'd never thought of that before had you? Inside he showed us lots of lovely things and how the stone floor and the step at the altar were worn down by people's feet which shows how long people had been coming to this little church to say their prayers.

When we got back there was an *enormous* tea spread on tables in the shade. We all had an egg except Uncle William who isn't very keen on them. Judith and Jimmy were too shy to eat much to begin with but presently they got better and we got worried about Judy who couldn't seem to stop.

This cottage had a very nice garden — quite different from the Moor End or the rectory gardens. Everything here grew very close together and there were some very smart, tall flowers on spikes called hollyhocks and some giant sunflowers too, looking rather like big faces. I mean you could easily have made them look like faces if you had painted a nose and eyes and a mouth on the dark part in the middle.

At the bottom of the garden there was a bush with fat hanging spikes of purple flowers. I thought they had a rather nasty smell but the bush was *smothered* with butterflies. There were two sorts and I can remember them. One was called the peacock which had two big eye spots on its wings when they were opened. When its wings were shut it looked all black so it was a great surprise when its wings opened wide to see such lovely colours. The other one Mr Herrick said was called the red admiral and this one was very bright and gay. Its wings were brown with strips of red and white spots. The back wings had red edges and black spots. The red admirals stayed on the flowers even when we came quite close and just opened and closed their wings very slowly and gently as if they were breathing.

There were apple trees in this garden too and I noticed that the apples weren't green any longer but when Richard and I tried one they were still jolly sour.

We had a lovely ride home and we pushed the roofs of both cars back and we all sang. It was a pity that Judy felt sick but I don't think she was used to cars.

Now it is too dark for me to write any more and I can hear the owl and I am so sleepy I can't stop yawning.

So good night darlings,
With love from
JANEY

✕

Moor End,
Wednesday

Darling Mummy and Daddy,

When I cycled up the hill this morning on the way to school I saw something very peculiar happening in the potato field. All the potato plants are up high and green now and some of the tops have purple flowers on them. Sidney was on the tractor which was pulling a thing like a small watercart and a spray was coming out behind and all the plants were covered with pale green when the water-cart had passed. It was very hot already and I would have liked to be sprayed by it if there had been time. I like my school very much but sometimes in this lovely weather I wish I hadn't got to go. But it will soon be the holidays and it is only three weeks before you come and we will have the loveliest holidays we have ever had. I have got a calendar in the kitchen and I cross off the days till you come.

In the hedges now the flowers that come before the blackberries are all out. I am looking forward to these. There is another flower too like a white bell which grows on a long thin stalk that twines through the hedge. It is difficult to pick and I must remember to ask its name. But there are two more Miss Wilson told me about at school that I do remember.

The first is called goosegrass and it isn't much of a flower at all but it grows by the ditch in the hedge and you know it because the leaves and the stem and the little flowers are all covered with tiny prickles. The prickles don't hurt, but if you pick it and throw it on anybody's clothing it will stick.

The other little flower is yellow and I found it on the common where it grows a lot. It has a narrow stalk and groups of little spiky leaves. The tiny little flowers grow in groups too. This is called lady's bedstraw.

I remember one more thing I wanted to tell you about. I found on a hawthorn leaf and then on the end of another leaf in the hedge a blob of white froth. There were lots of these blobs about which looked as if someone had been spitting. One day I asked Susan and she said that an animal was inside the spit. I didn't really believe her, so on the way home to-night I found one of these things which I know now is called a frog spit. I looked at it jolly carefully but couldn't see anything in it and thought Susan must have been laughing at me. But she wasn't because I got a pencil out of my satchel and poked the point into the froth and found a funny little yellow insect. If you look very closely at him it seems as if he has quite a nose and two dots for eyes. I don't know whether he makes the froth purposely or what it is for — I must ask somebody.

I have kept the most exciting news till the end like they do in stories. When I got home to-night Uncle was in the farmyard

Sally was very proud of herself and her four puppies.

with a bundle of straw in his arms. He called me over and showed me where he was making a bed in a dry corner of the big barn. When he had made it nice and soft he put some boards across the corner just to make it cosier and told me this was where Sally would have her puppies. So we got a dish of water and called Sally who is very fat now and I gave her a hug and she seemed to know that she was a most important person so we said good-bye to her and left her because Uncle said she would rather be by herself and that there wasn't anything to fuss about and that I could go and see her in the morning. So good night for now and I will write before I go to school how many puppies there are.

Thursday morning

There are four puppies! They are marvellous and all like Sally — golden colour with big ears. Their eyes are shut and Uncle would not let me stay long to look at them but I spoke to Sally and she is very proud of herself and was very pleased to see us. Isn't it marvellous? Now I must stop and will post this in Townsend on my way to school.

With love from
JANEY

✕

Moor End,
Sunday

Darling Mummy and Daddy,

You are not going to get a Janey letter to-day because I shan't have time. I had such an adventure yesterday that I must tell you all about it at once.

In case you don't know, yesterday was St Swithin's Day. On Friday I had a letter from Richard marked 'Secret' — of course

I can tell you about it now 'cos it isn't secret any more. The letter said would I wait for him after school because he wanted to see me specially before Saturday. He said too that perhaps I could cycle to meet him 'cos he goes by train to his school and cycles from the station which is a long way from the village. So I told Aunt Kate that I would be late home on Friday and she didn't mind because she says it does me good to be out of doors as much as I can. After school then, because I had plenty of time, I went into the rectory with Susan and told her about the puppies and played with her. She didn't seem to know anything about a secret with Richard so I didn't say anything either and when it was time I cycled out along a road I didn't know to meet him. It is a nice road and for some of the time it goes by a common which is not like ours at Moor End. It is not so tidy and there are gypsies on it and I thought they were filthy dirty and I didn't like the way they looked at me. The only flowers I saw were those tall pink ones that used to grow in the places where the bombs fell in the war. Do you remember Daddy that we used to wonder how these flowers could grow in all the rubbishy piles of dirt and dust and broken bricks? I'm sure this was the same flower but I forget its name now. I got off my bike to look at it and a yapping gypsy dog came up and I was glad when Richard whizzed along on his bike and shouted at the dog till it rushed back to a dirty caravan and started barking again. I asked him to tell me quickly about the secret because I had come all this way specially to meet him. He said he wouldn't until he had shown me the goldfinches and I couldn't make him alter his mind so we cycled back till we came to a gate into a field. We left our bikes and climbed over and it was the sort of field that looks as if it had never been any good. It was full of thistles which now were big balls of fluff breaking up in the breeze and drifting about like dandelion clocks.

Richard said he'd seen goldfinches in this field every day for a week and that if we kept still now we should see them again.

They soon came but we heard them before we saw them. Do you remember the canary Mrs Smith next door used to keep in a cage? The goldfinches' song was rather like a canary and every now and then it made a lovely little tinkling. Then we saw them flying and I cannot explain how dainty and gay they were. Their heads were red, black and white and their wings black and gold and they flew like fairies must fly when you can see them. And all the time they were on the thistle heads picking at the seeds.

Richard does all the things that other boys do and sometimes I hardly see him at all because he is with his other friends but he is different about birds. Sometimes he seems to forget everything else when he is watching them, and he was like that with the goldfinches so after a little I asked him why he wanted to see me so specially and what was the secret. Then he laughed and told me that to-morrow was St Swithin's Day and that if it rained on that day it would rain every day for forty days. He said it might be fun to go and see the old witch woman in the pine wood who told us to come and see her again when we went on Midsummer Eve. Do you remember I told you about her? I didn't know whether Richard was joking but he said he wanted to see whether the old lady could do any spells to make it rain on St Swithin's Day and we might as well go and see her anyway. So although we knew she wasn't a witch we thought it would be fun to go, and Richard said he had asked another friend from his school called John and his sister Rosemary to come too because they had never seen a witch. Then he winked at me and I saw it was going to be a joke and I said I would call at the rectory for them in the morning. And that's all I can write now after all 'cos I'm tired of writing. More to-morrow.

✕

Monday

When I got out of bed on St Swithin's Day I looked out of the window and it didn't look as if it was going to be fine. I wondered why of all the days in the year it must look like raining on this day and then at breakfast Aunt Kate told me a little rhyme about St Swithin without me asking. I wrote it down after and here it is. This is what she said her mother had told her when she was a little girl:

> Saint Swithin's Day be thou fair,
> Twill rain for forty days no mair.
> Saint Swithin's Day if thou dost rain,
> For forty days it will remain.

and then she told me what I hadn't understood before — that if it was fine to-day it would be fine for forty days which would mean that it would be grand for your holiday.

Then Uncle came in and said it would be a wet St Swithin's and that if I was going out for a picnic with Richard we had better not go too far and I should take a mac. I looked out of the window and the sun was shining now. It was very hot and didn't look like rain but Uncle is generally right so I put my mac in my bike basket on the top of the sandwiches and the big bag of fat yellow gooseberries that Aunty gave me.

It was stuffy out of doors and I was out of breath when I got to the beech trees. By the time I reached the rectory the sun had gone but it was hotter than ever. Richard and John were having a slow bicycle race in the road which was rather stupid particularly as Richard fell off. Rosemary was as old as me and nice. She had fair plaits longer than mine. John was not quite as old as Richard and had red hair and freckles and was rather cheeky and when I thought about it afterwards it seemed as if he and Richard punched each other whenever they had a chance. I think boys are silly sometimes.

'Are you really going to show us a witch?' Rosemary asked. 'What fun knowing one. I'm longing to see her.'

I didn't tell her that this witch was not real because Richard might have been cross.

Rosemary and John hadn't got macs because the sun was shining when they left home and Richard said he wasn't going to bother anyway so we started off. It was very hot on the way and I think we all felt how stuffy it was. It began to get dark too and there was no wind at all not even when we free-wheeled downhill. Just before we got to the pine wood on each side of the road John got a puncture. His back tyre went quite flat and he was very funny because he got in a temper and kicked his bicycle. Richard had a puncture set, so the boys got the tyre off and Rosemary and me cycled back to a cottage we had just passed for a jug of water which was difficult to carry. They found the hole in the tyre easily enough but it was nearly half an hour before we were ready again. The weather was most peculiar now and I was jolly sure it was going to rain hard for St Swithin's. Richard wanted to make a camp fire on the side of the wood by the witch's house and cook some potatoes he had brought. He said we could spy on the witch at the same time and everybody agreed that this was a good idea. When we reached the wood where the trees came right down to the road it was very dark indeed and Richard said that was because we were near the witch and she was casting a spell over us. His voice sounded very loud and when we stopped outside the little white gate nobody spoke because everybody was quiet and waiting.

I didn't like it and I know that Rosemary hated it too. There was no wind to move the trees, no birds sang and nobody came along the road to cheer us up. I don't think anybody dared to say we ought to go home but I thought p'raps we should 'cos I was sure that we were going to get wet through soon.

Richard said that we had better go on and we could have our fire at the far side of the wood. We left our bikes in the hedge and went right into the wood. John whistled very loudly and Rosemary whispered to me, 'I think this a hateful place.'

When we came out of the trees the sky was a horrid sort of yellow in one part and black in another. Richard showed the others the chimney of the witch's house and said we would light our camp fire just where we were so as the witch couldn't see us.

We gathered lots of fir cones and some twigs and Richard and John had a punching match but at last we got the fire going. We had just put the potatoes in the red ashes when the first thunder came although it was a long way away.

Richard said, 'She's doing her spells ... Just you watch and you'll see her come out of that chimney on a broomstick ... I expect she'll do another magic any minute. Jane and me know this is a very wicked place and I'm going to ask my father to come and take the curse away.'

Of course it was very naughty of Richard to talk like this but the peculiar thing was that something like magic *did* happen but I'll tell you about that tomorrow 'cos I'm too tired now to write any more.

Wednesday

I couldn't write any more last night, but now I'll finish this adventure and post it all to you at once. Just after Richard said that he knew something magic was going to happen there was a most horrible sort of screech from over our heads and then the air was full of screaming birds with big black wings, whirling and flying so fast that they were all mixed up together. They swooped round our heads and over the little cottage screaming so loud that Rosemary put her hands over her ears.

Richard stared up at them and then said, 'They're swifts! I'm sure they are but I've never seen so many … Why are they doing this?'

And John said with half a laugh, 'Magic, I suppose.'

Then there were two more bangs of thunder and some horrid great flashes of lightning and a wind started to shake the trees. Before we could do anything else there was another crash and we couldn't see anything for hail. Great marbles of hail hit our heads and faces, put out the fire in a twinkling and made the ground white.

'Come on,' Richard shouted. 'Down to the cottage. We mustn't go in the wood 'cos of the lightning,' and he started to run down the hill.

'We can't go *there*,' Rosemary yelled clutching at my arm but I knew that the old woman wasn't a witch and that it was the only thing to do. As we ran after Richard the hail stopped and the rain came and I'm sorry Mummy but I seemed to be soaked before I could put on my mac. Richard was in front and he tore down the hill and through the little white gate with us just behind him. Streams of water were already rushing down the hill into the tiny garden and while we waited — all of us puffing and blowing — in the porch the door opened and there was the old witch.

Richard was very polite to her.

'I'm so sorry,' he said, 'but I do hope you won't mind if we shelter till this is over … Do you remember that Jane and me came to see you on Midsummer Eve?'

Then she looked at us all with little, black, sparkly eyes and smiled at me without any teeth and told us to come in. Rosemary was afraid but I whispered that she wasn't real and that we must get dry anyway and we all squeezed into a little room where everything was shining. The big black cat got up from a hearthrug made of coloured scraps of cloth and arched its back at us and spat. The old witch, who said her name was Martha Hawkins, made some tea on the fire in the tiny grate and while we were having it the rain got worse than ever and the lightning and thunder were terrible. Suddenly Richard jumped up and said, 'Quick! Your broomstick, Mrs Hawkins. Look at the water.' We looked and saw brown water coming in under the door and the broom couldn't sweep it away properly 'cos a stream of water was rushing down the garden path. Then Richard called to John to help him and what do you think they did? They took off their coats and shirts and socks and shoes and dashed out into the awful rain and slammed the door. From the window we saw them make a dam of earth and turf across the doorstep to stop the water coming into the room. Then they scooped out a little ditch with their hands so that the stream coming in at the front gate went into the garden and not down the path. Mrs Hawkins was pleased about this and so were the boys who were now terribly wet and covered with mud. After they had washed themselves under a pump in the scullery and put on their clothes again John asked her about the screaming birds that came so suddenly and then disappeared as soon as the storm broke. She was rather deaf and he had to shout, and then she nodded her head and said something about 'Devil Birds' and 'Flying Demons' and that it was bad to be here when they flew like this. Then I thought she seemed quite witch-like and I began to wonder whether maybe we had been wrong in thinking she was an ordinary old lady 'cos she kept on muttering about 'bad birds' and looked rather peculiar. She gave us more tea though, and the rain got worse than ever and came spattering down the big chimney. Rosemary tried to make friends with the cat but it wouldn't and I wished we were at home.

After a bit I said could I take off my sandals and dry them. Then the old lady stopped muttering about 'bad birds' and pushed the boys in the scullery again and got Rosemary and me a towel and

'I do hope you don't mind if we shelter here till the rain is over,'
said Richard politely.

made us undress and dry ourselves by the fire. Our clothes weren't very wet now but she made us do it and we had some more tea and we weren't a bit shivery any longer.

Then suddenly the sun came out and Richard shouted from the back that there was a big rainbow and we all went out into the garden. Even Mrs Hawkins came to the door and smiled again without any teeth. Nearly all the flowers were knocked down or washed out of the soil and the path down the side of the hill was nearly a ditch with water still pouring down it. Everything was shining now and the birds — the nice birds — began to sing again and all the earth was steaming. The sky was blue again and the rainbow was the biggest I have ever seen.

Old Mrs Hawkins laughed with a sort of cackle and said, 'Look for the crock o' gold m'dears! You'll find it at the foot of the rainbow!'

Then Richard said we had better clear up a bit so we shovelled away the mud from the doorstep and swept it as clear as we could. When this was done Rosemary — who is really very sweet — thanked Mrs Hawkins for sheltering us and for giving us tea and said we would bring her a new packet of tea one day. She was very pleased about this and laughed again and said something rather funny. She said, 'And next time you come don't bring the rain like you did to-day for St Swithin,' and she said it just as if *we* had made a magic and brought the rain.

We walked back up the hill and through the wood. I'm sorry again Mummy but our shoes were wet through long before we had scrambled up to the trees. The water was still splashing out of the branches and we were glad to get back to the road and our bikes. John felt his back tyre but it was still hard so we went straight back to the rectory. In some places, at the bottom of the hills, the road was under water and everywhere the gutters were running and the ditches full.

When we got there Mrs Herrick was in the garden cutting lavender and I have put a piece in this letter for you. Mrs Herrick says she saves all the trimmings from her lavender and rosemary bushes. Sometimes she throws them in the porch where visitors' feet crush them and make them smell and sometimes she saves them until the winter when she throws them on the fire. I shall ask Aunt Kate to do that.

That is all my adventure and *I haven't got a cold*.

With love from
JANEY

August

Jane woke soon after the sun was up. There was no special sound to awaken her for the dawn was very still. No bird sang and the world outside her window drowsed in a haze of heat. She woke because she was too excited to sleep any longer. So excited that she hated the idea of breakfast and only wanted the hours to slip by until her mother and father arrived at Crossmarket this afternoon for a fortnight's wonderful holiday.

No good getting back to bed now so she dressed and slipped quietly downstairs. The grandfather clock in the hall said half-past five and for the first time since she had been at Moor End she was up before her uncle and aunt.

In the kitchen, Simon, the old black cat, stretched on his chair and purred as she tickled him under the chin. She found a pencil on the dresser and, on the back of an old bill, wrote

Dear Auntie,

I have got up and gone out 'cos I couldn't sleep. Back to breakfast.

Janey

Then she slipped the bolt on the back door and went out into the farmyard. It was very still and quiet here too, for the horses had been in their field since May and were not stamping and fidgeting in the stable as they did in winter.

She sniffed the lovely, cool smell of early morning in the country — the smell of mist, the smell of a farm and of animals, the scent of growth in the hedge and of distant blossom — and then ran over to the barn in which Sally slept with her babies. The spaniel whimpered with pride as Jane fondled her and played with the puppies who were scrambling over each other in their excitement.

As Jane crossed the farmyard and climbed over the gate, Sally stood in the doorway of the barn slowly wagging her tail but would not follow her. As she jumped down a fairy thread of gossamer clung to her face and when she looked carefully she saw countless strands of silvery webs stretched along the hedgerows and drifting from the trailing branches of blackberry to the bracken above the ditch. When the sun caught them she saw that each tiny thread was loaded with minute but gleaming dewdrops.

The dew was heavy on the grass too and Jane kicked off her sandals and ran barefoot through it along the edge of the ditch. Her feet and legs were now as tanned as her face which had filled out and glowed with health and happiness. She laughed to herself as she thought how shocked her mother would be to know that she ran about now without shoes or stockings and never even caught a cold! Then she stepped into some nettles, put her sandals on again and trotted on up the hill until she came to the gate into the root field. She was out of breath now so she climbed up and sat in her favourite position on the top bar of the gate and watched the wheat and oats down in the valley change colour as the sun climbed up the sky. She tucked her toes under the second rung to keep her steady and sat with her chin on her hands and her elbows on her knees. As the sun warmed her cheek, the mists below her fled and the colour of the wheat changed to a deeper, golden brown. The oats in the next field were a much lighter colour and she knew the differences between them now. 'Three or four more days and we'll be cutting,' her uncle had said yesterday and Jane knew now that August was the busiest month of all the year on a farm when the farmer saw the results of all his work. She knew too that everybody helped at harvest and that Aunt Kate would not have much time to look after Mummy and Daddy but that they understood that too and would do all they could to help. Jane smiled as she thought of her mother helping and hoped she would bring some country shoes this time!

The glowing grain at the foot of the hill looked very inviting so she jumped off the gate and walked down between the rows of swedes towards it. Two rabbits jumped out from almost under her feet and with a flick of white tails dashed down the hill and disappeared into the standing corn.

Then Jane remembered what Mr Herrick had told her only yesterday when she had met him in the village. He had asked her when her father and mother were coming and then told her that the first day of August was a special day in the Church's calendar called Lammastide. He often told Jane interesting things like this and when she asked what Lammas meant he said that it was the festival of the first fruits or Loafmas.

'Once upon a time, Janey,' he went on, 'when life was altogether simpler and when men and women in this country came to Church to say their prayers and to give thanks, they offered to God on this day a loaf baked of the newly gathered grain … So when you say your prayers to-morrow, remember to be thankful for the bread you eat every day and to ask that the harvest everywhere may be safely gathered in.'

Jane remembered this as she ran down between the big, fleshy leaves of the swedes and thought of all the excitement of the next few weeks and what fun it would be to help to get the harvest home.

She stood on the rough track that divided the fields and looked at the wheat standing straight and heavy-headed in front of her. It was wonderful how straight and regular it grew. Every seed which had been sown eight months ago must have come up. She picked one of the ears and rubbed it in between the palms of her hands as she had seen her uncle do. It was prickly at first and then the ripe grains rolled out and, with one puff, she blew away the chaff and popped the corn into her mouth.

Although there was no wind Jane was suddenly aware of a tiny rustling noise and she thought some of the stalks a few feet away swayed very slightly. She went down on her knees and very gently parted the stiff, tall grain just in time to see a tiny, red-brown mouse climbing up to a little round nest, which was fixed to several of the stalks. Jane had never seen a nest made by a mouse before, but this one looked so delicate and frail that she was afraid to see if it contained any babies. The mouse which had slipped into it was so very small and helpless and was probably very frightened so she moved her hands and the stalks slipped back into place.

Then she wandered on along the path and looked at the oats which did not stand so tall and straight as the wheat. The sun moved up the sky and chased the early morning mists away and the cock in the Moor End farmyard began to crow as if he had not been awake for hours. Jane looked back at the house and saw a plume of blue smoke above the kitchen chimney and knew that Aunt Kate was up and boiling the kettle for her husband's first cup of tea. But breakfast would not be ready yet so she strolled on and wondered why she had never got up so early before. She thought of home — real home — and of how hot the pavements would be in this weather and of how the High Road would smell of petrol and of hot tar and of how the little gardens would all look so tired and dry. Mummy and Daddy would be getting up soon because they would have a lot to do to-day and she knew how Mummy would fuss about leaving the house and locking everything up.

It would be difficult to leave Moor End when the time came but she knew she would have to go back. She wondered why anybody chose to live in the towns but she supposed people had to do so. Two butterflies fluttered up from the oats to greet a new day and then, very faint and far away, she a heard a church clock strike. As she counted seven strokes she felt hungry and turned back along the path to Moor End. At the farmyard gate she met George who stared at her with open mouth.

'And what have you bin a'doin', young miss?'

Jane laughed.

'I like getting up before breakfast ... I always do! ... My mummy and daddy are coming to-day, George ... They're coming for their holiday.'

'Holidays!' George snorted. 'No holidays for the loikes of me at this time o' year.'

'What are you going to do with that great knife thing?' she asked, pointing to the scythe which he was carrying.

'I be going to cut the oats ready for binder,' he said and he went on to explain that he cut by hand round the edge of the field so that the tractor had a clear path to haul the binder. Jane did not quite understand how the mysterious binder worked but when she asked her uncle at breakfast he told her that she should see everything on Tuesday morning when they would be ready to start.

'And you might ask young Richard and any other youngsters big enough to help,' he continued. 'We'll be wanting all the help we can get for the next fortnight and I pay well for stookin.'

This sounded rather weird to Jane also, but she didn't ask what 'stookin' was and just pretended that she understood.

'I'll ring him up if I don't see him to-morrow,' she said. 'Why aren't you going to start on Monday, Uncle? Because it's Bank Holiday?'

'Sometimes we all work on August Monday but not if we can help it, for 'tis important day at Townsend. There's the flower show and the cricket too and I thought maybe your ma and pa would be liking to see both … Now I must be off … Be ready for station at half-past four, Janey … I s'pose I've got to spare the time to take you …!'

Jane found it difficult to make the hours pass until tea time. She telephoned the rectory but Richard and Susan were out, so then she went to watch George scything. He seemed to do it very well and for a time she was fascinated to see how he swung the big blade from right to left and brought the golden grain tumbling down. Every few minutes he stopped and sharpened the blade with a long, grey stone, and she liked the ringing noise of this too. At dinner time it was so hot that they took their meal out of doors and had it under the apple tree. Aunt Kate did not often do this.

'I don't hold with picnics and the like,' she had said once, 'and I can't see the sense of carrying food all over the countryside and sitting on the hard ground and getting bitten by insects … I reckon the Almighty meant us to have our meals indoors at a table in a proper, civilized way.'

After dinner, Jane fidgeted so much that she broke a glass when she was helping her aunt and was sent out of the kitchen. In the farmyard the pair of swallows were particularly busy and as Jane looked idly up at the eaves of her granary she saw that four new fledglings of the second brood were perched on the edge of the rain-water gutter. The four babies were huddled close together while the parent birds flashed to and fro round the yard swooping for the flies which they brought to their children. After a little the mother began to jostle the baby at the end of the row from the gutter and Jane stood entranced to see the little birds take their first proper flying lesson. Twice she chased the lurking farm cats away and once was quite cross with Joan the dairy maid when she crossed the yard with clattering pails and frightened the swallows.

At last it was time to go and put on a clean frock and, because it was so hot, she took her sunbonnet too and wondered if her mother would notice it.

Uncle William was in a great hurry to-day and his wife did not insist on him changing so he drove off in his open-necked khaki shirt and his old straw hat. They pushed the roof of the car back and were in Crossmarket almost before Jane realized that they had passed the forge and the friendly blacksmith.

'I've got some jobs to do, Janey,' he said. 'Train's due in ten minutes and I'll try and be back by then. If I'm not, wait for me outside in the yard.'

So Jane smiled at the old porter and went on to the platform. She remembered how she had waited here at Easter when the weather was very different. To-day the heat was stifling under the station roof and beating up from the platform. Then a bell rang sharply in the signal box and the level crossing gates swung open and closed the road. Above the gleaming, silvery rails the heat shimmered and against the black palings of the fence at the back of the platforms a row of giant crimson hollyhocks stood like sentinels. She strolled up and saw the big, fat, furry bumblebees buzzing from flower to flower. Then she heard the distant whistle of her train and ran back to the exit. The old porter knew all about Jane now and even remembered the dark, cold night in January when she had first come to Crossmarket. He had a grand-daughter of his own — younger than Jane — and when youngsters didn't get in his way and clutter up his station he liked them. He gave her a friendly grin and clipped his ticket clippers within an inch of her freckled nose. Her eager little face laughed up at him as she flicked back the two black plaits tied so tightly and neatly with new green ribbon in honour of the occasion.

Then with a roar the long train slid into the platform and she saw her father waving to her. He was on the platform before she could reach him and then he pretended not to know her.

'It can't be our Janey,' he said to Mummy. 'This is a girl about three years older pretending to be her … I wonder where we shall find our Jane? Shall we ask her?'

But after that none of them could pretend any longer and they were all still admiring each other on the platform when the train went out and Uncle William in his old shirt and farm boots came clumping up to meet them.

That evening, after supper, they all sat under the apple tree again as the sun set the western sky afire. The two men lit their pipes to keep the midges away and Jane sat on a cushion on the grass and leaned against her mother's knees.

Overhead the bats fluttered blindly. Before she went to bed Jane took her parents to see Sally and her puppies. She did not go to sleep quickly for she was too excited. The reflection of the sunset died out of the eastern sky before her mother left her and then the night, like grey-blue velvet, slid up outside her window and while she watched a star blinked — and then another and another until the summer sky blazed with the light of distant worlds.

※

The weather held. Sunday was so hot that they stayed at home in the garden. The common opposite the house shimmered in the heat and Uncle William rubbed his chin and said, 'Maybe we ought to start cuttin' to-morrow.'

But when to-morrow came everyone was in holiday mood and after an early lunch they all squeezed into the car and rode down to Townsend. Jane had often played with the others over the village green and had even paddled in the rather muddy little pond in which a few white ducks used to stand on their heads. She had never thought much about this patch of grass round which the houses of the village were built but to-day it looked very different. At the rectory end were three big white tents and this, Uncle said, was the flower show. At the other end of the green was another white tent for the cricketers; for to-day was the most important match of the year and as they got out of the car the umpires in their white coats came out on to the pitch.

Then Richard and Susan came running over to greet them. After they had shaken hands with Jane's mother and father, Richard said: 'You haven't forgotten the sports, have you, Janey? I put your name down for three races, so you owe me one and sixpence.'

'You *didn't* Richard! I've hardly ever run in a race. What are they?'

'Egg and spoon and hundred yards and two-twenty yards under twelve.'

'But Richard,' Jane's mother broke in, 'it's very nice of you to think of Janey but I don't think she ought to run races. I don't think she's strong enough. She's been ill you know.'

Mr and Mrs Watson looked at each other and smiled as Jane said:

'Oh, but Mummy, I'm better now and I'd like to try.'

So they left the cricket and went over to the field behind the rectory where the sports had started. Some small children were, at that very moment, running in the first race. Several of them paused to looked round at those still behind them and others looked anxiously for their parents lining the course.

Susan glanced towards the plodding runners and said suddenly in her deep little voice:

'Peter will win. We've been training for this.'

Then Jane realized that Peter, in short-legged blue dungarees — and not very much else — was already well ahead. He was running with his head up and his eyes fixed on his mother who had the foresight to stand by the winning post.

He won easily amidst sympathetic applause.

Next came the egg and spoon race and Jane did her best but it was not a very good best. She was in too much of a hurry and kept on dropping the egg. Then there was a hundred yards race for boys and Richard won this. He was a very good runner. Jane's hundred yards followed. There were twelve runners and she knew most of the girls but she felt very shy and nervous and her heart was banging uncomfortably against her ribs as they all lined up waiting for the pistol. The bang came almost before she was ready and suddenly all the others seemed to be in front of her. She lost her nervousness then and had passed two girls when she realized that the race was over and that Richard was waiting and laughing at her.

'You start too late Jane,' he said. 'But you finished well. You'll win the two-twenty yards if you do as I say. Don't worry if the others get ahead at the beginning but keep just behind until you come to where I'll be standing and then go for all your worth!'

'But I can't win Richard if I'm behind for all that time.'

'Yes you can. You were hardly puffed when you finished just now. It's just that you're no good for short distances ... I bet you'll win, Janey.'

They went back to the others then and Jane's mother fussed and looked worried and wanted her to wear a coat but her father winked at her and said:

'Well tried, darling. Would you like an ice?'

Jane was about to say 'Thank you' when Richard interrupted. 'Not till she's won her race, if you don't mind sir,' and everybody laughed very loudly at this and Jane went pink and then laughed too. They went back to look at the cricket match for a little while and were thrilled because Mr Herrick was batting and doing very well. They watched him make twenty-six in twenty minutes and then went back to the field again in time for Jane's big race.

Some of the girls waiting round the starter looked *enormous* to Jane. Two of them who were whispering together stared at her and said rudely:

'What's she running for? She must be in the wrong race. Look at her skinny little legs.'

Jane looked at their legs and was glad that hers were not so fat and at that very minute she made up her mind that she was going to win. She glanced up and more than halfway round the bend she saw Richard, in his bright green blazer, by the ropes. She raised her hand and he waved back and pointed to the winning post where her mother and father and uncle and aunt and Mrs Herrick and Susan and Peter were standing.

Jane felt her cheeks redden and then she clenched her teeth. She *must* win just because the ones she loved most expected her to do so.

When they lined up she found herself next to one of the big girls with the fat legs. As the pistol cracked the girl's elbow nudged her shoulder and, for a second, threw her off her balance so that she half stumbled. Then the others were all ahead again and Jane, in a furious temper, forgot Richard's advice and began to race. She passed two girls quite easily, but the winning post was still a long way off, when, out of the corner of her eye, she saw Richard's blazer and her anger died and she began to think coolly and to run more steadily without straining. Far ahead the two big girls were thudding along together so Jane, without quite realizing what she was doing, lengthened her stride and caught up three others. As soon as she reached them she saw that Richard had been right for all three of them were very red and out of breath while she was beginning to feel that she could go on for ever. She was halfway now and running quite easily when she saw Richard running *towards* her on the other side of the rope.

'Now, Janey!' he was calling, 'Now you can do it.'

She put her head back and felt the wind on her hot cheeks as she passed her three companions and crossed to the inside of the track by the rope. Richard was running with her now and suddenly the air was thick with shouting. Two girls from her school were just ahead for an instant and then she had passed them. She did not realize that almost everyone in the field was cheering the quaint little dark girl with the two plaits who had been last at the start but was now running like a champion and passing all but the two big leaders.

Only thirty yards to go now and Richard was yelling almost in her ear.

'Only old fat legs, Janey! Go it, Janey! You can do it.'

And she *did* do it. She had really never admitted to herself that she would do anything Richard asked her but somehow she felt now that she could not let him down. She passed one girl ten yards from the post and the other by two feet and then she was in her father's arms and everyone was clapping and shouting and made such a fuss that she wanted to cry.

But all that Richard said was, 'I knew you could do it, Janey.'

Then they all went back to the flower show and had tea outside one of the big tents. Jane had three ices. When they were halfway through she saw Judith and Jimmy the twins, whom Mr Herrick had brought on the picnic last month. They were by themselves so Jane said could they come and have tea too and they did. They didn't say much but they did enjoy the ices!

After tea they all went into the big tents and looked at the piles of fruit and flowers and vegetables which were spread on long trestle tables. There were beans and potatoes and giant red carrots, cauliflowers and onions in one tent, flowers in another and honey, butter and eggs in another. Everybody there seemed to know everybody else and there were greetings in plenty for Mr and Mrs Watson and lots of jokes because the farmer had sent nothing to the show.

'I've no time for gardening and the loike,' he laughed, 'but maybe next year I'll get missus and young Janey here to start some bees !'

Next year! Jane wondered if her uncle knew what he was saying and it was as well that she did not see her mother's face.

Then they went over to see the end of the cricket match. The shadows were lengthening over the pitch and the rooks were now cawing round their nests at the top of the big elms. While they were watching the rector won the match for Townsend by catching the last two players of the opposing team off his own very innocent-looking bowling.

Then a very grand lady made a speech and gave away the prizes to the children who had won their races and then to the flower show winners. Peter went up boldly for his prize and was then led protestingly home to bed.

Richard and Jane both won savings certificates and when the former came over to the car to say 'Good night' Mr Watson said:

'Work to-morrow, Richard. Will you come and help me stookin' an' bring any more you can ... We'll be hard at it for a fortnight now.'

Richard grinned. 'I'll come — but I don't know if I'll be much good up against Janey ... She's so quick!'

✕

Next morning Jane slept later than usual and when she awoke the air was filled with a steady throbbing which puzzled her for a minute. Then she remembered! The big tractor of course and Uncle was already cutting the harvest, and she wasn't there! Downstairs the others had nearly finished their breakfast and her father teased her a little and said she was tired because of her running.

As she scooped the last grain of white from the bottom of her brown egg Jane said:

'Which field, Auntie? I want to be there all the time … You'll come won't you Daddy 'cos there's lots of work to do … Uncle said so … We've got to do what's called stooking … Auntie, darling, what *is* stooking?'

Mrs Watson looked surprised at the question but explained how the binder cut and bound the sheaves of corn and then threw them out on to the stubble.

'Then they've got to dry properly in wind and sun,' she went on, 'and stookin' is standing the sheaves up on end in fours or sixes with the tops leaning together … You'll soon see my lass but it's hard work and you won't be able to do it all day and every day. And you'd better be wearing those dungarees I bought for you else you'll scratch yourself to bits.'

Jane's mother looked up in horror.

'Dungarees!' she gasped. 'My Jane in dungarees like a … like a … *workman*! What *do* you mean Kate?'

Everybody laughed at this and Jane ran upstairs and took off her shorts and pulled on the new brown dungarees. Her mother, when she saw them, seemed to think there was something rather shocking about them but her father liked them and went out up the lane with her and along the track to the harvest field.

Jane never forgot this day. Somehow, all that she had learned and seen of farming since coming to Moor End seemed to have been waiting for this, and she was right because harvest is the end of the farmer's year.

Sidney was on the old red tractor that was now roaring up the field away from them. Behind him came the binder with its big wooden-bladed wheel beating down the standing grain on to the knives and then flinging out the tied sheaves on the other side as her aunt had explained. One of the farm boys was sitting on a high seat on the binder and as Jane watched she saw him suddenly raise his hand and shout. The tractor stopped and Sidney jumped down. Uncle William, who had just come up, explained: 'Sometimes weeds and the like jam the binder and it's young Fred's job to watch and see that it's running properly. If it sticks he has to shout out ... P'raps we'll let you try one day Janey ... But aren't you smart, Janey! Have you come to do some work?'

'Yes please, Uncle. I've come stooking and Daddy wants to learn too.'

Then there was a lot of shouting and ringing of bicycle bells and there was Richard and three other boys and Rosemary too all come to help.

Mr Watson soon put them to work. He showed them how to lift the sheaves and put them down hard on the stubble in pairs so that the tops were close together. Each stook was made of six sheaves with three on each side.

'Like a little house,' Jane said. But it was much harder work than it looked for the sheaves were bulky and often had thistles in them which scratched badly. Sometimes too the children were not very clever for the stooks would collapse and they would have to build them up again. Soon Jane's back began to ache and her hands got red and sore but she was glad of the dungarees because they did protect her legs.

Round and round the binder went and smaller and smaller became the rectangle of golden grain in the centre of the field. After half an hour Mr Watson signalled Sidney to stop and the lad on the binder changed places with Richard who had been hoping most fervently that this would happen! Jane had a turn too and screamed 'stop' so loudly when the binder jammed at the top corner of the field that Sidney pretended

Jane had a turn on the binder.

to fall off his own seat in surprise. Mrs Watson and Jane's mother came to the field just before dinner time with big baskets and bottles and they all picnicked in the shade of the hedge while Uncle William looked anxiously at the sky and shook his head.

'Thunder about I reckon. Maybe we should have started yesterday.'

Soon after the binder had started up again two friends of Mr Watson's arrived with guns and the children were then told to keep to the top of the field out of the way while the rabbits were shot. Jane was furious about this, particularly as her father was given a gun and posted at one corner of the still standing grain.

'If you kill *one* rabbit, Daddy,' she stormed at him, 'I'll never speak to you again ... I think it's absolutely *beastly* cruel of you all.'

But when the rabbits began to escape from the square of uncut grain which was getting smaller all the time they were not so easy to shoot. They dodged between the stooks and doubled this way and that in a most bewildering way and it was easy to see that Jane's father wasn't used to shooting, for all the bunnies which came his way escaped. But the other men got plenty.

'Don't fret yourself, m'dear,' Aunt Kate said as she saw her niece's white, set face. 'We have to kill them else they would ruin the farm. Rabbits and rats are the farmer's worst enemies and if we left the bunnies alone they would soon eat up the pasture and make gaps in the hedges with their burrowing and the like ... Don't worry, Janey! You'll like them in a pie.'

But Jane did worry and felt sick each time the guns banged and the rabbits tumbled over.

By the time the field of oats was finished Frank had cut a lane round the wheat the other side of the hedge and the binder started work at once. Jane was tired now and went to sit with her mother who was trying to look comfortable as she leaned against an oak tree in the hedge.

'You look so hot and dirty, darling. Do you really *have* to do all this? Are you sure you're strong enough … The sun is coming out now and I mustn't get sunburnt else I shall be in agony … And do look at your father, Janey! I do wish he wouldn't show his braces like that.'

But Jane wasn't really listening for she was watching Rosemary coming up the field. She did hope that Mummy wouldn't ask her if she was strong enough to help when somebody else was there. It was a pity but she did not seem to understand that she was growing up and just as strong as other girls now.

Then Mrs Watson called the children and took them back to the farm to help her carry the tea over to the field. They were all tired now and when the men went back to work after the break Richard and Rosemary and the others lay on the stubble.

'I should think I've done a thousand stooks,' Richard said dreamily, 'If I turn over on my front will you rub my back, Janey … This is the hardest work I know … Shall we go and have another ride on the binder?'

'I wish I'd got some dungarees like yours, Janey,' Rosemary said. 'My legs are scratched to pieces. But I do love coming here just the same. It was jolly good you winning that race.'

As they lay there under the hedge the sun came out for the first time that day and chased the clouds away. Jane put her hands behind her head and drowsily watched the sky turn blue between the leaves of the oak tree. In the next field the throb of the tractor died to a murmur as it breasted the top of the hill and went down the other side. Below her the stooked sheaves stood up like rows of little houses with their roofs glowing in the evening sun. A flock of birds came swooping suddenly down from the north and wheeled over the field.

She nudged Richard violently. 'What are they, Richard? Look! They're flying over the house now ... Richard! I think I know what they are. We saw them the other day at the witch's house.'

Richard jumped to his feet.

'They can't be swifts, Janey! There's not going to be any thunder now ... and yet they might be. Let's go and see ... Come on you others.'

Five of them cut across the stubble between the stooks, trotted down the hedge and climbed a gate into the far end of the Moor End rickyard.

Jane was right for the swooping birds *were* swifts and Richard remembered that they gathered together in great flocks at this time ready to fly south for the winter.

'But I don't know why they fly round this house like this,' he went on, 'I suppose old Mrs Hawkins would say it was unlucky ... I remember now that Father told me that they go back very early ... The swallows are later.'

The children did not go to the harvest fields every day although Jane found herself listening for the throb of the tractor wherever she was. She loved to see the grain fall under the wooden blades of the binder and to watch the bound sheaves shoot out the other side. Her father went out nearly every day and began to look so brown and well that both his wife and daughter pretended not to know him!

One night it rained a little but the sun was hot enough next morning to turn the rain drops on the stooks to mist in a few hours. Richard and the others did not come regularly either because Mr Watson said there was no sense in them tiring themselves out. But the farmer himself was hardly ever in the house or farmyard, and twice in one week he fell asleep over his supper. The weather still threatened, so now the men hurried to build the ricks and this was work that the children loved. The three horses were harnessed to the big-wheeled carts and Richard, Rosemary and Jane were each given charge of one. They led the horses out to the distant parts of the field and then helped to load the carts with sheaves. When the cart was almost overflowing — and they made a competition of every load to see which team could finish first — they rode their horses back over the stubble to the stack which was being built. Here the sheaves were tossed on pitchforks up to old Frank and another man who built the stack around them. And they *were* round too because Uncle William told them that Frank was an expert in making round stacks and that Jane would like the look of them when their pointed roofs of straw were put on later.

Along the track between her uncle's fields Jane watched the ricks grow until they looked like a row of little round houses in a village street. She noticed how, in the other fields, the stacks were built near the gates against the hedge but in their own rickyard there was no room because the stacks left there after the threshing in March were of straw which would be used for the cattle presently.

And so the days of the holiday slipped by and Jane's mother began to get used to the country and stopped worrying as to whether it was too hot or too windy or too wet or too tiring to go out of doors. The lines on her forehead disappeared and without realizing it she got a little sunburned and looked much nicer for it!

As for Jane's daddy, he decided at the end of the first week that he had been doing the wrong sort of work for over twenty years and shocked his wife deeply by asking Mr Watson at supper one night if he could give him a job on the farm and a cottage to live in.

'I'd make a good tractor driver, William,' he said.

'That's the trouble nowadays,' the farmer replied. 'Everybody wants to drive the tractor but nobody wants to learn how to look after animals. It be stockmen I want but maybe Janey here will come back and help us at Moor End one day when she's finished her schooling!'

One day Jane's family and Richard and Susan spent a day together and explored the brook again. After they had enjoyed their picnic lunch they found a narrow part of the stream where the banks were quite deep, and dammed it. This was tremendously exciting and all of them except Jane's mother got very wet and muddy. First they got together some heavy stones and old bricks from a corner of the field and started to build a wall over which the water rushed. Then they tore turf and clay from the banks higher up and working together piled these in front of the stones. The water rose quickly but whenever a leak started Richard rammed clay into the crack while everyone else worked frantically to strengthen the wall on the other side. At last, for a few brief minutes, the stream below the dam ran dry and then Richard got panicky because

Jane watched the ricks grow until they looked like a row of little round houses.

a farmer lower down might be wanting water for his cows! So they waited until the stream overflowed the rim of the dam and loosened some of the stones and then they watched it burst and send a dirty, tidal wave roaring down the drying channel.

'I 'member some ducks down at the farm,' Susan said. 'Won't they be surprised?'

On the way home after that lovely day they saw how the blackberries and the hips on the briars in the hedge were changing colour as they ripened. In the same hedge too among the briars Jane found those odd-looking bunches of fibre which look like scarlet sewing silk. Richard said these were called 'robin's pincushions'.

They came down to Moor End through the wood and passed a patch of rosebay willow herb glowing rosily in the evening sun. Already, the base of each spike of bloom was white with the fluff of the bursting seed pods, and as they watched, these pods broke away and sailed like fairy parachutes gently in the soft breeze across the glade. On the Saturday morning when Jane's father and mother were to go home the weather broke.

'Never mind, darlings,' she said. 'It has stayed fine for you and that's all that matters. This is the loveliest holiday I've ever had and I do hope they'll ask us again next year ... If you promise that you'll come at Christmas I won't mind you going back now so much.'

Uncle William and Aunt Kate then made it clear that whatever happened there must be a reunion at Christmas and so, this time, Jane went to the station with her parents and said 'Good-bye' without a tear — or a without a tear that anybody saw!

Uncle William was very quiet as he drove back to Moor End through the puddles and under the dripping trees. When they were nearly home Jane said,

'Thank you for having them, Uncle, when you were so busy ... But we did help some of the time, didn't we ?'

He shifted his pipe.

'Can't think how we ever did without you, Janey girl! Can't think what we shall do after Christmas ... Here we are! Run in and give your aunt a hand with the plum jam and ask that young rascal Richard if he'd like to come over to-morrow and help me dig out that wasp's nest in the garden .... I'm putting poison in to-night!'

September

Jane stirred uneasily and turned over in bed. Drowsily she wondered why she had wakened so early. Then she realized that her back was cold so she snuggled her knees up to her chin and pulled the bedclothes round her and slept again until her aunt came in at seven.

'Why, Janey! You're like a little dormouse curled up for its winter sleep … but 'tis colder this morning and to-day is the first of September.'

The bathroom at Moor End overlooked the farmyard and Jane often opened the window wide when she had finished washing and dressing and called 'Good morning' to George. This morning a slight mist still covered the ground and on the roof of the barn there was a suspicion of frost.

George was watering the horses and smiled up at her as she leaned from the window, but his words were drowned by the roar of the tractor as Sidney drove in through the farmyard gate.

'What are you going to do to-day, Sidney?' Jane yelled but he couldn't hear her and only shook his head and laughed.

At breakfast her uncle told her that they were starting ploughing again to-day and that if she was not doing anything else she might come and watch.

'And there's plenty for you to be doing next week or two before you go back to school, my lass,' he said as he wiped his moustache. 'You can help your aunt pick some blackberries and the hedges are full of nuts this year … And there's a special surprise for you a week come Saturday and the harvest festival at church the day after and then I'm told it's school again for you … Are you coming with me now, Janey?'

The Herricks were away on holiday and a strange parson had come to the rectory, so for another week Jane was by herself but she was never lonely or bored. She knew that her uncle liked her with him when he went round the farm and as she never tired of his company either she agreed at once.

'We'll go and look at Sidney's ploughing afore long,' her uncle said, 'but I want a word with George first.'

The sun had driven the mist away now and in the distance Jane could hear the faint throb of the tractor. First they went round the farm buildings and met Aunt Kate on her way to feed the chickens. This reminded Jane of her ducks which were now growing fast and had long ago forgotten their foster mother. Jane was still allowed to look after them herself so she ran back to let them out of their little house, fill their water trough and give them a dish of mash. She remembered that as ducks always lay their eggs in the early morning it was as well to keep them in their house until they had laid. Although Jane's 'duckery', as she called them, would not be ready to pay their keep for at least another six weeks, she was already training them. She knew the drakes now because of the curl in their tails and these were to be fattened for Christmas. She always laughed to see how they all waddled out of their house in a procession and then dashed for the trough and as they seemed to prefer muddy water Jane didn't bother to change it too often!

Back in the farmyard Sally was jumping up at Mr Watson and even when Jane called her she only glanced at her and wagged her tail. Sally's first love was Uncle William and Jane knew it. All her puppies except one had been sold or given away and Jane had been allowed to choose which she would like to keep for herself. She chose the one which was most like Sally and called her Sheila. Sheila was to be hers for ever and her father had already written to say she could bring her home when she came.

So the farmer, the little girl and two spaniels set off through the rickyard where the stacks of straw still stood where they had been built at the time of the threshing. 'We'll be fencing this off and putting the cows in round the straw next month,' Mr Watson said as he unlatched the gate that led into the first of the stubble fields. The two dogs began to explore the hedge bottom as Jane and her uncle stood for a moment looking down the hill. This was the field where Jane had first learned stooking and it sloped down to the rough track beside which this year's stacks had been built. On the other side of the path the potato and root fields stretched up a steeper slope to a wood. Next to them was the biggest wheat field of all which was now marked with four thin, brown parallel lines running from up the track to the trees. Sidney, on his tractor — and looking from this distance rather like a mechanical toy — was pulling a plough which was widening one of the brown lines as they watched.

'He's a good ploughman,' Mr Watson muttered, 'but not so good as old George with his horses … Come down and see him.'

As they trudged through the stubble Jane realized that they were treading on flowers. Some she knew already and had them in her collection — there were blue speedwells and gay scarlet pimpernels and dead nettles, for instance. She recognized the lovely miniature pansies in blue and yellow too, and bent to pick some while she waited for the two dogs. Poor Sheila hated the feel of the sharp stubble on her soft paws so Jane picked her up and ran down after her uncle. Suddenly there was a whirring noise and with a great hullabaloo a big flock of birds lifted into the sunshine and stampeded through the air up the hill in front of them. Each bird flew low and Jane saw Sidney, on his tractor, look up as they passed.

'Partridges, Janey,' her uncle said. 'Good to eat. Now let's look at Sidney.'

Sidney was doing well. The great plough had three shining blades which were leaving three new, rich brown furrows behind it as it was pulled down the hill. Jane watched the earth sweeping over rather like water at the bows of a ship and sniffed delightedly at the smell of the fresh turned earth. Many big black rooks were already pecking among the furrows and Mr Watson pointed out two black and white magpies enjoying an unexpected feast higher up the hill.

'Useful birds at this time o' year, Janey. They eat slugs and grubs and do us farmers a lot o' good … There'll be seagulls over the field afore long and it always puzzles me to know how they seem to know when there's a bit of ploughing going along … What are you going to do now, lass?'

'I've been thinking Uncle, that maybe I could give Auntie a surprise and get her some blackberries. Do you think they'll be ready yet?'

'Plenty in the wood. Take a crooked stick and cover up your arms and legs and see what you can get on your own. You've only to show a blackberry to your aunt and she'll bottle it … Just think of all the blackberry tarts we've had on Sundays since you've been with us.'

So Jane ran back with the dogs and, when her aunt was out of the way, slipped up to her room and put on her dungarees. Then she tiptoed down to the hall for one of her uncle's sticks with a crooked handle, borrowed a basket from the kitchen and within five minutes was running up the hill to the wood with Sally at her heels.

The wood was not frightening to-day and Jane was beginning to recognize all its changing moods. She loved it this morning for it looked green and friendly. Two big pigeons cluttered up from the trees ahead and the sun was hot on her cheeks as she trotted up by the hedge. When she stopped for breath halfway up the track she was surprised to hear some little pops and cracks. She looked round but could see no animal or bird which might have made such a noise unless it was hiding in the gorse bushes on her left. She crept over quietly and tried to look inside the nearest bush and was startled by a sharp pop above her head. She laughed at herself then for being so stupid when she realized that the heat of the sun was breaking open the seed pods of the gorse flowers and scattering the little black seeds. She watched carefully until two more exploded and then, whistling Sally, went on up the hill. She noticed next that the rowan tree which had been easy to recognize all through the year stood out in the September sunshine in a blaze of scarlet. The creamy blossom which she had seen in May had now turned to fruit and, as Sally barked, a flock of birds flew up from its branches and crossed the wood.

Once inside Jane soon found the blackberries. They were not easy to pick as the bushes were very thick and she was not tall enough to reach the best ones which seemed always to be just out of reach. Soon her arms were criss-crossed with long, angry scratches and she wished she had worn her old raincoat but before long she put every berry she picked into her basket and none into her mouth. By dinner time she had picked two or three pounds and Aunt Kate was delighted.

'They're good this year Janey I can see. I'll be up there with you this afternoon and to-morrow we'll make jelly ... Now hurry up with your dinner you two else I shall never get away … It's work, work, work for me from morning to night in this place and nobody seems to care!'

They had just finished dinner so Jane slipped off her chair and put her arms round her. 'I care, darling. I care very much and just to prove it I'll wash up and then we shall be quicker starting.'

Mr Watson winked at his niece as he pushed back his chair and went out.

That afternoon they saw the dead shrews and the remarkable battle between the stoat and the thrushes. Jane saw the shrews first when she went off on her own to find a bush where nobody had been before. She was walking along a little grassy path between the trees when she noticed the dead bodies of four little shrews. At first she thought they were mice and then remembered that Mr Herrick had told her once that a shrew had a long snout and a hairy tail. He had told her too that shrews always seemed to be hungry and they would eat anything alive or dead — even each other!

Jane put down her basket and knelt to look at the tiny furry bodies. They had no mark on them. No animal or bird could have touched them and it seemed that they had just laid down and died. She went on a few steps and then squealed as she stepped on something soft. It was the body of another shrew and now when she looked more carefully the path was covered with tiny bodies. Suddenly she forgot the sunshine dappling through the trees around her and the blackberries too. She hated the wood again and all these horrid little dead shrews all over the path. There must have been hundreds of them and she was almost afraid to move for fear of treading on them.

'Auntie!' she called. 'Please come. I've found something beastly.'

Mrs Watson must have realized that her niece was frightened for there came a mighty crashing in the undergrowth as she burst through the bushes and brambles and came to her as quickly as she could.

'Why, bless the child! What's the matter, Janey?'

Jane gulped and pointed at her feet. Her aunt followed her glance and then smiled.

'Tis only the shrews child! Some years they seem to die like this in September though generally 'tis later in the month than this. 'Tis nothing to be frightened about.'

'But *why* Auntie? *Why*? Why do they all die like that at the same time? I hate it!'

'Nobody seems to know why, Janey. Ask the rector some time for he knows more about birds and beasts than anyone I know … But some say that no shrew can cross a pathway trod by humans without dropping down dead … Come back with me now my dear and help me finish this bush.'

They saw the stoats by a big tree in the hedge on the far side of the wood. They had just come out of the shadow of the trees into the open when Jane dragged at her aunt's sleeve and pointed. Two big birds with speckled breasts — she thought they must be missel-thrushes — were flying low and attacking three little brown animals which were squirming on the ground round the roots of the tree. Time and time again the thrushes swooped and attacked and then some swallows joined in the battle and Jane clapped her hands as the stoats were routed and driven away from the wood across the field. As soon as they were in the open one of the birds fluttered on the ground in front of the stoats as if it was injured and Jane remembered that this was what the peewit did sometimes. The stoats made a few attempts to catch him but without success and then the swallows swooped again. Jane held her breath in excitement as the three soundly defeated stoats doubled back and dashed for the shelter of the wood.

'I'm jolly glad about *that*,' Jane said decisively. 'I don't like stoats but I never thought they would run away from birds.'

'And I've never seen that afore in all my life,' Mrs Watson said, 'and if you'd told me you'd seen it happen, doubt if I'd have believed you … Now tea Janey and we'll pick some more to-morrow.'

The next few days were very busy because Mrs Watson began her jelly making and this meant several more visits to the wood and Jane began to dislike the taste of raw blackberries. Nothing really exciting happened except that she had a postcard from Richard saying that they were coming home next Friday 'because of the fair'.

'What does Richard mean about "because of the fair"?' she asked Mr Watson one evening after supper just before he went to bed. She was sitting on the top bar of the farmyard gate watching the blue smoke curl up from her uncle's pipe. It was a lovely evening and the setting sun was lighting up the gold of the newly thatched stacks by the track at the foot of the hill. Jane was hoping that nobody had noticed the time and that she would be able to stay here until the Moor End owl drifted over in the dusk. Uncle William leaned comfortably against the gate and looked up at her.

'The fair, Janey? Ah! Now that was the surprise I was keeping for you on Saturday but if young Richard has let the cat out of the bag I shall have to tell you now … Every year for a hundred years I believe, a fair has come to Crossmarket on the second Saturday in September. We call it the Statty fair and I don't rightly know why. Afore your aunt and me were wed we used to go to the Statty and we've never missed one since. We thought maybe you'd like to come with us … Rector always goes and fills his car up with Townsend folk and as young Richard will be coming we didn't feel we ought to leave you behind' … but before he could finish Jane flung her arms round his neck, hugged him and then slipped to the ground.

'I've never been to a proper fair, Uncle … I think Saturday will be the most wonderful day of my life.'

But when Saturday arrived it brought rain, and Jane rather miserably went up to the granary and pushed open the big door so that she could look out over the farmyard. All the gutters round the barns were gurgling happily and the puddles danced as they were tickled by the gentle raindrops. The rain was warm and steady and it looked as if it would never stop.

At lunch time Jane asked:

'How do they build a fair in all this rain? Will they start do you think? Can we go even if it is raining?'

They surged over the bridge and looked down on the fair ground.

Mr Watson explained that the fair would be put up whatever the weather and Aunt Kate made it clear that Jane would not be allowed to go if it was pouring this evening and at this terrible threat she felt the tears so near that she just stared hard at the plum stones on her plate.

Then, almost as if he wanted to help, the sun peeped through the scurrying clouds and by four o'clock the sky was clear. At five o'clock Richard telephoned and Jane had to listen while he told her all about their holiday.

'Susan's been sick in the car,' he added. 'She often is so she won't be coming to-night. Rosemary is coming and some others too I expect … See you soon Janey.'

Mrs Watson gave them a big supper which Jane was too excited to eat properly and before they had finished it the Townsend party arrived. The rector was very brown and jolly and had a special hug for Jane and a joke for Aunt Kate about the fair and then they all bundled into the two cars and set off along the now familiar road to Crossmarket.

On the other side of the town beyond the station there is a triangle of grass edged with trees and with a few gorse bushes at one end. For three hundred and sixty three days of the year nothing much happens on this little remnant of a common but in the afternoon of the three hundred and sixty-fourth day the 'Statty' arrives and on the morning of the three hundred and sixty-fifth it spreads itself over the common and blossoms like a rare and extravagant flower which only blooms once a year. Although it pretends to work in the afternoon it is only an apology of a fair until dusk when the crowds come and the lights flare and when the brazen music from the roundabouts drowns the shouts of the men at the booths and when the riders in the dodgems scream as the rattling cars collide.

Just before they reached the blacksmith's forge, Jane saw the glare in the sky over the roof tops of Crossmarket; and once, when they stopped at the traffic lights, she heard for the first time the music and clamour of the fair in the distance.

The Townsend and Moor End parties left their cars in the market square and soon joined the hurrying crowds on the pavements. Jane, with one hand grasped in her uncle's and the other on Richard's sleeve, held on tight as they surged over the bridge and looked down on to the fair ground.

Jane never forgot the first sight and sound of the 'Statty'. Against the darkening sky she saw a feathery plume of smoke from the little chimney in the centre of the roundabout's roof. Below, the brightly coloured horses glowed in the orange lights of the lamps and careered gaily round and round to the loud and lilting music. Men were shouting, children calling and girls laughing, but louder than all the clamour of human voices was the brazen thudding clangour of the roundabout's song. Round the sides of the meadow they saw the mysterious shapes of tents which were lit from within, and many booths with open fronts and flaring lights. In one dark corner strange oblong shapes swung upwards against the sky, blotted out a few stars and then slid down into the gloom again.

'Come on a swing-boat with me, Janey?' Richard asked. 'Do come. I love them.' Before she could answer — and she didn't think she was going to like swing-boats very much — Mr Watson loosed her hand.

'You'll be wanting some cash, Janey,' he said as he produced two half-crowns from his pocket, 'but we'd better all keep together if we can … What are you going to do first?'

'You keep with me, Janey,' Richard said. 'I'll show you the fair … I know everything about it 'cos I come here every year … Roundabouts first then, if you're not keen on the swings.'

After that everything became rather confused for Jane. She found herself lifted on to the lowest step of the roundabout as it came to a standstill and then pushed by Richard on to the back of a black-and-white painted horse with a wicked look in his eye. Richard climbed up behind her and she clutched the horse's head hard as laughing, shouting people swarmed round her on to the other horses which suddenly began to move up and down as well as round and round. The music blared louder than ever and a dirty man with a wet and rosy face winked at her from his place by a shining engine in the centre. Louder and louder the music crashed and faster and faster the horses careered. Jane saw her uncle's face laughing up at her from the crowd but she did not dare lift a hand to wave to him. She began to hate the movement. People's faces moved up and down and so did her tummy. Another man in a blue jersey and with rubber shoes on came swaying along between the horses collecting the sixpences as he came. Jane did not dare leave go to find her purse in her pocket but Richard paid for her and then the horses began to slow down and she soon felt better.

'Do I look green?' she whispered to Rosemary as she jumped to the ground. 'I felt *awful*.'

'You look all right, Janey, but I don't like them much either. Let's go on the mat slide.'

After one try, Jane would have liked to spend all her money on this! They climbed up a ladder to a little platform which was higher than everything else in the fair and then, before she could protest, she found herself sitting on a mat with Rosemary at her side and shooting down a polished slide to the ground. The air rushed by and blew her pigtails out straight behind. The lights rushed towards her and, as she opened her mouth to scream, she found herself on her back and Richard laughing down at her.

Then her uncle took her on the dodgems and the rector took Richard in another car. The music started, sparks flashed and crackled from the wire netting above them and

Louder and louder the music crashed and faster and faster the horses careered.

the cars crashed into each other as they raced round the black, gleaming track.

There were stalls where brown-faced girls wearing big earrings stood in the centre of sloping tables and urged passers-by to 'try their luck' by rolling pennies down a grooved slide. The pennies rolled and wobbled down the tables and sometimes they ran off the end and were lost; and sometimes the girl would smile with a flash of white teeth and throw over two or three more pennies to you because your penny had come to rest on a lucky, coloured square painted on the table.

There were coconut shies too and both Mr Watson and the rector spent some time at the shooting range where they aimed with air guns at tin cats sitting on a wall! As it got darker more and more people crowded into the fair. Jane's feet were tired now and her head began to ache with the noise and the glare and the smell of trampled, wet grass.

Outside one tent was a notice which said that you could see the 'Fattest Woman in the World' for sixpence, but Mr Herrick would not let them go in. On a platform outside another much bigger tent stood an enormous negro with bulging muscles on his bare chest and arms. He was ready to box any challenger for £5 and men were almost fighting each other in their haste to get inside the tent to see him do it.

Jane was never quite sure how Mrs Herrick and Aunt Kate spent their time because sometimes they were with the others and sometimes not; but it was the latter who noticed how Jane was feeling and suggested that it was nearly time to go.

'But you haven't won a prize yet, Janey,' the rector said. 'You can't go home without a prize ... You come with me and I'll win one for you,' and he led the way to the darts booth where the boards like big dark targets stretched in a row behind the barrier. On a shelf underneath the boards was an assortment of rather horrible-looking prizes — glass vases, green water jugs and china ornaments. But among the ornaments Jane saw a china dog in black-and-white and she knew at once that she must have him. He was a 'sitting down' model of an unknown breed but he had one black ear up and another down and his head was on one side and he had a delicious, lolling pink tongue.

'What do you want, Jane?' Mr Herrick asked as he paid his money and took up his darts. 'The dog? Right! You shall have him.'

It cost him a lot of money to get the dog but after quite a long while the prize was put into Jane's arms and they went back to the others. On the way home Jane fell asleep, but she never forgot the Statty Fair at Crossmarket.

⁂

The next day was Harvest Festival and the church was as full as it had been at Easter and looked nearly as lovely. There were fat sheaves of corn tied to the pulpit and a colossal marrow on each side of the altar steps. Rosy apples, brown eggs and shining tomatoes were piled neatly below the choir stalls and Jane wouldn't have been surprised if one of the choir boys had reached forward and helped himself. They sang some hymns which she knew, and the rector preached a 'thank you' sermon. She smiled to herself because although he looked very splendid up there she could not forget that she had seen him winning a china dog for her at darts only last evening! Then they all sang 'Come, Ye Thankful People, Come' and went out into a very blustery day, with the wind roaring in the tree tops and shaking down a few of the first tinted leaves. 'Autumn's nearly here,' Aunt Kate said as she passed the time of day with a friend at the churchyard gate and Richard made it worse by reminding them that there was only one more day left of the summer holidays.

'I don't care,' Jane said stoutly. 'I've had the best holidays I've ever had and I don't really mind going back on Tuesday.'

'I go Wednesday,' Richard said. 'Sometimes I think school is a waste of time because I learn lots more in the holidays ... Cheerio!'

When they got out of the car at Moor End Jane saw George in his garden and went over to speak to him. As she reached the big elm tree she stopped in surprise for it seemed as if the tree itself was singing with quite a high-pitched hum. She looked up into the branches but there seemed nothing special to see, although when she stood still the noise was louder than ever. So she asked George, who was busy picking runner beans.

'Um?' he said. 'What's 'umming?'

'That's what I'm asking you, George. Come and listen *please*.'

So very reluctantly George put down the old enamel bowl and muttering about 'his dinner' and 'his missus' came over to the tree.

'Now!' Jane said. 'Can you hear it? It's louder than ever.'

'Ooo-aye,' George replied at last. 'I reckon 'tis an 'um ... Bees and the like in the new ivy flowers ... Allus like that first day the flowers open,' and he stumped back to his bean picking.

And when Jane looked carefully again she could see millions of bees and insects moving among the clustered leaves of the ivy. It was not easy to find the flowers but after a little she realized that they were in yellowish green clusters at the end of each climbing stem. She went up the lane a little way and although she soon found some more ivy it was not in flower, which seemed very strange.

But it was on Monday evening that Jane had her strange adventure. Because it was her last evening she was allowed to stay up later than usual.

'I suppose you would be too tired to play a game with me, Uncle,' she pleaded at supper. 'I know Auntie will play but if you could just manage it for once I would like it very much ... *Please*, Uncle William!'

Sometimes, when she wanted a special favour, she called her Uncle 'William' and he seemed to like it and this time too, the charm worked.

'Well! Well!' he said. 'I'd got some figures to do but maybe a little game of rummy would be good for us all ... Mother! It's getting cold in the evenings now and we'll go in t'other room and light up the first fire of the season and then we'll play a game with our Janey ... If you're finished, Jane, you can run in and put a match to it.'

So Jane went into the sitting room which was mostly used at week-ends and moved the flimsy silk screen covered with painted flowers from the fireplace and kneeled down on the hearth rug. The fire was laid with crumpled newspaper covered with flecks of soot and a pile of fir cones which Jane herself had collected from the wood. She had been taught by her aunt never to come back from a walk in the country without cones or firewood and now she never forgot! She was trying to train Sheila and Sally to do the same but they were rather silly about it.

She struck the match and put the flame to the paper, which smouldered and went out. She tried again with one of the fir cones and at last, by coaxing and blowing, the tiny fame caught and the cones began to blaze. There were logs in a big basket by the hearth and as she tossed one on her uncle came in, wearing his 'going out' suit, and lit the lamp.

Jane loved an evening like this. She loved the summer, but it had been much colder to-day and as they had not seen the sun at all, a blazing fire was great fun. Mrs Watson was very fond of 'the cards' and took her rummy very seriously but Jane was lucky and always seemed to pick up black twos and all the other cards which she wanted. Sometimes she was so lucky that she felt really sorry for her uncle who never seemed to win. Aunt Kate won the first game and did not then say that Jane must go to bed, so she dealt again as quickly as she could. Surely nobody would be so brutal as to send her to bed once another game had started!

She had just proudly put down her first set of three when her aunt, who sat with her back to the fire, suddenly placed her cards on the table, put a finger to her lips and pointed over Jane's shoulder to the uncurtained window.

Jane turned quickly, and for a moment could hardly believe her eyes. At first all that she noticed was a few moths fluttering against a pane and striving to reach the light inside the room. Then she saw a little mouse run along the outside sill and suddenly stand upright and scrabble against the glass with its tiny paws. Then another came ... and another ... and Jane crept to the window and went down on her knees to watch them. As she was so close to the glass and the room was fully lighted there was no doubt that she could be seen; but the mice seemed quite unafraid and still ran swiftly up and down the sill and sometimes stood upright so that their white underneaths gleamed in the lamp light. But why? Was this some sort of strange mouse dance or ritual? Was it the sort of thing that happened to field-mice in September just as the shrews died mysteriously?

'Perhaps they want to come in?' Jane whispered as her uncle went down on his knees beside her and shook his head.

'They're after the moths,' he said. 'Watch!'

Then she saw a little moth come, with wings outspread, to rest against the glass and at once a mouse with specially long whiskers jumped up to reach it.

Jane laughed.

'He's like Samuel Whiskers! Do you think he'd come in if we opened the window?'

'Certainly *not*,' Mrs Watson protested. 'I'll not have Samuel Whiskers or any other mouse's whiskers in this room … Open the window one inch and I bring Simon in and he'll catch their whiskers for them!'

So, rather reluctantly, Jane came back to the table and finished the game. Often while they played she turned to watch the window but even after she had won, without thinking much about the cards, the mice went on with their dancing and prancing.

'Now for bed, my girl,' said Aunt Kate at last. 'You're much later and maybe you're too excited to sleep and that won't do you any good for to-morrow. Have you got your books and your satchel ready and did you remember to ask George to pump your tyres up and oil your bike for I know you won't have any time to spare in the morning?'

As she bent to kiss her uncle he put an arm round her shoulder. 'You're getting me into bad habits, my girl,' he said. 'Have you enjoyed your holidays? Not been too dull for you I hope down here with your old uncle and aunt.'

And the words she wanted to say would not come so she turned and ran blindly up the stairs to her own little room.

October

Moor End,
October 2nd

Darling Mummy and Daddy,

It seems a long time since I went back to school and longer still since you were here. I haven't written you one of these special Moor End letters for a long time but lots of things seem to be happening so I am going to make a special try this month when I have time.

First of all I want to tell you what I expect you know about Michaelmas daisies which grow in our garden at home just like they do here. Last Sunday Mr Herrick told us that they were called Michaelmas because their flowers are generally at their best on St Michael's Day which is September 29th. At church the purple and mauve flowers were everywhere and we heard how St Michael was the warrior saint and leader of all the good angels. I think it is a very nice idea to have a day when we can all remember the angels specially, and I never thought about it like that before. Mr Herrick knows a lot about exciting things like St Michael and I like going to church at Townsend very much.

Aunt Kate says that it is going to be a very hard winter because there are so many berries on the trees and in the hedges. She says the hips and haws are sent because otherwise the birds would starve when the snow comes. But I can't understand that because the birds are eating them all the time now and there won't be any left when winter really comes.

On Saturday Richard came over with Rosemary and John and we went out with the dogs. Generally when Richard comes we go along the stream because he seems to like water very much. This time we saw the kingfisher again and he looked very royal. We found some eating-chestnut trees too — not the conker sort — and picked up a lot of chestnuts. John had a knife so we split off the spiky outsides and took the brown shiny nuts home. We did try to eat some raw but they weren't very nice and though we chewed them like anything the taste soon went and I had to spit mine out.

We came home a new way and made friends with an old brown man who had been working in the woods. We walked down the lane with him and when John pulled some dead wood out of the hedge the old man said he ought not to take it indoors 'cos it was unlucky 'cos it was elder. It sounds rather silly but John dropped it just as if it hurt his hand and we all laughed at him except the woodcutter. We said good-bye to him outside his cottage. A big girl with very black eyes stared at us but Richard stared back and said, 'Why do you have those crossed bits of stick fixed up over the door? It looks like elder wood that you told us not to take home ... Is it a spell?'

But the man and the girl just didn't say anything so we went home and Aunt Kate let us all into the kitchen and we roasted the chestnuts on the grate after tea and they were jolly good although my tongue is rough where it got burnt.

One more thing. Richard says that there is a wood pigeon's nest in the conker tree on the lawn here — I know you will remember where it is — and he says he thinks there are eggs in it, which is silly. It was too late for us then to climb up and see and I have forgotten to look again but two pigeons did fly out of the branches when I came home last night.

I don't know if I shall be able to go to school if it snows or rains all day but I still like going on my lovely bike. All the trees are golden and the hedges are red but the leaves haven't fallen down yet. I must stop now because it is nearly eight o'clock but there is one more thing I must tell you. I stayed to tea at the rectory to-day and did not leave until after the Children's Hour. It was almost dark as I pushed my bike up the hill by the beech trees and before I got to the top I saw that the sky over the hill was red. I know that it was silly of me but I was afraid and thought there was a big fire somewhere near and that it must be home — here, Moor End, I mean. My heart banged very hard and I pushed the bike faster than I ever have before until I got to the top and could look down and see the farm safe and sound. Do you remember Daddy how we stopped at the top of the hill and looked down one day when you were here at Easter? But the sky was still very red and I couldn't think why because it couldn't be a sunset over there because that is where the sun rises. Then, just over the roof, came a great red rim like a red hot plate and I knew it was the moon. But it was an **ENORMOUS** moon and the reddest I have ever seen. And the funny thing was that while I watched it moved quite quickly up the sky and before I got on my bike it came up above the house. I wonder if it looked the same to you to-night?

I will post this to-morrow and write again soon.

With love from
JANEY
XXXXXX

Moor End,
October 4th

Dear Mummy and Daddy,

I have got a lot to tell you to-day. First of all I must tell you that I woke up in the night and it was very, very quiet. You know how sometimes you wonder why you have woken up and that was how I felt. The window was wide open and I couldn't see a moon and I was still puzzling about waking up like that when I heard someone or something *whispering* outside. I know it sounds silly but it was exactly like a little, clear, fairy whisper saying, 'Seek … Seeeeek…. Seek!' It was a bit ghosty being there in the dark and hearing this funny little whisper but I wasn't really frightened because, after a little, I guessed that it was a bird or an animal. I heard the little cry several times later but went to sleep again at last and in the morning I forgot to ask Uncle William about it.

But Mr Herrick told me that the whisper was the cry of the redwing which is a bird that flies to us from the north and that when they come it is the first sign of winter. He told me this after school but he came to our school too this morning and told us that to-day is St Francis's Day. I won't tell you all about St Francis now except that he was a very wonderful man who made great friends of all animals and birds and called them his little brothers and sisters. Mr Herrick said that St Francis loved birds very specially and that they would do almost anything he asked them. Everybody loved St Francis and I think I do too. He called the sun and the wind and the rain and fire his brothers and sisters which I think is a lovely idea.

Auntie says that because it gets dark early now I must come home *directly* after school so I shan't be able to go to the rectory for tea any more until the spring comes again. Now I want to tell you about the farm because if I don't you won't know what they are doing Daddy, and I remember that you said you wanted to be a farmer one day! When I have time I still go round with Uncle specially on Saturdays and he tells me most things. Sidney has nearly finished the ploughing which he began last month but they do other things to the fields before they begin sowing again 'cos you can't sow anything on the furrows which are full of great clods. Uncle says that he leaves the furrows for a little while and then the tractor comes again and pulls a thing called a disc harrow. (Don't you think I'm clever to remember all these names but Uncle has just told me again?). The disc harrow is a row of wheels with very sharp edges which cut up the ridges of soil and make it fine and ready for sowing. I called it sowing but Uncle says the right name is drilling. The driller is a long red box on wheels with little pipes leading down to the soil. The box is filled with seed and pulled up and down the field by the tractor though I s'pose one of the horses could have done it. George, who doesn't like it much, fills up the long red box with wheat seeds and then climbs up behind as the tractor pulls the driller over the smooth brown field. I got on the back with him once and we had to see that the shiny wheat ran down the little pipes to the soil. The driller makes little ditches for the seed to fall into. After the field was drilled George had to fetch Short and the ordinary harrow which is like a big rake with lots of spikes. The harrow is pulled over the seed in the open drills and covers it up smooth and cosy.

Now I must go to bed.

Sunday

I'll finish this off now and you'll have it instead of an ordinary 'Janey' letter 'cos I haven't time to do both this week. I am rather stiff because I was helping to get in the potatoes all yesterday. Uncle has to borrow a special machine to get them up and I will try and tell you about it. The tractor pulls it up and down the big furrows and some prongs go round and round at the back and whisk the potatoes out of the ground. They told us at school that anyone who wanted to help with the potatoes could have a holiday next week and quite a lot came to Moor End. We had big baskets given to us and had to fill these with the potatoes which the machine pushed out of the ground. George came up and down the rows with his cart and all the potatoes were taken to the edge of the field where there was a machine which made a lot of noise and sorted out the *very* small ones.

I didn't mind helping but it was jolly hard work and Auntie says I'm not to do any more. I like potatoes very much but I never knew before what a lot has to happen before they get on our plates. P'raps I could help with the machine that sorts out the small ones.

Do you remember that Richard said there were eggs in the wood-pigeon's nest in the conker tree? Well, there are two baby wood-pigeons and he climbed up to-day to see. The nest is in an easy place to find right in the middle of the big trunk where the branches start. We had to get the steps out of the barn and then Richard managed to pull himself up and there they were. I couldn't quite reach so he took one of the fledglings very gently out of the nest and showed me. It didn't look very nice but Richard said some new babies don't look nice either and that he remembered Peter very new and that he looked horrible which I don't believe. Then Richard said that I had better not tell Uncle William about them because he would want them killed as all farmers and gardeners hated pigeons. 'I expect they'll die anyway,' he said, 'because it's much too late for them to be hatched and p'raps the parents won't be able to find them anything to eat,' and then he put the ugly fledgling back in the nest and went home.

Up till now I haven't said anything to Uncle about them and I don't think he would really be very interested do you?

That's all for now,

With love from

JANEY

PS I'm rather worried about those baby pigeons. It would be very bad luck for them not to have enough to eat just because they were hatched out late. Maybe I'll have to feed them a bit.

✕

Moor End,
Saturday

Dear Mummy and Daddy,

I can hardly wait to tell you what an exciting time we have had since the storm started on Wednesday night. I expect you have had it too because the wireless says that it is everywhere but it has been TERRIBLE here and except for Uncle's car we are rather like being on a desert island because the telephone has broken and a great branch of the elm tree came smashing down in the night and broke up the gate of George's cottage and George says if he had been standing there he would have been killed dead as mutton but it was his lucky day 'cos he was safe in bed.

But I will start at the beginning and tell you all about it and it won't be very difficult because I did a composition on it at school to-day.

When I came home from school on Wednesday it was very windy. I remember this specially because for some of the way it blew me along and because I noticed how all the leaves were blowing off the road. When I came to the hill and got off my bike all the trees in the fields on the other side of the hedge were roaring and shaking and down came the leaves thicker than ever. There is a gap in the hedge about halfway up the hill and when I climbed up the bank to look through over the fields the wind came so hard that my beret came off and I was blown on to the road. Then I thought I would go to the beech trees and watch the wind which

The trees were roaring and shaking in the wind as Jane was blown down the hill.

sounds silly but I expect you will know what I mean. It was hard work pushing up the hill but I left my bike in the hedge at the top and tried to run along the track to the mound where I first met Richard and Mr Herrick. Now that I was at the top of the hill the wind was stronger than ever and tried to pull off my raincoat and push me back to the road. But I scrambled up the mound and under the trees and it was very exciting and I will tell you why. Up above the branches were crying in the wind and all the while the little brown leaves came pattering down; but when I got close to the grey trunk of the biggest tree and put my arms round it I couldn't feel the wind at all. Then I went to the other side and looked to see where the wind was coming from. I could see Townsend down in the valley and a train in the distance but not any smoke because the wind must have blown it away at once. All the trees were swaying and bowing to me up on the mound and the cows in the nearest field had all got their backs to the wind too and were staring at me. I stayed up there a long time alone with the wind, and the clouds came tumbling up till they filled the sky and it began to get dark. So then I thought I would go home and when I got on my bike I absolutely *FLEW* down the hill. In the rickyard straw was flying about and some corrugated iron on the roof of one of the cart sheds was loose and banging in the wind. Aunt Kate was rather cross because I was so late. Now my hand aches and it is supper time so I will write some more presently.

I was telling you about the storm. Uncle came in very worried and said somebody had done a bad job on one of the ricks because the thatch had been blowing away. So that was the straw I had seen when I came in. I think he and George had fetched a ladder and ropes and things and tied tarpaulin over the bad part of the rick but he grumbled a lot and hardly took any notice of me at all. Afterwards Auntie said he gets angry when the men don't do their work properly. While we were having supper we could hear the wind roaring all the time and sometimes the house shook. Then there was a crash and a banging outside and Uncle said something about the iron on the roof of the shed and went out in a hurry and I have never seen him so grumpy before. The chimney in the kitchen smoked very badly too and Auntie couldn't stop it and that made Uncle angry as well and I thought I ought to go to bed. Then I remembered Sally and Sheila who still slept in the barn and I thought it was jolly unfair for them not to be indoors out of the storm but I didn't dare ask if they could come into bed with me. I knew Sheila, who had never been in a storm before, would be frightened but I didn't dare ask.

When I went up to bed I was frightened too. I don't mind telling you now Daddy that I was frightened but I didn't say anything to Uncle and Auntie when I went upstairs. Do you remember the little stairs that go round and round up to my room? As I went up them they creaked and moved and almost talked and I hated it. When I got to my room I shut the door very tight but even then it kept on rattling in the wind. The windows were shut so I opened them a little and then the noise of the big elm tree and all the other trees was like the sea.

While I was undressing and saying my prayers the wind stopped suddenly and the quiet was most peculiar. I hopped into bed and hoped the storm was over but it wasn't because the wind soon started again and this time the rain came too. First it banged on the window and then I could hear it on the roof. It came splashing down the chimney with large plops and the wind got worse and I put my head under the bedclothes and presently I must have gone to sleep because when I woke up it was light and the wind was still roaring and the rain was still splashing down the chimney. When I got up I saw a pool of water in the hearth and the floor under the window was wet too. As soon as I heard Uncle going downstairs I got up too. Auntie had just made the tea when I went into the kitchen but they weren't grumpy this morning and Uncle said that if I put on my boots and raincoat I could go out with him and see what had happened. It was George who told us about the elm tree and we went to look at it but Uncle wouldn't let me go very close. 'Never trust an ellum,' he said and George said, 'Ay! That's right!'

It was still raining and the farmyard was one big puddle and the wind made little waves on it. Three of the pieces of corrugated iron had blown off the cart shed roof and some more pieces were flapping and when Uncle saw those he sent me indoors again. At breakfast I said how could I cycle to school and he said he would take me in the car but when he got halfway up the hill we were stopped because a big tree had fallen right across the road with its roots sticking up in the air.

So I couldn't go to school and I had a holiday! When we got home Uncle tried to telephone about the tree but the phone wouldn't work and he was very angry indeed and said that whenever he wanted the telephone most that was the time it broke down. And in the middle of his grumbling the postman arrived and we told him about the tree and he said the damage everywhere was very bad and if Mrs Watson had the teapot on the hob he could do with a cup. I like this postman who is called Fred because he always has a joke but he didn't stay long this morning because he had to tell them about our telephone and the tree.

In the afternoon the rain stopped and the sun came out so I put on my wellingtons and went out to see what had happened to the tree. I met it coming down the lane on a great flat truck pulled by a lorry with a crane on it. Rain water was still running down the hill but I saw that now all the trees were bare. There were no leaves anywhere any more except on the holly trees in the hedge, and on the road where they were very slippery.

Mr Herrick's car was at the top of the hill but he wasn't in it so I guessed he would be at the beech trees and so he was. I told him why I wasn't at school and about the tree and our telephone and the iron roof and he said a chimney pot had been blown off the rectory.

'It's the first storm of winter, Janey,' he said. 'Yesterday it was autumn but now the leaves have gone with the swallows and winter has come.'

Just as he said that about the swallows I remembered about the baby pigeons in the conker tree but I will tell you about them next time.

So good-night now and with love from

JANEY

✕

Moor End,
Saturday

Darling Mummy and Daddy,

I promised to tell you about the baby pigeons and it has been quite an adventure. On the day after the storm when I met Mr Herrick by the beech trees I told him that Richard had found some babies in the nest and that I wondered what had happened to them in the storm. He said he would go and look as he was on his way to see Mrs Smithson who wasn't so well. 'Though really I think she'll live for ever,' he said as we got into the car.

Underneath the conker tree amongst the wet brown leaves and lots of twigs was one of the baby pigeons quite dead. I told the rector there had been two so he got the ladder and climbed up to see and when he came down he had the other one in his hand. Its throat was moving a bit but it looked very wet and miserable and Mr Herrick said if I wanted to save it we must take it indoors. I didn't know what Uncle would say and I was sure that Auntie wouldn't be very keen but I know she likes the rector and maybe neither of them would know that it was a pigeon if I didn't say anything.

We went into the kitchen the back way and wiped our boots very carefully on the mat and Auntie looked up and said, 'And what's the matter with you two a'creeping in on me like that? How are you to-day Rector, and Mrs Herrick is well I hope?'

Then Mr Herrick explained very carefully that the baby bird would not live unless we could keep him warm in a box by the fire and that if Auntie didn't mind he wanted me to look after it. Auntie said, 'If it's an owl I can't abide them and I'll have no owl in Moor End but if it's kept in here Janey will have to keep Simon away. It's a cat's nature to catch birds and he'll get this one sooner or later.'

I had forgotten about Simon who is *hateful* about birds but Mr Herrick said we would just see if we could keep this one alive now and worry about the cat later and had Auntie got a cardboard box. I held the baby pigeon while he filled the box with straw and some scraps of cotton wool. It looked horribly ugly and wet and felt cold in my hand.

We put the box underneath the kitchen range and when it was warm and we were sure that Simon was not in the room we put the pigeon in but I was afraid it was dead. Then Mr Herrick said he had to go and see Mrs Smithson but I was the nurse in charge and that if I wanted to save the patient I had better give it some brandy. He said that he would ring up when he got home and see if it was still alive. Auntie wasn't very pleased when I asked her for the brandy and said it was all nonsense to feed birds with it but after I had *pleaded* with her she gave me some whisky in an egg cup. I didn't really know how to give it to the pigeon which now looked quite dead but supposed it was best to give it a few drops at a time and see what happened. I got its beak open somehow and dropped some whisky down its throat off a match stick. When I had put four drops right down it wriggled and its throat began to work again so I popped it back into its nest and sat down on guard while Auntie fussed about and laid the table. Twice I chased Simon out. Auntie said it wasn't fair to the cat but I was sure the bird was alive and when I gave it some more whisky it seemed to like it and opened its mouth for some more.

Then Uncle came in and asked me what I was doing under the range and I had to explain that I was saving a bird for Mr Herrick. When I had said that I knew it wasn't *quite* true so I said, 'I don't think it's a very rare bird but the rector said that if it was to live I must be its nurse and I've made it live with some of your whisky and thank you very much for it.'

He laughed rather a lot at this and came over and looked at the bird and said I was wasting my time but he wasn't cross so it was all right. Mr Herrick rang up after supper and I told him what I had done and he said that was splendid and I should give him some more whisky before I went to bed and some of my porridge in the morning. I thought he was making fun of me but he wasn't 'cos he said it twice and told me he had read somewhere that a bird's life was saved with porridge.

I didn't tell Auntie about this 'cos I thought they had been very kind about the whisky and breakfast time would do anyway but I was worried about Simon and the bird at night. Before I went to bed Auntie said Simon could sleep somewhere else but I don't think he liked it much. The bird was quite perky in the morning so I gave it some more whisky before breakfast and then some blobs of my porridge on the other end of the match stick after breakfast, and now if I can keep it away from Simon I know it will live. I would keep him safe in the granary but I think it is too cold for him. I shall be very busy now looking after the bird and I don't quite know what will happen while I am at school.

With love from

JANEY

✖

Moor End,
Saturday

Darling Mummy and Daddy,

It is a week since I last wrote and the most important news is that Simon caught the baby pigeon just when it was growing up fast. When I got home from school on Wednesday it had disappeared and then Auntie had to tell me the truth. I always hated this beastly cat Simon but now I shall never even touch it again. I don't know how it caught the baby pigeon and Auntie won't tell me.

It has been raining nearly all the week. Auntie has bought me a black sou'wester hat and a cape and I wear them both with my boots when I cycle to school but it is not such fun cycling with the wind blowing against me and this week it has seemed to be the wrong way whichever way I go. Uncle told George to clear out the big barn while it is raining so hard and George has done it. He says I could eat my dinner off the floor now but I don't want to do that.

Every day, at the top of the hill, I see some red berries like strings of scarlet beads in the hedge. Someone told me they are brionies.

There is a nut tree in the hedge too and it has some real tight, baby catkins on it already. And over the hedge in the field there were still some buttercups.

Now I must stop. I am sorry about the baby pigeon and am longing to see you at Christmas.

With love from
JANEY

November

When Jane woke on the first day of November the walls of her little room were glowing rosy red. As she turned over and burrowed into the soft pillow again she remembered thankfully that because it was Saturday she could stay longer in bed. Saturdays and Sundays were the days appointed by her aunt for a 'lay back' for Jane and now that the days were short and the mornings colder she did not mind obeying these orders. It was rather fun to lie back in the warm and think of what happened yesterday and what there was to do to-day.

The window was open a little and as the sun crept up the fiery sky Jane smelled the lovely scent of bonfire smoke. She remembered her uncle lighting the fire two evenings ago and it had burned slowly ever since. When she got back from school yesterday she had run out into the garden and watched the thin plume of blue smoke rising into the misty dusk and wondered how anything as damp as this mass of rubbish could burn so steadily. Then she put her hands into the smoke and felt the warmth of the fire underneath but when she got back to the kitchen Mrs Watson wrinkled her nose with disgust and told her that her hair would smell of bonfire for days.

Now Jane slipped her fingers from under the bedclothes, held them to her little freckled nose and sniffed hard. She could smell smoke, but was not sure whether it came from her hands or not. She liked the smell anyhow, and, oddly enough, it was almost the only country smell that reminded her of home, for a bonfire smells the same wherever it burns, though never so sharply sweet as on an October or November evening. She moved her hands behind her head again and watched the glow of the rising sun on the beamed ceiling. She remembered how her father came home from work for lunch on Saturday and then, as quickly as he could, changed into his old clothes and went to work in the garden. And in the autumn all the little gardens in their road would have a bonfire burning on Saturday and Sunday afternoons and Daddy and Mr Brown next door used to make jokes about the way the wind was blowing.

Perhaps, after all, it would be fun to go home again. In her last letter Jane's mother had told her that they would both be coming for Christmas and were going to take her home with them before the New Year. It would be lovely to be with them but she was going to miss Moor End just as much as she had missed her parents nearly a year ago.

Then her aunt's voice came shrilling up the stairs — 'Janey! Time to get up, sleepyhead!' So without more ado she jumped out of bed and ran, as she always did, to the window. The sky was still aflame and Jane knew now that the old saying about 'red sky at morning is the shepherd's warning' had some truth in it for as often as not storms or wind followed such a fiery sky.

Jane had her breakfast by herself on Saturday mornings but her aunt sat down by the fire while she ate and had an extra cup of tea with her.

'And did you hear the witches riding by your window, m'dear? I warned you last night that 'twas All Hallows Eve!'

'No I didn't,' Jane said solemnly looking up from her porridge. 'And I don't really understand about All Hallows. What are they?'

'To-day is All Saints as you will hear if we go over to church in the morning for the rector is a rare one for saints and the like. I reckon All Hallows be another way of saying All Saints but I remember when I was your age, and for many a year after, we would be having a Halloween party last night. Many special games we used to play like bobbing for apples with our teeth in a pail of water. We had to peel the apples all in one piece and then throw the peel over our shoulders.'

'What happened then?' Jane asked with wide eyes.

Her aunt laughed.

'Peel was supposed to make the initial of the man you were going to marry but I don't recollect that mine ever made a W!'

'But what's all that to do with witches, Auntie?'

'I don't rightly know that either 'cept that my mother always told me 'twas the one night in the year that all the witches in the world rode through the wild darkness to their meeting places.'

'What meeting places?'

'Tops o' hills they liked 'tis said and wherever a gibbet stood in olden time was a favourite place.'

'And have *you* ever seen a witch riding on a broomstick on Halloween, Auntie?'

'No, nor never will … Get on with your porridge, child, or 'twill be cold, and take no notice of my old-fashioned notions.'

Five minutes later Jane looked up from her plate again.

'I want to ask you something special. You know you said I could go to the rectory firework party on Wednesday and that Uncle would fetch me in the car? Well, it's not much fun going to a firework party without fireworks is it, Auntie. I wondered if I could cycle into Crossmarket this morning and buy some to take with me? Most of the others are going to do that.'

After some argument Mrs Watson agreed that if Uncle William said yes she would not say no, so Jane knew that she would be able to go.

Her uncle was standing in the farmyard watching George unload a cart of swedes. It was a cold, damp morning now and already the sun was hidden behind low clouds.

'Why do you bring the swedes all the way from the field to here. Why can't you pile them up at the sides of the field like you do the potatoes?' Jane asked.

'Because George wants them here for feeding the cattle. Cattle won't grow fat and come through the winter just on the old wheat straw ... George will cover these swedes up with straw to keep the frost off 'em but he cuts some up every day ... Potatoes stay in a clamp outside till they be wanted next spring. Besides there's no room here for so many spuds. There's many tons of 'em outside now — and besides we allus puts the swedes in this corner and I reckon George will always do it whatever I tell him ... Come and look at the heifers with me, Janey?'

'But can I go to Crossmarket on my bike to get some fireworks, please, Uncle? Auntie says she doesn't mind if you don't and I'll be very careful.'

Mr Watson looked down at her doubtfully for a moment and then nodded.

'But you'll take care, Janey, and think what you're doing and watch the traffic lights and come back as soon as you can ... I'd take you in the car if I had the time this morning which I haven't.'

So Jane ran off without looking at the cattle and got out her bicycle. She cleaned the mud off it and polished it until it began to look almost new again and then set out along the road over the common. Crossmarket seemed much farther away on a bicycle than it did in a car and her legs were aching by the time she reached the blacksmith's forge on the outskirts of the town. She got off here and went into the murky warmth. Her friend the smith looked up and smiled a welcome while his hand moved like lightning between his mouth and the hoof which he held between his knees. Thud, thud, thud, thud, went the nails but the great horse never moved although a cloud of bitter smoke rose from the hot shoe. She watched while the bellows roared and the sparks flew and another shoe was whipped glowing from the furnace.

'I'm going to buy some fireworks with my own money,' she told the smith.

'Fireworks!' he laughed as he removed the last nail from his mouth. 'Fireworks! Reckon I get all the fireworking I need right here in my own place. When I knocks off here little miss I don't want to see no more fireworks!'

Jane wasn't sure that he understood what she meant but supposed he was joking.

Just then the carter came back for his horse so she slipped out while they were still talking together in their slow voices. The streets were very crowded now so she pushed her bicycle up into the town and leaned it against the kerb whenever she came to a shop with fireworks in the window. She spent a lot of time gloating over what she saw before going in to buy. At last she found a shop where there was a nice boy who said he was helping his father because it was Saturday morning. The boy knew all about fireworks and told Jane which sort whizzed round and round and which shot up straight into the air and which jumped and cracked, until she wished she had brought some more money. This shop was the ironmonger's into which her uncle had taken her once before and was full of the most exciting things. She noticed a card of 'pot menders' hanging over the counter and bought one for her aunt as a little surprise but there didn't seem to be anything at the same price which would be appreciated by Uncle William so she said good-bye to the friendly boy and went out to her bicycle. When she had put her purchases into the basket she noticed that it was getting dark and that the street was thick with a white, damp fog. Two shops opposite switched on their window lights and as one of them was a baker's Jane crossed over and bought two buns with what she had left in her purse. The buns were very good indeed — fresh and hot and sticky — and if she had had another penny she would have done still more to spoil her dinner! She munched them on the way home but the fog was getting thicker all the time so she knew she ought to hurry. When she rode into the farmyard and whistled to the dogs Uncle William came out of the stable to welcome her.

'Just in time, Janey! If you'd have been much longer I was coming out to look for you. Fog will be bad to-night.'

As usual Mr Watson was right about the weather. After dinner it was not possible to see the farmyard gate from the kitchen window. All the world was shrouded in a thick, damp, grey blanket. All was hushed and still and when Jane put her head out of the back door the only sound was the steady drip, drip of a leaking gutter round one of the barns. It was an afternoon for staying in and Mrs Watson lit the fire in the front room and Uncle William took his boots off and came in to sit with them. Jane made toast for tea and was allowed to go on reading while they ate it and when bed time came she was ready to go without argument, for she had been yawning for an hour.

Next day the fog was thicker.

On Monday it rained so hard that Jane was taken to school in the car. On Tuesday morning before it was light Jane was wakened by the cold and had to get out of bed for her dressing gown. When her aunt called her later she said that the first real frost of winter had come early. The frost held all day although the sun rose fiery red again and on Wednesday morning it was still as cold although clear and bright.

Jane set off earlier than usual because she had to walk all the way to school this morning. The fireworks were in a parcel with a string handle and her satchel bumped on her back as she walked fast up the hill. When she reached the top and looked back her cheeks were tingling and her feet and hands were beautifully warm. It was rather fun walking, particularly as Aunt Kate and Uncle William were coming over in the car this evening to see the fireworks and then to take her home. She looked back and saw the smoke rising from the Moor End chimneys and then glanced down the hill into the valley below her. Her friend the weathercock on the church tower glowed red as the sun found him looking out over the village of Townsend.

The only tree to which any leaves still clung was the big oak halfway down the lane. The elms were stripped bare but their naked branches made a lovely tracery against the sky and Jane remembered how she had noticed the pattern of the Moor End elms nearly a year ago in the snow.

The hedges were thick with the white blobs of 'traveller's joy'. Jane always remembered this name because Mr Herrick had told her that these light and airy 'snowballs' were the seeds of a climbing plant called white vine or virgin's bower. When she had asked him why 'traveller's joy' he had said it was probably because a traveller would have some happiness in seeing these gleaming feathery masses when everything else in the hedges was dull and dead. But Richard had said 'I call it Old Man's Beard and so do all the chaps I know.'

After dinner at school she went into the rectory paddock and watched Peter and the old gardener building up the bonfire for to-night. It looked as if it was going to be a good one.

Most of the children in Jane's class were coming to the firework party and the afternoon seemed very long for them all. At last it was four o'clock when they ran out into the road the air was dry and frosty, and, as Rosemary said, it was cold enough to make a bonfire really worth while.

They all had tea together in the old nursery upstairs and Peter was allowed to let off indoor fireworks of his own which sparkled and smoked but did not burn if you put your hand against the sparks. When they went down to the garden the night was lovelier than the day had been for the moon was already rising into a blue velvet sky and the stars were bright and clear.

'Do you know the stars, Janey?' Richard asked as they stood round the great pile of brushwood and rubbish waiting for the rector to come and start them off. 'Do you remember how keen Bevis was on them in the book I gave you?'

Jane didn't know anything about stars really so Richard showed her the great Pole Star which is always in the north. He showed her too the seven stars nearby which are called the 'Great Bear' or the 'Plough' but then Mr Herrick arrived with an oil-lantern and some tapers and the fun began. Every child had brought some fireworks and the smaller ones were all mixed up together in a big clothes basket while the more important ones were sorted out and let off separately. The rockets were stood in upside-down flower pots and the rector went down the row lighting each as fast as he could so that one after another spluttered and whizzed up into the sky. Then the catherine wheels were pinned to a board and made a brave show and next the roman candles threw up their coloured balls of fire.

Jane had never been to a party like this before and when the great bonfire was lit in four places and began to crackle and roar they all joined hands and danced round it. Higher and

When the bonfire began to roar and crackle they all joined hands and danced round it.

higher the flames sprang — lovely, wavering fire-flowers of bright orange and red. The sparks were flung as high as the roof before the heart of the fire glowed so that it hurt their eyes to look at it and was so hot that they all broke the ring and scattered. Jane blundered back into a grown-up whose laugh seemed familiar and turned round to find her uncle and aunt. Soon after this they all crowded into the big hall and Mrs Herrick had a cup of hot soup ready for everyone before they all went home in the moonlight.

The frost held for two more days and then broke suddenly and the next Saturday was bright and warm.

'St Martin's Summer or Martinmas,' Mrs Watson said at dinner time, 'tis often the same round about mid-November and you'd best be out of doors while you can.'

'Richard and the others have gone to the pictures this afternoon,' Jane said. 'Shall I come round the farm with you, Uncle? If only you'd let me cycle in the dark I'd go out on my bike but it's not worth it if I can't.'

'You can't,' said her uncle wiping his moustache, 'but you can come with me.'

As Jane had been quite certain that she would not be allowed to go out with a bicycle lamp she was not very disappointed!

Although the sun was already low it was warm enough to be without a coat. The farmyard glowed with a soft, golden light as she whistled up the dogs and went over to join her uncle in the rickyard where the cattle were now fenced in round the straw ricks. He showed her the troughs into which George threw the chopped-up swedes and explained that wheat straw was being trodden into manure which would be carted back to the fields next year.

'And so you see Janey how 'tis that everything that comes from the soil goes back into it at last. These heifers will stay here for the winter but I reckon you know that the milkers are in the other byre and how, because they be milked twice a day, the floors must be kept clean and washed down and the muck taken out … Let's be going over the fields.'

As they plodded through the carpet of mucky straw to cross the rickyard Jane smacked a frisky young Red Poll on her behind and made her move. She wasn't afraid of cows now! The dogs were already exploring the hedge at the side of the field when they climbed the locked gate and looked down the hill to see the first faint blue-green tinge of the wheat sown only a few weeks ago. Thousands upon thousands of rows of neat little blades were already pushing through the brown soil and Jane remembered how she had walked through the stubble not long ago and seen a few flowers still blooming. Now she could only find one flower in the shelter of the hedge — a tall weedy-looking sort of plant with lobed leaves and a crown of bright yellow flower heads gleaming richly in the fading sunlight. She asked her uncle what it was but he could not remember.

'Tis ragwort m'dear,' he said. 'It grows in bad ground and the seeds fly everywhere.'

As he spoke a great flock of birds flew up from the hedgerow which was bright with scarlet haws. As the birds passed over Jane noticed that they looked like thrushes because of the speckles on their breasts but that their sides were pinkish red. She was sure that these must be the redwings which Mr Herrick had told her about and which she had heard one night last month when she was lying awake in the dark.

Presently, on another field she saw the fieldfares which were bigger than the redwings. They looked like thrushes too, but their backs and tails and wings were dark brown and their heads grey. When they flew over they had a rather ugly cry which sounded like, 'Chak-chak-chak'.

Over in the sheep field they saw that old Frank was already getting ready to build his lambing pens.

'It's just that he's been taking his time carting some straw over,' Uncle William explained. 'There be plenty o' time o' course. February or back end of January they'll be here and I well remember your going to see them this year Janey ... You'll not be seeing our new lambs next year, my dear, but maybe you'll be down at Easter to see us.'

Jane said nothing. She felt too choky.

They came home a new way in the dusk and in a narrow, sunken lane which was little more than a cart track Jane was just wondering what had happened to the dogs when her uncle stopped suddenly and pinched her arm. She glanced up at him in surprise and saw him put his finger to his lips and then point ahead. About thirty yards in front of them a fox was sitting on his haunches with his back to them scratching himself in a bored kind of way. Every now and then he put his nose up and sniffed but apparently he could not smell them for he made no attempt to move until, in the distance, Sally barked and Sheila yelped in sympathy. Instantly he stiffened and looked round but although he must have seen them both very clearly he flattened his body against the grass so that he was nearly invisible. Sally barked again — much nearer this time — and only then did the fox move and set off down the lane at a loping trot.

'They get mighty hungry and bold this time o' year, Janey,' Mr Watson said. 'We must tell your aunt to be sure to see that the fowls are locked up to-night.'

'I must do the ducks too, Uncle. Did you know we're making Charlie and Clarence fat for Christmas? I think it's awful but Auntie says that's what they're for ... I don't think I shall be able to eat them.'

Mr Watson chuckled. 'Don't worry. You'll eat 'em.'

Then the dogs came up, excited and panting, and made a lot of noise when they scented the fox.

And so November slipped by. St Martin's Summer was short lived and Mrs Watson had been wise to warn Jane to make the best of it, for after but three more days the rain came and never seemed to stop. Day after day Mr Watson used the car to take Jane to and from school and the lanes were slippery with dead and fallen leaves and all the country smelled of damp decay.

Shorter and shorter were the hours of daylight as the year prepared to die and Jane began to love the welcome of firelight and lamplight as she rushed down the hill in the old car on each afternoon. The days were now too short for anything but school and Moor End.

December

When Jane woke it was dark. Although the curtains were drawn back she could not even see the position of the window and yet she felt that it must be nearly time to get up. When she turned over in bed towards where the door should be she knew that she was right about the time for suddenly a line of orange light showed the crack between the door and the floor boards. The light moved and brightened and Jane heard her aunt's foot on the stairs as she came up with the lamp. Then the door opened and the warm lamplight gushed in and chased back the darkness.

'Awake Janey? Hurry my dear for I'm late for once and 'tis the darkest morning I remember. 'Tis as dark as the inside of a cow!'

Jane laughed. 'Why a cow, Auntie? And why is it so dark? Is it raining?'

Mrs Watson put the lamp down on the dressing table and the shadows stopped chasing each other round the walls.

''Tis not raining but it's near the shortest day and don't you break up for the holidays to-day Janey? Or had you forgotten?'

Jane slipped out of bed and hugged her aunt.

'I had forgotten … This is my last day of school at Townsend. I don't think I like it.'

She hurried her breakfast and while the morning light was still grey fetched her bicycle from the barn and set off up the hill for the last journey to school. As usual, she stood on the pedals for one of the specially steep parts of the hill and then got off by the gate into the root field. She could hear George coughing somewhere near and when she climbed to the second bar she could see the old man cutting the big fleshy stalks and leaves of the green kale and tossing them into a farm cart drawn by the patient Short.

'Is that the cow's breakfast, George?' she called. 'You'd better be quick with it else you'll be late.'

He straightened his back. And how well she knew now the gesture with which he pushed his hat back on his head. To-day he looked very tired and Jane knew that she was going to miss him badly when she did not see him every day.

'This is my last day at school, George. We break up before dinner and then after Christmas I'm going home.'

But all he said was, 'Be off with you, young miss,' as he had said so many times before.

She waved to him, got off the gate and pushed her bicycle up the last and steepest part of the hill to the beech trees. Over to her right a big flock of rooks flapped lazily out of three elms in which they had been roosting and flew down wind to the ploughed land to look for their breakfast. She knew now that rooks were among the farmers' best friends for they ate many of the caterpillars and pests which make their homes in the soil.

There was no sun to gild the weathercock this morning and indeed the short day seemed ended almost before it had begun as she rushed down the hill to Townsend.

All the girls knew that she was leaving of course and even before the register was called her desk was piled with little presents brought by her special friends. There were pencils and crayons and paints and a jay's feather and a silver bangle and many other treasures as well, and everyone was so sweet that poor Jane felt rather weepy.

There were no proper lessons but their teacher read poetry to them. Everyone was allowed to choose what they would like to hear but when it was Jane's turn she felt too miserable to say anything.

'Never mind, Janey! I'll choose one specially for you,' and this is what she read:

Farewell to the Farm
by
Robert Louis Stevenson

The coach is at the door at last;
The eager children, mounting fast
And kissing hands, in chorus sing:
Good-bye, good-bye, to everything!

The house and garden, field and lawn,
The meadow-gates we swang upon,
To pump and stable, tree and swing,
Good-bye, good-bye, to everything!

And fare you well for evermore,
O ladder at the hayloft door,
O hayloft where the cobwebs cling,
Good-bye, good-bye, to everything!

Crack goes the whip, and off we go;
The trees and houses smaller grow;
Last, round the woody turn we swing:
Good-bye, good-bye, to everything!

Jane knew that she was being silly but the tears just *would* come into her eyes and it was even worse when the teacher closed the book and said, 'We shall miss you, Jane. You won't forget us will you when you go back to London.'

Later, outside the gates, there were more good-byes but some of the girls were in the carol singing party which was being arranged by Richard and Rosemary for Christmas Eve, so that Jane would see them again. But in spite of all the partings it was fun to go home on a Thursday in time for dinner and even more fun when four of her friends walked up to the top of the hill with her.

'See you before you go, Janey!'

'Come and see us in the holidays when you come to Moor End!'

'Happy Christmas, Janey!'

'See you at the carols, Jane!'

Then they turned and went back to Townsend and Jane stood on the crest of the hill with her back to the farm and watched her friends grow smaller and smaller, turn and wave, and then disappear round the bend of the lane. A pale and watery sun slipped from behind a cloud and for a few minutes a faint, golden radiance lay over the bare countryside as Jane freewheeled down the hill to home.

Thursday was her aunt's day for cleaning out the kitchen. She was rather behind to-day and Jane realized that she was not particularly welcome and that dinner would be late! So she wandered out into the garden where a robin was singing bravely and found the buds of two real roses.

'I'll save them for Christmas,' she thought. 'P'raps Mummy and Daddy could have them in their room.'

Tuesday was Christmas Day but her parents were not coming until Monday and the carols, after a final rehearsal to-morrow, were to be sung round the village and neighbourhood on that same evening.

Then there was holly, mistletoe and evergreens to be picked; but Richard, who broke up that afternoon, had promised to come over to-morrow and help with that job.

'I know where there's mistletoe,' he had said on Sunday when they had last met, 'and not many people round here know that. And the hedges are full of holly so that won't take us long … I'll get Father to come over in the car and collect it 'cos we need a lot at home.'

And Jane, who suddenly felt rather lonely out in the Moor End garden in the pale December sunshine, hoped that tomorrow would soon come. She had bought most of her presents but if it was fine she was going to cycle into Crossmarket directly after breakfast and finish her shopping.

She wandered up into the orchard hoping that her aunt would soon have dinner ready. The sun had gone in now and she shivered as she looked sadly at the four ducks who came waddling towards her in solemn procession. The drakes had disappeared yesterday and Jane knew that she would meet them next on the dinner table on Sunday.

'Silly ducks!' she said affectionately. 'You're my babies really but I've nothing for you. Did you all lay an egg for me this morning?'

Then she heard Mrs Watson's call and ran in thankfully to dinner. 'So you've finished with school at Townsend, Janey?' her uncle said.

'You've had your fun there I'll be bound even if you haven't learned much … I've to go to Crossmarket this afternoon and your aunt has just decided that she wants to do some more shopping so you had better be coming along with us.'

So the afternoon was a hundred times better than she had expected. Mrs Watson was a magnificent shopper when she really started and apparently she had not thought of Christmas presents until to-day. Jane trotted along behind her rather like a small tug in the rear of an ocean liner. Her father had sent her money for presents, but her list was still a long one and Mrs Watson proved a great help. Uncle William met them at four o'clock in the little tea-shop where Jane had once poured out for him, and they all sat down thankfully with parcels piled on the floor around them. It was a splendid tea. Jane loved meals out and especially in a little town like Crossmarket. Somehow the people seemed friendlier than in London but perhaps that was because here everybody seemed to know everybody else. Many, that afternoon, stopped for a word with Mr and Mrs Watson and a smile for Jane.

'Tis strange,' Aunt Kate said after their tea had been interrupted the third time for a greeting, 'I've not the time to come gallivanting here often but when I do it's as much as I can do to get round the place for interruptions ... and a very Happy Christmas to you Mrs Smithson my dear and thank you kindly for enquiring but I thank God for my health every day of my life ... And how is your George? ... Yes! This is our niece Janey who's been with us this year nearly past and going home after Christmas to Lunnon ... Thank you kindly again and our best wishes to all ... And what are you sitting there grinning at, William? What is there that's comic about greeting old friends I'd like to know. And if you would pay the bill and carry all these parcels for us we could get on our way instead of wasting our time in this place!'

Uncle William winked solemnly to Jane. 'Women,' he said, 'will be the death o' me.'

It was freezing hard as they drove home and the night was very dark. Jane went to bed early and slept until she was called late the next morning.

After breakfast Jane walked up the hill to meet the others. George and another man were trimming the hedge and she stopped to watch them. Each had a short handled chopper with a curved end which George called a brummock and they cut out the straggling brambles and trimmed back branches that had grown out of the top of the hedge. Both men wore thick leather gauntlets and it was wonderful to see how they tidied the hedge into a neat shape and trained the live wood so that it grew *along* the hedge and thickened it. Three piles of trimmings and clippings were already heaped just inside the hedge and while Jane watched George set fire to them. The wind was blowing steadily from the west and soon fanned the fire into wicked life. Jane watched fascinated to see how the flames were beaten flat by the wind and seemed to chase the smoke that was whisked away through the hedge to the old hayfield to the south of the lane. Soon the brambles and the smaller branches were turned to glowing ash and Jane was

George and another man were trimming the hedge and Jane stopped to watch them.

just thinking what fun it would be to roast potatoes in the embers when a red car which Jane knew to be the Herricks' swished down the lane.

'Good-bye!' Jane called as she ran after the car. 'I'll come and see how you've got on presently.'

'Father had to go to Crossmarket,' Richard explained, 'but he'll fetch us and all the holly and stuff about tea time … I borrowed some secateurs out of the tool shed and you'd better go and get some thick leather gloves like us, Janey. I've got some string … Did you know your auntie has asked us for dinner? I hoped she would!'

Jane ran in for an old coat and the gloves and Sheila followed her out of the yard. The puppy was now getting too old for Sally who was often very annoyed with her daughter's playful ways. Mr Watson said more than once that it was time Janey took her away with her.

They went up by the hedge to the wood with solemn Susan holding Jane's hand and soon came to the first holly tree. The best berries were at the top of course but somehow Richard managed to climb up a little way and, by holding on with one hand, clipped down some fine crimson bunches.

'The leaves up here haven't got any prickles,' he called. 'I wonder what's happened to them?'

'Perhaps they haven't growed them yet,' Susan said. 'I've got a bit here I'm going to keep for the Christmas pudding.'

Further up under the shelter of the hedge they found some young green sprays rather like ferns.

'They look like carrots to me,' Jane said brightly, 'but I s'pose they're not.'

'Fancy you knowing a carrot now Janey!' Richard laughed as they tied up the first big bunch of holly. 'You wouldn't have known a carrot by sight when you first came, would you … And I'm jolly sure you don't now 'cos they're the new shoots of wild parsley.'

'Don't be such a rude beast,' Susan said firmly. 'I think they look like carrots too anyway.'

Up in the wood they saw a magnificent green woodpecker. They were walking quietly in single file along a grassy track when Richard stopped suddenly and turned with his finger to his lips. About twenty yards ahead a handsome green bird with a gorgeous crimson crest was hopping over the turf and looking about him eagerly as he hopped. Suddenly he would stop and thrust his long bill into the ground and sometimes he seemed to be plucking off the grass blades. When Susan shifted slightly and trod on a twig he turned his lovely head to look at them and then, without a sound, flew off into the wood. And as he flew the faint sunlight lit up the bright yellow feathers on his back so that he looked almost like a great canary.

'I wonder why he wasn't up a tree?' Jane said. 'I heard him in this wood in the summer ... Do you know what he reminds me of?' she added suddenly. 'Robin Hood! That's what he's like in his bright green coat with a scarlet feather in his cap.'

Richard found the oak tree for which he was searching soon after and pointed up to a big branch on which three bunches of mistletoe were growing.

'I come here every year,' he told them, 'and there's always some to pick but that branch looks nearly dead now ... I think I can climb up if you will just start me off.'

He put a foot on Jane's interlocked hands, grabbed for a branch and scrambled up. Then he had to lie on his stomach along the old branch and snip off the green, woody branches of mistletoe which Jane and Susan caught as they fell.

'Mistletoe is magic, I believe,' Richard gasped as he cut off the last piece and at that moment an ugly, harsh call echoed across the wood as a jay flew over.

'It's making that noise 'cos you've done an omen or something,' Susan said as she dropped her mistletoe in alarm.

'I hate those birds.'

They went to the little dell which Jane and Richard had discovered last February. Under the hazel bushes by the stream Susan stooped to find some half-hidden primrose plants with the tiniest buds deep in the centre of the leaves.

'Ricky!' Jane said suddenly. 'I know it's awful of me but I don't want to go home. I want to be here when they come out.'

Richard looked at her in surprise.

'Why not?' he said. 'Why don't you come at Easter? They'll be out then.'

'I'll send you some, Janey, anyhow,' Susan promised; but they all had less to say as they went back down the side of the wood clipping holly as they went.

After lunch they walked the lanes until they had enough evergreens for both households. While they were waiting for Mr Herrick and their tea Richard fixed Jane's bird table a little higher up the trunk of the chestnut tree because Simon often jumped up and killed the birds who came for food.

'The tits are best,' Jane said. 'They're not afraid of him and he never catches them either. They like that horrid piece of fatty skin I hung up … Here comes the Rector at last so now we can have tea and fill up the car with the holly. When are you going to put it all up, Susan?'

'Sunday, I expect. In the afternoon.'

And that was what the Watsons did too for after the Sunday dinner was cleared away and washed up, Uncle William was cruelly awakened from his nap by the fire and sent for string and tacks while his wife went up to the attic for strings of last year's paper chains.

Mrs Watson did not believe in doing anything by halves.

'If we're going to have decorations let's decorate handsome,' she said as she thrust a great bunch of holly behind the faded photograph of her parents which hung over the mantelpiece … 'Now William! It's no use trying to read the paper and tack up that paper chain! Janey, my darling! Where would you like the mistletoe to hang when young Master Richard comes to pay his compliments this Christmas?'

And when Jane muttered something which sounded like 'Don't be silly, Auntie,' Mrs Watson roared with laughter and collapsed into a chair while the tears streamed down her face. 'Nothing like a bit of mistletoe about the place,' she gasped as she set to work again. They did not finish until supper time. By then the house was transformed and Uncle William said, 'Tis the same every year, Janey, even when there's only the two of us. There's never much room in this house at best o' times but this Christmas we shall all get pricked every time we sit down to eat … You'd better be off to bed early to-night, my lass, for you'll be late to-morrow with your carols and your mother and dad coming too …' He turned solemnly to his wife and Jane did not see him wink as he said, 'Have they let us know what time they'll be coming, my dear? Had no word from them have we? Reckon I shall be too busy to get into Crossmarket to-morrow to hang about for trains from Lunnon …'

Poor Jane's eyes were almost as round as her mouth until she caught sight of her aunt's twinkle. 'It's two o'clock, Uncle, and you know it is,' she said as she ruffled his hair, 'and you know you promised to take me. I'll be sitting in the car waiting for you to come all the morning.'

But to-morrow came at last with a heavy white frost and bright sunshine.

'Just like a Christmas card,' Aunt Kate said as she went to take the letters and parcels from the postman. 'And the parcels I'm hiding till to-morrow … William! Did you arrange for George to bring in the Christmas tree to-night when Janey is out singing?'

Mr Watson nodded because his mouth was full but Jane was too excited to eat much. It was hard to wait until dinner and harder still to eat any dinner but at last it was time to go, and for the third time in her country year she made the thrilling journey to the station to meet her father and mother. The wheels of the car sang on the black, frosty road and Jane felt like singing too as they passed the familiar landmarks. First they crossed the common which sloped up on their right to the wood she now knew so well. Then they turned into the main road and waved to someone they knew at the bus stop. Then past the Hawkins' farm where a lad swung out into the road with his tractor and made Uncle William mutter as he swerved to avoid him. Then the ancient inn called The Marquis of Granby which usually had some very old men sitting on a bench outside; then another farm and the humped bridge over the stream; the crossroads where they turned left and from where you could see the tall spire of Crossmarket's church against the skyline and then, almost before you realized it, you were passing the forge.

The same old porter was still in the station booking-hall and still had a smile and a word for Jane when she wished him a Happy Christmas. The bell in the signal box clanged, the signals fell and the level-crossing gates swung back. Jane's mouth went dry and her heart thumped so loudly that she thought her uncle would ask her if she could hear the noise as well! She felt shy too and suddenly ran up the platform towards the train as it came gliding round the curve. The smutty-faced engine driver grinned at her with a flash of white teeth as he leaned from the cab and Jane noticed that he wore a sprig of mistletoe in his peaked cap. The train slid gently to a stop and for a terrible minute she thought they had not come. But they were in the front this time and Uncle William found them first while Jane pushed and wriggled frantically through the crowds.

'I'm never going to let you go away again, Jane,' her mother said as she hugged her. 'This is the very last time. It's been too long.'

The ride back to Moor End was as much fun as usual. The last time they had all come this way together the harvest had made the country golden; but now the trees were bare, the hedges thin and all the land was brown and ridged except where the wheat already showed a tinge of green.

Aunt Kate was waiting to welcome them and there was a lot of kissing under the mistletoe hanging in the hall. Jane's mother admired the decorations at once and her father asked Uncle William how long it had taken to turn the house into a flower shop!

At tea time Mr Herrick rang up to ask them *all* to come and join the carollers and Jane was astonished when Aunt Kate and her mother agreed. They went over in the car and the moon came up and the frost glittered and sparkled in the hedgerows. All the singers met at the rectory first and then toured the village collecting for the Crossmarket hospital. They carried old oil lanterns and the rector stood in the centre of the big circle and led the singing. They sang all the old favourites like 'Herald Angels', and 'It came upon the midnight clear', and some new ones as well. Jane's favourite was 'O little town of Bethlehem', and as she sang:

Above thy deep and dreamless sleep
The silent stars go by.
Yet in thy dark streets shineth
The everlasting light:
The hopes and fears of all the years
Are met in thee, to-night.

she could almost imagine herself looking down on the little town of white, flat-roofed houses with a great, shining star hanging proudly over a dirty old stable. She shut her eyes tight to make the picture clearer but Richard spoilt it by tickling her neck as he sang in the sweetest voice she had ever heard,

> We hear the Christmas Angels
> The great glad tidings tell.
> O come to us, abide with us,
> Our Lord Emmanuel.

Richard had a very beautiful voice which was the success of the evening when they all trooped into the bar of the Three Black Crows and sang 'Good King Wenceslas' with himself as the page.

They were asked into some houses and sang in halls and drawing-rooms, but although the party had four cars the children soon got very tired and Jane fell asleep on her father's shoulder on the way home.

Christmas morning was so cold and clear and still that Jane awoke to hear the church bell ringing for early service in Townsend. She jumped out of bed and opened her bedroom door. Faintly from below came the clink of china, so she reached for a dressing gown and slippers and ran down to wish Aunt Kate a 'Happy Christmas' and ask if she could take tea up to her mother and father. And then because it was Christmas Day and because she hadn't seen them for so long she squeezed into bed beside her mother and chattered while they sipped their tea.

They had presents with their breakfast. It would take too long to tell the contents of all the parcels but nobody was more thrilled than Jane to see the look on her mother's face when she undid the little parcel containing the embroidered purse which she had made for her at school. And Jane had a paint-box, a bicycle bell, a scarlet leather lead for Sheila and a dog licence for her as well from her uncle, so that the puppy was now really her very own.

Then Uncle William drove Jane and her father over to church while the ladies stayed at home to cook the turkey.

Never had there been such a wonderful morning. Every twig and every blade of grass was covered with a film of sparkling hoar frost. Even the two rose buds in the garden which, in her excitement, Jane had forgotten to pick were coated so thickly that they looked almost like the fruits crystallized in sugar that we used to enjoy at Christmas time before the war. While Uncle William was getting out the car Jane ran across the road to the common. The turf crackled under her feet as she went over to look at the hedge. Every twig had its covering of ice too and when they drove up the hill later the sun had warmed the tree tops and the ice was falling and tinkling on to the road.

At the back of the church on a low table was a model of the stable at Bethlehem. Jane had never seen anything like this before. It was a little like a tiny model theatre for an electric star hung over the stable roof and in the doorway sat Mary in her blue dress with the baby on her lap. By her side, so very humbly, stood Joseph, and on their knees and wearing their fine robes and their crowns the three great kings who had followed the star offered their gifts. Gently Jane put out her finger and touched the donkey and the cow that stood at the nearby manger, almost expecting them to look up or whisk their tails. Then the church filled, the choir and the candles came in and Richard grinned wickedly at her when he was sure that his father wasn't looking.

After church they were all asked into the rectory and the grown-ups stayed downstairs while Jane went up to the nursery with the others. She had given books to Richard and Susan and crayons to Peter but had not yet had their presents to her.

'Open the others first, Janey,' Richard said. 'I want you to see mine last. Buck up … Oh! Let me cut the string for you.'

227

Whether it was because none of the rectory children had much money or whether it was because Mrs Herrick had always encouraged them to make things and to use their hands whenever they could, it was always true that their presents were wonderful surprises. To-day, Peter's present was a tin of home-made toffee.

'It's for the train when you go home, Janey,' he explained. 'Mummy and me done it last week. I had a bit 'fore I put it in the tin. Do you mind?'

Susan's offering was a gaily embroidered pencil case. The stitches were big but her fingers were small and she loved Jane better than needlework.

But Ricky's present was the best of all and the greatest surprise she had ever had. When she had praised and thanked the two little ones for theirs Richard went to the top shelf of the cupboard and, very carefully, lifted down a roll of brown paper and carried it to the old table under the window!

'I'd better help you, Janey. If I don't hold one end they'll spring up!' This sounded mysterious and exciting enough; but when she undid the paper and saw what Richard had made for her she could not find a word to say and did what she had never dared do before — she flung her arms round his neck and kissed him. He flushed scarlet but instead of shouting at her he grinned rather sheepishly and ran his fingers round the inside of his collar.

'Do you like them, Janey? I thought they would remind you of Moor End and the places we know.'

He had drawn and coloured for her two maps — the first of Moor End farmhouse and garden and the other of the country round about — and Jane could see at once that they must have taken him weeks to finish. There had never been a present like this!

'Let me see them properly, Ricky! Hold one end and I'll hold this ... Aren't they marvellous, Susan?... Let's look at the country one first … Richard! You've got everything in. Here's the wood … and our dell where we found the anemones … and right over in the corner here is the witch's house … You are *clever*, Ricky!'

Richard fidgeted.

'Oh well,' he muttered. 'That's all right, Janey. Thought you'd like them and I enjoyed doing them … Matter of fact I cheated a bit with the witch's house 'cos it's much farther away from us than that and the paper wasn't big enough!'

Then the grown-ups came in and the presents were shown again and Mr and Mrs Herrick saw the maps for the first time because Richard had worked on them in secret.

Down in the hall Mrs Herrick slipped her arm round Jane's shoulders as she stood rather mournfully wondering whether she would have to say good-bye now.

'Not good-bye yet, darling,' she smiled. 'You're *all* coming to our big party here to-morrow night.'

So home they went to Moor End again and found the house full of the smell of roasting turkey. And when they all sat down flushed and happy at last at the loaded table the turkey tasted even better than it had smelled. After all had been cleared away they sat round the fire and ate chestnuts, although Jane could not manage many. Just before tea, Jane's father said that unless he had some fresh air soon he would fall asleep and would anyone come for a walk with him.

Jane ran for her coat and when they opened the front door the cold made them both gasp. It was nearly dark but the moon was coming up and the stars were bright and clear. They walked sharply up the hill and their footsteps rang on the road until they reached the track to the beech trees.

Jane took her father by the hand and pulled him up the mound.

'It all seemed to start here, Daddy,' she said. 'This is where I met Ricky and the Rector and saw the little bramblings eating the beech mast ... There aren't any nuts this year though. Whenever I think of Moor End I shall remember the beeches ...'

'You won't mind coming home now, Janey, will you? And you'll have Sheila to remind you of the farm and we'll often come and see them here.'

Jane's fingers tightened round his hand. 'I want to come with you but it's difficult to go ... I never knew I could feel as well as I do now, Daddy, and I'll be able to help you in the garden on Saturdays and do all sorts of things I couldn't do before. What fun we're going to have! ... Come on! Tea will be ready.'

As they crossed the farmyard Jane noticed that the stable door was open. Silhouetted against the orange glow of a hanging lantern was the figure of an old man leaning against the doorpost while from within came the sound of shifting hooves and a contented munching. Jane felt her father's hand on her arm and, when he pointed upwards, she saw right above the stable a great shining star.

'Christmas Day, Jane,' he whispered. 'A stable and a star. I shall remember this too.'

She always remembered the brightly lit Christmas tree waiting for them when they went indoors again and she remembered too the lovely smell when her aunt tossed on to the glowing fire handfuls of lavender and rosemary cuttings until the house was rich with the essence of summer sunshine again. They sang some carols together too and then played games until Jane fell asleep.

Jane did not remember much about the rectory party except that it helped her to forget that in a few hours she would be gone. They played all the usual games and finished up with Sir Roger de Coverley. And when the time to say good-bye came it wasn't so difficult after all because although she was

The brightly-lit Christmas tree was waiting for them when they went indoors again.

leaving the best friends she had *ever* had, she was going home to be with her mother and father again.

Everyone — even Richard — kissed Jane under the mistletoe in the hall and she went out to the car with 'Come and see us again soon' and 'Happy New Year' ringing in her ears.

Next morning she was awakened by her mother instead of Aunt Kate and then after breakfast there was the flurry and excitement of packing. While the trunks were being locked Jane ran out to talk to her friends. Old Frank the shepherd had come over for something so she saw him too. George was tossing swedes into a cart and seemed astonished that she was going, although she had been telling him about it for weeks. Sidney came in on the tractor and when she had shaken hands very shyly with him he said, 'I'll be saving you a peewit's nest again, Janey. Come and see it Easter time. They all be flying over fields again this morning.'

Then, before she could run up to the wood as she had hoped to do, Uncle William sounded a warning from the car and she had to dash indoors.

The luggage was strapped on and Jane stood awkwardly in front of Aunt Kate, who was not coming to the station.

'We shall never forget what you've done for her, Kate,' her mother was saying when there was a tinkling of bicycle bells and Richard and Susan came rushing down the hill.

'Gosh!' Richard gasped. 'We thought we'd never make it … Mother sent you these, Janey. They're from the garden,' and from his bicycle basket he passed her a bunch of lovely waxen-white Christmas roses.

Before she could say anything Uncle William sounded his horn again and Jane found herself lifted and squeezed and kissed by Aunt Kate. Next she found herself in the car with an excited Sheila licking her face. The door slammed. Richard and Susan banged on the windows. Aunt Kate waved and blew a kiss as the car started and Jane turned to look through the near window as the old tractor roared out of the farmyard gate.

They were moving now. The house was behind them. Smaller, smaller. A dip in the road as it crossed the common and Moor End had vanished.

Jane brushed her fingers across her eyes and then turned to smile at her mother.

Notes on the text

BY KATE MACDONALD

January

stayed at home in the morning: it was common in this period for many professions to work on Saturday mornings.

van: trains used to have a special luggage compartment for large cases, kept secure by the train guard.

brick copper: a large deep metal (often copper) vessel built into a brick housing, with space for a fire underneath to hear the water that was poured in from the well. This would have been the main source of hot water for a house without central heating.

rainwater pump: a pump to bring up water from an underground cistern that collected rainwater.

February

mangold: mangelwurzel, a kind of beet grown for animal fodder.

best blue coat and hat: girls and women routinely wore hats with their smart coat in this period.

But she didn't: the rectory children have been brought up on Bible stories, but Jane had missed Sunday school due to her months of illness. Samson was a great hero famed for his physical strength.

red lightning: red squirrels were more common than grey squirrels in the mid-twentieth century, though they are now rare.

March

warm knickers: in this period before central heating thick flannel underwear would be worn in the winter as an essential insulating layer, even though children went bare-legged and boys wore shorts all year round.

khaki shirt: Joe's remnant of army uniform is one of the very few reminders in the story of the recent war.

telephone: the telephone was not a common installation on people's houses at this time, and children would have had few opportunities to use it.

scarlet fever: a bacterial infection of the throat and tongue, which before antibiotics were widely available was a common childhood killer. There is still no vaccine for it.

licked his pencil: before the ballpoint pen became common in the later 1940s lead pencils were used as the cheap and handy alternative to fountain pens. Licking the lead was a common substitute for sharpening it, to make the lead darker. It was also potentially poisonous, routinely forbidden in schools.

hedge-sparrow: also called a dunnock.

Mrs Tiggywinkle: the hedgehog washerwoman from Beatrix's Potter's children's story, who wears a lace cap and an apron.

June

fairy bombers: an understandable imaginative leap for a child who has grown up during wartime.

This was the world and I was king: from Robert Louis Stevenson's 'My Kingdom' (1913), published in *A Child's Garden of Verses*.

July

form: a long bench.

hurdles: wooden fences to make a sheep pen.

gypsies: Saville was writing in a period when Gypsies were considered to be a threat to property, and their lifestyles challenged those of mainstream society.

tall pink ones: rosebay willow herb, bombweed or fireweed.

jug of water: to find a puncture, inflate the leaking tyre, and then put the tyre in water to see where the bubbles come out.

coats: their jackets.

October

Children's Hour: long-running daily BBC radio programme for children.

December

Sir Roger de Coverley: a country dance for sets of four couples, similar to the Virginia Reel.